Caz Finlay lives in Liverpool with her husband, two children, and a grumpy dog named Bert. A qualified probation officer, Caz has always been fascinated by the psychology of human behaviour and the reasons people do the things they do. However, it was the loss of her son in 2016 which prompted her to rediscover her love of writing and write her first novel, *The Boss*.

cazfinlay.com

facebook.com/cazfinlayauthor
twitter.com/cjfinlaywriter
bookbub.com/authors/caz-finlay

Also by Caz Finlay

The Boss

Back in the Game

Head of the Firm

Liverpool Loyalty

Traitor in the House

PART OF THE FAMILY

CAZ FINLAY

One More Chapter
a division of HarperCollins*Publishers* Ltd
1 London Bridge Street
London SE1 9GF
www.harpercollins.co.uk
HarperCollins*Publishers*
1st Floor, Watermarque Building, Ringsend Road
Dublin 4, Ireland

This paperback edition 2022
1
First published in Great Britain in ebook format
by HarperCollins*Publishers* 2022
Copyright © Caz Finlay 2022

Caz Finlay asserts the moral right to be identified
as the author of this work

A catalogue record of this book is available from the British Library

ISBN: 978-0-00-846335-9

This novel is entirely a work of fiction. The names, characters and
incidents portrayed in it are the work of the author's imagination. Any
resemblance to actual persons, living or dead, events or localities is
entirely coincidental.

Printed and bound in the UK using 100% Renewable Electricity
by CPI Group (UK) Ltd

MIX
Paper from
responsible sources
FSC™ C007454

This book is produced from independently certified FSC™ paper
to ensure responsible forest management.

For more information visit: www.harpercollins.co.uk/green

For Finlay – we did it, son.

Prologue

I put the gun on the table in front of me and stood up, ducking slightly so I didn't bang my head on the ceiling. Picking up the empty takeaway carton, I stuffed it into the overflowing rubbish bin, pushing it down with my fist so it didn't spill back out onto the floor. The smell of rotting food jumped out at me as the boxes were squashed into the small space. I should probably take it down to the huge recycling containers out at the front of the park, but I could hear the rain hammering on the roof of the caravan and it was a five-minute walk. I could cope with the smell until the morning.

Turning on the old television, I flicked through the channels to find something to watch before settling on reruns of The Big Bang Theory. I'd seen every single episode countless times, but I could watch them over and over again. It was my go-to programme – the television equivalent of chicken soup. And I deserved some comfort, didn't I? After everything I'd been through, I deserved more than an old leaky caravan and a crappy twenty-four-inch telly.

I had nothing.

I had no one.

I choked back the tears. The time for feeling sorry for myself was over. Because time was the only thing I had left and I would use it to carefully plan my revenge. Everyone thought I was stupid, but I was cleverer than all of them. And soon they would learn that truth.

I might not have strength or brute force on my side, but I had more brains than the lot of them put together. I eyed the Baikal handgun on the coffee table. It was a beautiful piece of kit. I loved the way it felt in my hand. I liked the way it made me feel. Powerful – as though I could take on anyone. I kept it close to me at all times – just in case someone found me. I'd even fired it a couple of times. A few practice shots to make sure I knew exactly what to do when the time came.

And my time would come soon. I just had to find out a little more information about my target and figure out the best time to strike. I needed him to be alone, for obvious reasons, but I also wanted there to be no one there to help him as he felt his lifeblood seep from his veins. I'd enjoy watching him – helpless and incapacitated, and in pain. Then they would all feel the pain of losing him too – and they would know exactly what it felt like to have someone you loved ripped away from you.

I sat back against the old sofa cushions and smiled to myself, content in the knowledge that Michael Carter's days were numbered.

Tick, Tock, Michael.

Tick, Tock.

Chapter One

Grace Carter opened the passenger door of Luke Sullivan's car and climbed inside.

'Thanks for picking me up,' she said with a smile.

'No problem. You ready for this?' he asked her.

She nodded. She'd thought about nothing else all weekend. 'Ready as I'll ever be. You?'

'I'm looking forward to getting some answers, but I'm not especially happy about who we have to see to get them.'

'Well, I don't suppose we have much choice, do we?' Grace asked.

'Unfortunately not,' he said as he pulled out of Grace's driveway.

Grace leaned back against the soft leather headrest and closed her eyes. It had been a little over a week since she'd discovered that Luke Sullivan was her half-brother. He'd been born three months after her father died and neither she nor Luke had had any idea of their connection. That was until Glenda Alexander, the mother of Luke's best mate,

Danny, had surprised them with the information eight days before. Glenda had even produced a photograph of Luke's pregnant mother and Grace's father, looking every inch the happy expectant couple, as proof.

Grace had refused to believe it at first. The photograph had knocked the wind from her, but it wasn't absolute proof. They could just have been friends. But unbeknownst to all of them, her father-in-law, Patrick, who had known Grace's father, Pete, in his younger years, had seen the resemblance between Luke and Pete immediately and had done some digging of his own. His source had found some old financial records and discovered that Grace's father had a secret will and had left Luke's mum, Maggie, a large sum of money. That seemed to prove beyond all doubt that Pete Sumner had indeed been Luke's father too.

The truth of the revelation had completely floored Grace. She had always idolised her father. There had only been the two of them when she was growing up, and they had been incredibly close – or at least that was what she'd thought. Now she knew that her father had been lying to her, she wondered what other secrets he had kept from her. Did she have any other half-siblings out there in the world? To think that all she had ever wanted was a brother or sister, and she'd had one in Luke for the past twenty-eight years.

Why hadn't her father told her that he'd met someone else? She liked to think he would have known she'd have been thrilled about the possibility of their family becoming more than just the two of them. Hadn't he known her at all? Had he been ashamed of her? Or ashamed of Luke's mother Maggie? None of it made sense to her. She had discussed the situation over and over with Michael, who had tried to assure her that her father would probably have told her when the time was right, had he not died unexpectedly. But Grace wasn't so sure. She wished she could believe him but there was no escaping the fact that for whatever reason, he had kept it from her.

The one thing Grace did believe was that Luke had been as in the dark as she was about the whole thing. It begged the question why his mother had never told him who his father really was either. Had Maggie known about Grace, and if so, why hadn't she told Luke that he had a half-sister? Or why hadn't she come to find Grace to tell her about Luke? And most puzzling of all, why did Glenda Alexander have the only photograph of Grace's father and Luke's mother together? Glenda had hardly known Luke's mother. Luke's friendship with Glenda's son Danny had been the only connection between the two women. Whatever the case, it seemed that Glenda Alexander was the only person who might have answers to their many questions. And whilst Grace believed Luke and Danny when they told her Glenda couldn't be trusted, what other choice did she have?

Grace opened her eyes and looked across at Luke. He was the one good thing to come out of the whole sorry mess. She smiled – her brother. The two of them had spent the last week trying to process this new information that had been landed on them, and they'd grown even closer as a result.

'How is your throat now?' she asked as she noted the fading bruises on his neck. When Glenda had revealed that

Luke and Grace had a relationship of some sort, she had done it in a way that had made Michael think she and Luke were having an affair. His response had been to grab Luke by the throat and try to strangle the truth from him. Fortunately, Grace had arrived in time. Michael felt bad about the whole thing now and had apologised to Luke and Grace, but at the time he had believed himself to be entirely justified.

Luke rubbed at his neck. 'Not too bad,' he said with a soft chuckle. 'But remind me never to get on your husband's bad side.'

'Well, don't worry, you've got your big sister to look out for you now,' she said, starting to laugh.

Luke laughed too. 'Fucking hell. Grace Carter is my big sister. I wish I'd known that when I was in school and Fat Barry used to try and steal my dinner money.'

'Fat Barry?' she asked.

'Yeah. He was a horrible fucker. The school bully. Until me and Danny fought back one day, anyway. He never messed with us, or anyone else after that, actually.'

'Maybe you don't need a big sister to look out for you after all then?' she said with a smile.

'Still nice to have one though,' he said quietly.

'Yeah,' Grace replied softly.

Suddenly, there was too much emotion in the confines of the car to deal with.

'So,' Grace said with a wicked grin, in an attempt to change the subject. 'Who did you spend the afternoon in a hotel with then?'

He laughed again. 'What?'

'You heard me. Michael said you were acting all cagey about a mystery woman—'

'Who he assumed was you,' Luke interrupted her.

'Yes. So, who was she?'

He shook his head. 'I'd rather not say. Not yet.'

'Aw, come on, Luke. You can tell me anything.' She gave him a playful nudge on the arm.

He took a deep breath and she thought he was about to tell her when they were interrupted by Grace's phone ringing.

'Saved by the bell,' he said instead.

Grace answered the phone to Jake. 'Hiya, Son.'

'Hiya, Mum. Is Michael with you? He's not answering his phone.'

'No, I'm with Luke. We're on our way to see Glenda.'

'Oh yeah, I forgot.'

'Have you tried the house phone?' Grace replied.

'Yeah. There's no answer.'

Grace checked the time on her watch. 'Maybe he's at the gym?' she suggested.

'I'll try him again in a bit.'

'Is everything okay?' she asked.

'Yeah. Everything's fine. I just need to ask him about something, that's all,' he replied.

'Okay. I'll let you know if I speak to him.'

Grace ended the call and tried Michael's number herself but it went straight to voicemail. He was probably at the gym like she'd said, and sometimes the reception there was sketchy. She'd try him again later.

Chapter Two

G race stood next to Luke as he knocked on the door to the flat above the nail salon in Huyton. He flashed his eyebrows at her as they heard the chain on the door being drawn back. Two seconds later, Glenda Alexander's wizened face appeared through the crack. She looked them up and down before a semi-toothless smile stretched across her face. She had been expecting them, and no doubt expected some recompense for her trouble. Grace was prepared to bung her a few quid if she provided any useful information.

Glenda opened the door fully and Grace and Luke stepped inside the narrow hallway before following her up the stairs. The flat was thick with cigarette smoke and Grace fought the urge to ask Glenda to open a window. It was probably best not to piss her off too soon.

'Come through,' Glenda said in her croaky voice. 'Can I get either of you a drink?'

'Not for me, thanks,' Grace replied.

'Nor me,' Luke added.

'Suit yourselves,' she said with a shrug as she sat on the worn leather sofa in her living room and lit up a cigarette.

Grace sat on the edge of the armchair and Luke perched himself the chair beside her. It was either that or sit next to Glenda on the nicotine-stained sofa.

'So? You two finally decided to listen to old Glenda, eh? Not as daft as I look, am I?' she cackled.

Grace fought the urge to roll her eyes and she felt Luke's body tense beside her. From the little she knew of Glenda Alexander, she was something of a drama queen, who thrived on being the centre of attention. She'd do anything for the promise of a few quid. As far as Grace was concerned she was lower than pond-life. What kind of mother left her two children to live with a monster who abused them? Grace knew little of Danny and his sister Stacey's backgrounds. They didn't disclose much and she respected their privacy enough to know that they would tell her if they wanted her to know. But she did know that their stepfather had been cruel and violent towards the two of them. One day Danny had fought back, hitting him over the head with a toaster and killing him outright, which had landed him three years in a young offenders' institution for manslaughter. But despite her intense dislike of the woman, Grace knew that the way to deal with the Glendas of the world was to make them feel important – at least until Glenda pissed her off enough to make her resort to other tactics.

'No, you're not daft at all,' Grace said with a fake smile.

'It seems you're the only person who can help us get to the truth, Glenda.'

Glenda sat back and crossed her legs. She lifted her cigarette to her lips, lapping up the attention.

'Can you tell us how you came to have the photograph of Maggie and my father?' Grace asked.

Glenda pursed her lips. 'I told you. I found it in her things. Remember, I came back after she died? I came to your house to pay my condolences. But you told me to clear off,' she spat at Luke.

Luke clenched his fists at his sides. 'Why were you even going through her things?' he hissed. The atmosphere in the room changed in an instant and Grace knew she had to do something to defuse it before Luke and Glenda had a massive row and Glenda refused to speak any further – or, worse, lied just to get her hands on some cash.

Grace placed her hand gently over Luke's fist. 'Why don't you nip to the shop over the road and get Glenda a packet of ciggies?' she suggested.

He frowned and she nodded at him.

'Fine,' he said with a sigh as he stood up. 'But don't let that old *witch* fill your head with a load of shit, Grace,' he spat as he pointed a finger in Glenda's direction.

Glenda was about to retaliate when Grace interrupted. 'Anything else you'd like him to get you, Glenda?' she asked sweetly.

Glenda glanced at her before turning back to Luke and grinning. 'Yeah, how about a nice bottle of whisky too. And not that cheap stuff either. Get me a good one.'

Luke scowled at her as he turned to leave her flat.

'Make it a litre,' Glenda shouted after him.

The next thing they heard was the thump of footsteps on the stairs and then the front door slamming shut.

Grace settled back against the chair and smiled at Glenda. 'Right, now that Luke's out of the way, how about you tell me what Maggie Sullivan was *really* like?'

Glenda smiled back, the twinkle in her eye giving Grace a glimpse of the woman she had been in her youth.

'Well, she was a stuck-up cow for a start.' Glenda started to cackle again.

Grace laughed too, but not for the reason Glenda thought. She laughed because she realised she had the woman right where she wanted her. The thing with people like Glenda was that they thought that everybody shared their dim view of the world. They thought that everyone was out for themselves just like they were.

'I can imagine,' Grace said.

'Always looking down her nose at me, she was. Like she was better than me just because she had a nicer house and a car. My Danny used to go on about her all the time. Drove me mad, he did. Wittering on about how nice her cooking was and how nice Luke's bedroom was. Maggie Sullivan was a snooty cow who thought she was better than the likes of me,' Glenda spat before taking a long drag on her cigarette.

'That must have been annoying,' Grace said sympathetically.

'Fucking right it was. Couldn't believe it when I found out where the snooty mare had really got her money from.

Lady Muck was a gangster's moll,' she snorted. 'No offence,' she quickly added as she looked up at Grace.

'None taken,' Grace assured her. 'I bet you wished you'd known that earlier?'

Glenda nodded emphatically. 'Yeah. Would have taken her down a peg or two, wouldn't it?'

'No doubt. People like that really get my goat too. Pretending to be something they're not,' Grace said, aware of the irony of that statement, but she had to make Glenda believe they were allies, and Maggie Sullivan was their shared enemy right now as far as Glenda was concerned.

'Exactly!' Glenda said with a smack of her lips. 'At least people like you and me don't pretend we're something we're not, do we, girl?'

'No. I can't abide false people, Glenda. And you're right, at least we're honest about who we really are. It's a pity Maggie didn't see things like that. Seemed like she was happy enough to take my dad's money, but she was too ashamed to tell his own son who he was. It's disgraceful.'

Glenda sat forward in her seat. 'I told you, she was a snooty cow. And she took your dad's money all right. Over two hundred grand he left her, you know?'

'Two hundred grand? I had no idea it was that much,' she lied. Patrick had found out how much Maggie and Luke had been left in her father's will, but she had the feeling Glenda was on the verge of revealing more information. 'How do you know_that?'

Glenda grinned at her. 'I went through her stuff, I told ya. I visited to pay my respects and when Luke nipped out to the bank I had a little rummage through her knicker drawer to see what I could find. I was down on my luck, you see. I didn't have a penny to my name, truth be told. I had an idea that might be where the stuck-up mare would keep anything of value, and I knew that Luke wouldn't have gone through her undies like that.'

'You found money?' Grace asked.

'Nah.' Glenda shook her head. 'But I found a letter addressed to Luke, with that photograph and some paperwork. I didn't know what it was. Thought it could have been worth something. So, I slipped it into my pocket. I was gobsmacked when I read it,' she said and sucked air in through her teeth.

Grace closed her eyes and took a deep breath, fighting the urge to tell Glenda what she really thought about her and slap that smug grin from her face. How *dare* she have deprived Luke of that letter from his mother, and the truth about his father, for all those years? 'What did the letter say?' she asked.

'Just a load of crap about how sorry she was and who his dad was. Why she'd never told him.'

Grace swallowed. That letter could have the answers she and Luke were looking for.

'Do you still have it?' Grace asked.

Glenda stared at her, her beady eyes narrowed. 'Maybe. How much is it worth?'

That was the final straw. Grace had gone in there prepared to pay for information if she had to, but she'd be damned if she was going to pay this vile old witch to get Luke's letter from her.

Grace stood up and crossed the room in two quick

strides. She towered over the older woman. 'Consider the fags and whisky that Luke has gone to buy you your payment. God help me, Glenda, if you don't bring me that letter right now, I will have my men come in here and tear everything in this place to shreds until they find it. And when they're finished with this shit-hole, they'll start on you!' Grace hissed.

Glenda stared up at her, her mouth open in shock, their fake camaraderie now vanished. 'Okay, keep your knickers on. I'll get it,' she snapped.

Grace glared at her as she got up from the sofa and wandered into her bedroom. A few moments later, she came back with a small yellowed envelope. It simply said *Luke* on the front. Glenda handed it over and Grace took it from her, placing it in her coat pocket. She was desperate to open it and read the contents, but it wasn't hers. It was for Luke to read and he had been denied that right for far too long already. She just hoped it would contain some answers for her too.

Just then, Luke came back into the flat. He placed a blue plastic carrier bag on the coffee table, dropping the flat keys he'd taken next to them. Grace could see a bottle of Grant's whisky poking out of the top. 'There,' he snapped to Glenda before turning to Grace. 'Did you get anything from the old cow? Are we done here?'

'Yes, we're done,' Grace replied. She didn't want to give Glenda the satisfaction of seeing the pain in Luke's face when he realised what she'd done all of those years before. 'Come on, let's go.'

They headed towards the door when Glenda shouted. 'I

want to see my children, Luke. You'd best have a word with them and persuade them to come and see their old mum if you don't want them finding out about what you did.'

Luke turned on his heel, but Grace put a hand on his arm and stopped him from storming back into the room. Instead she turned and walked back over where the older woman stood. At least Glenda had the good sense to take a step back.

'You know who I am, Glenda. And you know who Luke is to me. Whatever it is he's done, Danny and Stacey will never find out about it. Because if they do, you won't live to see the light of another day, never mind your children. Do you understand me?' she snarled.

Glenda sniffed. 'I just want to see my kids,' she said, shaking her head.

Grace glared at her.

'I won't tell them nothing,' she said with a roll of her eyes.

'Make sure that you don't. I'll be watching you, Glenda,' Grace said before turning on her heel. Together, she and Luke left the stinking flat, slamming the door behind them.

They were walking along the street when Grace spoke again. 'What the hell did you do?'

Luke raised an eyebrow. 'I appreciate you going to bat for me even though you didn't know what you were defending me for.'

Grace shrugged. 'You're family. There's not a lot I wouldn't back you over, Luke. But what did you do?'

'My mum died a couple of months after Danny got out

of prison and just before Stacey got out of that kids' home. Glenda turned up at my house claiming she wanted to pay her respects. She also started making noises about seeing Danny and Stacey and how they could all be one big happy family again. But she was off her head on crack and all she really wanted was her next fix. Danny was just getting his life back on track, and although Stacey was still in that hell-hole, it was only a few weeks before her sixteenth birthday. I knew she'd be getting out then. My mum had left me some money, so I paid Glenda off,' he said with a sigh. 'I gave her five grand if she'd agree to leave Liverpool and stay away from Danny and Stacey. I know it wasn't my finest hour, but I was doing it for them. I should have told them, and I always planned to, but the timing never seemed right.'

Grace understood completely where Luke was coming from and why he'd made the decision that he did. But she also knew first-hand the damage that secrets and lies could do, and she knew that Danny and Stacey would be hurt and angry if they found out.

'I understand why you did it. Even if it wasn't your decision to make, I know that you made it for the right reasons,' she said to him. 'I don't think any good would come from them finding out now, but in my experience these things have a way of coming out, no matter how hard we try and bury them.'

'Well, let's hope Glenda keeps her trap shut then,' he said.

'I think Glenda is going to be a pain in our arse for some time to come, Luke,' she said with a sigh.

'Well, did you at least get something useful from her?' Luke asked.

'Actually, I did,' Grace replied quietly as she slipped the letter from her pocket and held it out to him.

Luke took it from her. 'What's this?' he asked as he turned the envelope over in his hands.

'It's from your mum. Glenda took it when she found the photograph.'

Luke stared at her for what felt like an eternity, his eyes searching hers.

'I know,' was all she could she think of to say.

'I'm going to fucking kill her,' he seethed as he turned back in the direction of Glenda's flat.

Grace put her hand on his shoulder. 'Whilst I agree with the sentiment, I'm not sure that's a good idea. Besides, don't give her the satisfaction of knowing that she's hurt you.'

He frowned at her but then he nodded. 'I told you she was evil.'

'Well, on that point, I'm in full agreement,' she said as they walked towards the car.

'Have you read it?' Luke asked.

'Of course not,' Grace replied. 'Why don't we get out of here and you can read it when you get home?'

Luke looked at her, suddenly appearing somewhat dazed.

'Want me to drive?' she asked.

He took his keys out of his pocket and handed them to her. 'Yeah, thanks, Grace.'

Grace smiled at him. 'Come on then.'

Chapter Three

Luke was lost in his thoughts as he walked up the path of his house. Grace had driven them both to her house and then he'd driven home himself, but he could barely remember doing it. He'd planned to read his mother's letter when he got home, but he had felt the weight of it in his pocket and had ended up reading it in the car whilst Grave was driving. He could hardly believe that Glenda had had stolen it from him.

Still lost in thought, he didn't even notice the front door opening as he reached it. He held out his key to put in the lock and then jumped when he saw her standing there with an anxious look on her face. He'd given her a key to his house so that they didn't have to keep sneaking around in hotels. He didn't know why he was so surprised to see her there. She'd been just as anxious about his visit to Glenda Alexander as he was.

'Stace!' he said as he jumped back, placing his hand over his hammering heart.

'Sorry. I didn't mean to startle you. I saw your car pull up.'

He shook his head. 'It's okay – I was in a world of my own. Sorry.'

Stacey stepped back and he walked inside. He put an arm around her waist and pulled her to him for a kiss. She leaned into him, kissing him back, and for a few blissful seconds, all thoughts of her evil bitch of a mother were purged from his mind.

'How did it go?' she asked when they stopped for breath.

Luke wasn't sure how to answer that. He was still processing what had happened that afternoon himself. The fact that Glenda could be so cruel as to steal that letter and keep it from him for all these years was incomprehensible to him. But then he looked at Stacey and thought of the misery and pain that woman had inflicted on her own children, and realised that stealing his mother's letter was one of her lesser crimes. He brushed Stacey's cheek softly with his knuckles. How anyone could ever hurt this woman was beyond his reasoning. 'Not great,' he admitted. He would tell her about the letter later, when he'd had a chance to read it again. Besides, he wasn't quite sure how he would explain the fact that Glenda had come to be in possession of the letter without revealing the fact that she had come back all those years earlier. 'She wants to see you and Danny,' he said instead.

As expected, Stacey didn't take that news well. She rolled her eyes. 'As if! Deluded old cow! Did she know anything about your mum and Grace's dad though?'

'Not a lot more than we'd already pieced together ourselves.'

'Oh. I'm sorry. I'd hoped she might have some answers for you.'

'Me too. But I don't feel much like talking about your mum right now,' he said with a grin as he ran his hands down to her behind and pressed his body into hers. He wanted to change the subject and he also wanted to stop thinking about it all for a few hours. It made his head hurt.

'Oh? What do you want to talk about then?' Stacey replied with a grin.

'Actually, I don't want to do much talking at all.'

'Well, I can arrange that,' Stacey breathed as she pulled his head to hers and kissed him again.

Luke ran his fingers through Stacey's dark curls as she lay facing him in bed. His heart had only just stopped pounding in his chest after their afternoon exertions. She smiled at him and he studied her face. She was the most beautiful woman he had ever seen in his life. She made him laugh like no one else could, except maybe for her brother.

At the reminder of his best mate, Luke groaned inwardly. Any time he spent with Stacey was always eventually overshadowed by the fact that they were keeping their relationship hidden from Danny. At first, it had made sense. He and Stacey had ignored their attraction to each other for as long as they could. They'd both known Danny wouldn't be overly thrilled about it, and also it would have been too awkward if things didn't work out between them. They had decided to wait until they were sure they had something worth telling him about, before they poked the proverbial bear. But that had been two months ago now and Luke was sure that Stacey was the woman he wanted to spend the rest of his life with.

'We need to tell Danny about us.'

Stacey groaned and buried her head in Luke's chest. 'Really?' she asked.

'Yes. Really,' Luke said. 'I can't keep lying to him, Stace.'

'Well, we're not exactly lying to him. We're just not being forthcoming with the truth. That's different.'

'I'm not sure Danny will see it in quite the same way,' Luke said with a flash of his eyebrows.

'Oh, God,' Stacey said as she put a hand over her eyes.

Suddenly, Luke was worried that there was more to her reluctance than Danny's disapproval and the inevitable interrogation they'd both be subject to. Although he was only four years older than her, Danny had practically raised Stacey. He was going to be pissed off, but it was nothing they couldn't handle. It wasn't like they were just fucking around.

'Don't you think we should tell him?' He placed his hand under Stacey's chin and tilted her face to look at him.

She blinked at him. 'Of course we should,' she said with a sigh. 'But you know he's going to overreact.'

'I'll tell him if you like,' Luke offered.

'No, you won't,' she said. 'I'm not leaving you to deal with him alone.'

Luke laughed. The fact that she was fearless was another

reason he loved her so much. 'Okay. Let's tell him as soon as we can then, eh? I'm working with him all week and I want to get it out in the open. Then he can kick me in the nuts and get it over with.'

'He won't hurt you. I'll protect you,' Stacey said with a smile.

'Oh, well, I feel much safer now.'

'I'll just tell him how much I love you, and then he can't stay angry for long,' she said with a flutter of her eyelashes.

'You love me?' Luke asked, raising his eyebrows. She'd never said that to him before.

She blushed and looked down, as though she'd been caught off guard. He tilted her chin up towards his face again. 'I love you too, Stace.'

Chapter Four

Grace was making Belle and Oscar a snack when Michael walked into the kitchen. He gave his two youngest children a kiss on the head as he passed them before making his way to Grace. He slipped his arms around her waist and kissed her on the lips.

'Hi, babe,' he said, his brown eyes twinkling.

'Hello, handsome,' she replied before she turned back to the kitchen counter.

Michael took a glass from the cupboard beside her and ran the cold water tap.

'Did Jake get hold of you?' Grace asked. She'd almost forgotten about her earlier conversation with Jake after the eventful afternoon with Luke.

'Yeah. He'll be here in a minute. He left the club just behind me. Him and Danny want to have a look through my old CDs.'

'Oh? Why?'

He shrugged. 'Some old-school night at the club or something.'

'Doesn't the DJ usually bring his own music to these things?'

'Nobody has a collection like mine though, do they? I've got bootlegs that don't even exist anymore,' he said with such a sense of pride that Grace couldn't help but laugh. He had insisted on bringing his huge collection of dance music CDs to their new house, despite her saying they should bin the lot of them. She had to admit they did sometimes come in handy for parties. Michael and his brother, Sean, had been massive dance music fans back in the nineties and their scouse house collection was unrivalled, but almost three decades later Grace wasn't sure it still held the same kudos. Michael however, refused to part with it. She was surprised he was allowing Jake to borrow any.

'What?' he said with a grin.

'Have I ever told you how much I love you?' she said as she pulled him back to her.

'Not often enough, Mrs Carter,' he said with a growl.

They were interrupted by the sound of the kitchen door bursting open.

'Jake!' Belle and Oscar screeched in excitement. They adored their big brothers and although Jake and Connor were regularly at the house, a visit from either of them was always a major event to Grace's youngest children.

'Hello, little monsters,' Jake shouted.

They ran towards him, but Belle's excitement was about to go into overdrive when she saw who walked into the kitchen behind her big brother.

'Danny!' she screamed.

Grace smiled at her daughter. She had taken quite a shine to Danny Alexander and in return he was great with both her and Oscar.

'Hello, little Bella,' he said with a grin as he scooped her up into his arms.

'Hi, Mum,' Jake said.

'Hiya, Son,' she replied.

Danny smiled and nodded an acknowledgement.

'Can we look at those CDs then, Michael?' Jake asked.

'Yeah. They're in the garage. Knock yourselves out, lads. You'd better take these two with you though,' he said, indicating his two youngest children.

'Come on, you tiny terrors,' Jake said as he shepherded them out of the room.

'Your toast is almost ready,' Grace called after them, but they paid no attention. She shrugged. They preferred their toast cold anyway.

She turned her attention back to Michael.

'Did you go to the gym?' she asked.

'Yeah. Me and Sean had a spar. Then I nipped to the club to see the lads. How was your afternoon with Zelda?' he asked with a flash of his eyebrows.

Grace rolled her eyes. He insisted on referring to Glenda as Zelda because he said she resembled someone from *Terrahawks*, a programme he and Sean used to watch when they were kids. Grace hadn't watched the show herself but Michael had shown her a picture on the internet and she had to admit the resemblance was uncanny.

'Make us a brew and I'll tell you about it,' she said as she finished slathering peanut butter onto the children's toast.

'Coming right up.' He gave a mock salute.

A few minutes later, Grace and Michael were sitting at their kitchen table with fresh mugs of tea. Grace told Michael about their visit to Glenda and the letter which she had stolen from Luke's mother's bedroom and kept from him for the past eight years.

'What a nasty piece of work,' he said as took a swig of his tea. 'Did Luke read the letter?'

'He was going to wait until he got home, but he read it in the car. I think it was burning a hole in his pocket. He was quiet. It was hard to know what was going through his head. I didn't ask to see it but he told me I should read it, so I did. It was basically an apology for not telling him about his father, or about me. They had a whirlwind romance and she fell pregnant. Who knows what her real reasons were for keeping her secret? She said they had always planned to tell me about their relationship, but then my father had died unexpectedly and she hadn't wanted to intrude on my grief. As time went on, she felt it got harder to tell either of us the truth – so she didn't. It's a shame, but that's what it is. I'm not sure there's any more of the story to know,' Grace finished with a shrug.

Michael placed his warm hand over hers. 'At least you know they were planning on telling you. Your dad wasn't planning on keeping you in the dark.'

'But she was six months pregnant when he died. He should have told me before then. Was he waiting until the baby was actually born?'

'I don't know, love. But I do know that your dad adored you. Nothing else that happened changes any of that.'

Grace looked at him and smiled. 'I know you're right,' she said with a sigh.

'But it fucking hurts when someone we love and trust lies to us,' he finished for her, pulling her up and onto his lap. 'Give yourself some time to wrap your head around it all. Less than two weeks ago you thought you were an only child, and now you have a brother.'

He was right. She didn't have a chance to tell him about Luke's other little secret before Jake and Danny came barrelling back into the kitchen, each holding a toddler under one arm and a stack of CDs under the other.

'God, we've only been gone for ten minutes. Can you two get a room?' Jake said with a laugh.

'Erm, we have a room. Plenty of them. But you lot are always hanging around,' Michael replied good-naturedly.

'Well, we'll sod off and leave you in peace then.' Jake winked at Danny. 'Do you two want McDonalds?' he asked Belle and Oscar, who shouted their agreement loudly.

'Don't keep them out too late,' Grace said. 'And not too much sugar,' she added as they were retreating out of the door.

'We'll have them back by seven. See you both later,' Danny said as he closed the door behind them.

'Looks like we have the place to ourselves for a couple of hours,' Michael said as he nibbled Grace's neck. 'I was going to grab a shower. Why don't you join me?'

'You have sex on the brain,' she said, wrapping her arms around his neck.

'Well, I happen to find my beautiful wife completely irresistible,' he said with a grin. 'So it's not really my fault, is it?'

Chapter Five

L uke Sullivan walked down the corridor of The Blue
Rooms towards the offices at the back. He was
looking for Danny, who always seemed to be in the place
lately. They had some business to take care of, but Luke also
wanted to see what kind of mood Danny was in. After their
discussion the previous day, he and Stacey had decided to
tell Danny about their relationship.

The club was closed to customers during the day but
Jake and Connor used it as a base for their operations.
Although Luke and Danny ran Cartel Securities, they also
worked on any job that Jake and Connor needed them on.
He and Danny were effectively hired muscle, and they were
paid well for it. The four of them worked well together and
Luke trusted the three of them with his life. They felt much
more than just friends and business partners – they were
family.

Luke walked past some of his bouncers who were
milling around in the hallway. They worked security on any

job that Jake and Connor needed them. It hadn't taken Luke long to figure out that Cartel Securities was the legitimate front for the entire Carter/Conlon empire and along with the usual security work, his bouncers were required on any number of different jobs. As he approached Jake's office, Luke saw the door was open and was surprised to see Connor and his fiancée Jazz inside.

'All right, mate?' Connor said.

'Hi, Luke,' Jazz added with a smile.

'Hiya. I was looking for Danny. Is he here?' Luke asked.

'Nah, mate. Him and Jake went to meet a contact over some new vans or something.'

'Vans?' Luke said. He hadn't heard any talk of needing new vans.

Connor shrugged. 'Something like that. They shouldn't be long though. They've been gone a few hours. You can wait in here if you like. I've got some stuff to sort out with the lads and then me and Jazz are off home. Paul is staying at his nan and grandad's for the night.'

Luke smiled at him. Connor's face always lit up like a Christmas tree whenever he mentioned his son, Paul, who was only five months old. He was Connor and Jazz's first child, but Luke sensed they'd be adding to their brood pretty soon.

'I'm looking forward to an early night,' Jazz said with a yawn.

'Yep. Me too,' Connor said with a wink.

'Connor! Behave yourself,' Jazz admonished him although Luke got the feeling she didn't mean it at all.

'Help yourself to a drink, Luke,' Connor said as he

started to walk out of the room. He stopped and gave Jazz a kiss on the lips on his way past her. 'I won't be long, babe. Don't give Luke a hard time while I'm gone.'

'As if I would,' she purred as she placed her hand on Connor's cheek.

Luke grabbed himself a can of Coke from the fridge in the office and offered Jazz one. She shook her head, indicating the coffee on the desk beside her. Luke sat on the small sofa in the corner of the office. 'How's things, Jazz?'

'Great. Paul's started to sleep much better now so I feel vaguely human again,' she said with a laugh.

'He's staying with Grace and Michael tonight then?' Luke asked. Jazz's parents were both dead, and he doubted that Connor or Jazz would be happy leaving their son with Connor's mum, Cheryl.

'Yep. It's his first time away from me though. I miss him already,' she said, pulling a sad face.

'Not enough to go and pick him up though?' Luke laughed.

'God, no!' She laughed with him. 'I am sooo looking forward to my lie-in tomorrow. Besides, I think Michael and Grace might refuse to give him back to me if I did. They've been asking to have him overnight for ages. So, who am I to deny them their beautiful grandson?'

'You might be right. Grace was only telling me yesterday how much she was looking forward to having him.'

'Everything okay with you, Luke?' Jazz asked as she took a sip of her coffee.

'Yeah. Why?' He avoided her gaze as she studied his face intently.

'You just look like there's something on your mind, that's all. Woman trouble?'

'Jesus, are all you Carter women mind-readers?' he asked with a shake of his head.

'Well, I'm not a Carter just yet,' Jazz said as she fingered her engagement ring. 'But I have been learning from the best.'

'My sister been teaching you all her tricks of the trade, has she?' he asked – realising that he'd called Grace his sister and for the first time it hadn't felt completely weird.

'She certainly has. But back to my question. So, it is woman trouble then?'

'You could say that.'

'Anything I can help with?'

Luke looked at Jazz. She was an incredible woman. She always looked stylish and well groomed. If you passed her on the street you might think she was arrogant or stuck up because she carried herself with a confidence that he'd rarely seen in a woman, but actually she was down to earth and warm. And, much like his sister, she had a way of making you want to spill your darkest secrets. 'I don't think so, thanks, Jazz. I think I need to sort this out for myself,' he said.

Suddenly, she sat forward in her seat. 'Oh, is this the secret hotel woman Connor told me about?'

Luke shook his head. 'Bloody hell! Is anything sacred in this family?'

'Nope,' Jazz replied with a smile. 'Not unless you specifically ask it to be. But we can all keep a secret when we need to. You don't have to tell me, but I bet I could help,' she offered. 'I've pretty much done it all when it comes to relationships. I give great advice. Try me?'

Luke looked up at the office door and then back at Jazz. 'I'd have to ask you to keep it secret and I don't want to put you in that position.'

'I'll keep your secret,' she said with a grin. 'Except from Connor. If I can't tell him, then it's probably best you don't tell me.'

Luke thought about it for a moment. He trusted Connor and didn't think he'd have a problem with him and Stacey seeing each other. He realised he could do with a woman's perspective. A woman who knew both him and Danny. 'The girl I've been seeing. It's Stacey,' he said quietly.

'Danny's sister Stacey?' Jazz asked. 'Your best mate's little sister?'

'Fuck, don't say it like that, Jazz,' Luke sighed.

Jazz started to laugh. 'Relax. I'm just messing with you. What's so bad about that? You're both consenting adults. You seem like you'd make a good couple, actually.'

'But you know how protective Danny is of her,' Luke said.

'He is. But I'm pretty sure he realises she's a grown woman and she has grown-up relationships. There is no one Danny trusts more than you. If you think about it, you're the perfect choice,' she replied with a shrug.

'I'm not sure Danny will see it that way.'

'Of course he's going to be a bit put out at first. Especially if you two have been keeping this from him for a while. He'll be worried that he's going to lose one or both of you, so just reassure him that won't happen. He'll get over it soon enough. I promise you. But you should definitely tell him sooner rather than later.'

Luke frowned at her. 'You sound very sure of yourself.'

Jazz leaned forward in her chair and stared at him. 'Luke,' she purred. 'If there is one thing I know, it is how men's minds work. I know exactly what makes them tick.'

As if to prove her point, Connor Carter, one of the most powerful and dangerous men in the North West, walked into the office. 'Are you ready, babe? Can we go home?' he asked as he planted a kiss on her forehead.

'Yes. But can we stop by Antonelli's for a takeaway? I know you wanted a curry but I really fancy Italian. I'll phone ahead and ask Steph to get it ready.'

'Anything you want, babe,' he replied.

Jazz grinned as she stood up and picked up her handbag. 'Bye, Luke,' she said.

'See you later, mate,' Connor said with a grin as he wrapped his arm around Jazz's waist.

'See yous,' Luke replied and watched as they walked out. Maybe Jazz did know what she was talking about after all.

Chapter Six

Luke and Danny sat in their office at Cartel Securities discussing Luke's visit to Danny's mother two days earlier. Luke left out Glenda's threats to expose him for paying her off all those years earlier, but he told Danny everything else that had passed between them, including the fact that she wanted to see him and Stacey.

'Stacey won't see her,' Danny said when Luke finished speaking.

'I know. But what about you? Are you going to?'

Danny looked out of the window. He didn't know what to do. His relationship with his mother was far more complicated than Stacey's was. Danny had been fourteen when their mother had left, and Stacey had only just turned ten. Danny was burdened, in a way that Stacey wasn't, with memories of the woman Glenda had been before drugs and drink had taken over her life.

Until he was seven, Glenda had looked after him and Stacey well enough. She was never a contender for mother

37

of the year, but she'd always made sure they were fed and clothed. She had ensured they went to school and were always clean and healthy. They even had the occasional day trip to Southport and New Brighton. But Stacey didn't remember any of that and Danny wished that he didn't either, because the knowledge that she had been capable of loving them but had chosen not to was more painful than anything else.

Glenda had met their stepfather, Steve, on a night out at the local pub. Danny had been home looking after Stacey, who had been three years old at the time, when their mother had arrived home with this strange man. Danny was used to his mum 'just popping out' for a few hours and leaving him in charge. He might have only been seven but he was a sensible kid and was used to spending the odd evening on his own. His mum would put Stacey to bed and then leave him with a couple of videos, a bag of crisps and a Lion Bar, and he would entertain himself until she came home. He always waited up for her and when she got back, she always gave him an extra long hug and called him her 'Danny Boy'. He could still recall the sickly sweet smell of the alcohol on her breath mixed with her cheap perfume. It was a scent that had always comforted him. She was always a little bit happier when she'd been on one of her evenings out.

But the night she came back with Steve was completely different. She'd ignored Danny when he'd called her name and had gone straight to the kitchen instead. He'd heard hushed voices and had followed her out there. He'd seen her pressed against the kitchen counter by a large man who had his hands on her in a way that had made young Danny feel unsettled. Instead of greeting him with a hug like she usually did, his mother shouted at him to get out. Even at seven years old, Danny could see that there was something wrong with her eyes. They were glazed over in a way he'd never seen them before.

'Yeah, get out, you little scrote,' Steve had hissed.

Danny had scarpered and crawled into bed with Stacey. He never slept in her girly bed usually, but something had warned him that Steve wasn't to be trusted. From that moment on their lives had changed completely. Steve never left and Danny would later discover that the reason for his mother's glassy-eyed look was heroin. She was an addict within the month and soon nothing of his or Stacey's was safe. Their toys, their clothes – anything that could make her or Steve a few quid was flogged.

Danny had needed to start looking after Stacey more and more. Making sure she had food and that she was clean and went to school. By the age of eleven, he was stealing food and anything else he could get his hands on so he and Stacey could eat. Then he met Luke and his mum Maggie, and she took Danny under her wing, trying to look after him as much as she could. She used to pick up second-hand clothes and toys for Stacey too – nothing too fancy so it wouldn't be a target for Steve or Glenda's thieving. Danny often wondered if he and Stacey would have managed as well as they did if it hadn't been for Maggie.

But what Danny had hated the most was the fact that Steve was a cruel bastard who thought nothing of giving him or his mum a slap, a punch or a kick whenever he fancied. Anything could set him off and Danny took the worst of his beatings. He was emotionally cruel too and enjoyed causing Danny, his mum and Stacey misery. Their mum finally had enough and walked out when he was fourteen and Stacey just ten, leaving her children to the mercy of a sadistic prick.

By the time Danny was fifteen, though, he had learned to fight back – and he was good at it too. Steve started to leave him alone after that. But when Danny came home from school one day and found Steve with his hands around Stacey's throat, Danny finally snapped. He picked up the nearest thing he could find, which happened to be a toaster, and smashed it over the back of Steve's head with every ounce of strength he could muster. Steve had never put his hands on anyone again and Danny had got six years for manslaughter. Every day of the three years he spent inside had been worth it to end that fucker's life.

'So, are you going to see her, or what?' Luke asked again, interrupting Danny's train of thought.

'I don't know, mate. I kind of feel like I should.'

'Why? You owe her nothing, Danny,' Luke said.

'But she's my mum, isn't she? I feel like I should at least hear her out. I mean, why has she even come back? It's been fourteen years.'

'Probably because she heard you've just taken over the biggest security firm in the North West. She's following the money, Danny. That's why she's back. To see what she can get from you.'

Danny looked at his best mate. Luke had always looked out for him, and for Stacey too. Luke hated their mother almost as much as they did and he understood his best mate's feelings on the matter. But Danny had other motives too. Maybe she would finally give him a reason why she left them? Maybe there was a reasonable explanation that he'd just never considered? And if there was even the slightest hope of that, then he had to take the chance.

Chapter Seven

Danny turned off the engine of his BMW 3 Series and looked out of the window at the small row of shops. His mother's flat was the one above the nail salon with the garish pink neon sign. He'd spent the night tossing and turning and wondering what to do about her request to see him. He still didn't know if he was making the right decision.

He took his phone out of his pocket and unlocked the screen before opening his list of recent calls. His finger hovered over his two most recent ones – Jake and Luke. He toyed with calling one of them although he didn't know why. Perhaps to convince him he was a grown man and capable of spending ten minutes in the company of the woman who had given birth to him? Or was he hoping they might talk him out of going through with it? He imagined Luke would do the latter.

Danny slipped the phone back into his jacket pocket with a sigh. If his mother was back in Liverpool, then he would have to face her eventually – so he might as well get it out of the way. He stepped out of his car and onto the street, kicking an empty Strongbow can out of his way as he walked across the pavement. The women in the nail salon looked at him as he walked past the window. One of them waved and winked at him and the two girls either side of her started laughing. In usual circumstances, he would have winked back, but he could barely focus on anything other than the sound of his heartbeat thumping in his ears.

He reached the door at the side of the salon and took a deep breath before ringing the bell. He looked down at his finely tailored suit and his expensive shoes and silently admonished himself. The watch he was wearing probably cost more than a year's rent on the whole building he was standing in front of. This was how he usually dressed for work during office hours, but he should have worn something a little less flashy. Either his mother would resent him for trying to show off or she would have pound signs in her eyes every time she looked at him. Neither of which was particularly appealing to him.

Danny shoved his hands into his trouser pockets and waited for what seemed like an eternity. He was about to turn around and leave when he heard the rattling of the door chain. A few seconds later the door opened and he was confronted by Glenda Alexander. He blinked at her. Time had not been kind to her. Her looks had once been her most treasured possession, yet now they were long gone – no doubt ravaged by her years of drug and alcohol abuse. Still, there was no denying it was her. He felt a swell of emotion in his chest as she looked at him. He wondered if she even recognised him, but after a few seconds her face broke into a gap-toothed smile.

'Hello, Danny Boy,' she said, opening the door wider. 'I was wondering when you'd turn up.' Then she stepped back to allow him inside.

Danny entered the undecorated hallway and followed his mother up the stairs. When they reached the living room, she signalled him to sit down. He looked at the stained sofa and his toes curled. As a kid, he'd had to live in partial squalor and he'd hated it. He'd never been able to take friends home because he was too ashamed. He'd always kept his own room spotlessly clean and tidy, and as an adult he was a clean freak. He hated uncleanliness. He always showered twice a day. He hated the smell of stale food and unwashed bodies. Here in his mother's flat, the smell might not be overly strong but it was lingering. It made him want to retch, and the bile burned the back of his throat before he swallowed it back down.

'You fancy a drink, lad?' she asked him.

He shook his head.

'Fair enough. You going to sit down then?' she said as she sat on the sofa.

Danny chose the armchair, which looked slightly more appealing and wondered how long he would have to scrub his skin clean before he could get the smell of this place from his nostrils later.

Glenda boldly looked him up and down, appraising him. When her eyes landed on his watch, her tongue darted out of her mouth and over her bottom lip. He took a deep breath and willed his heart to stop hammering in his chest.

'So, what brings you here to see your old mum then?' she asked.

He shrugged, not knowing how to answer her. Telling her that he knew she wanted to see him might somehow give her power over him. He was a grown man now, not a little kid. He didn't need her approval. He didn't have to do anything she asked him to.

'Cat got your tongue, Danny?' she cackled.

He frowned at her. Why the hell was he here? 'No,' he said. 'Why did you come back? It's been fourteen years. Why now?'

She opened her mouth as though she was going to say something and then closed it again. She took a cigarette from the table in front of her and lit it. 'Where's your sister?' she snapped.

'She doesn't want to see you.'

At this, Glenda snorted. 'Well, that's charming, isn't it? I only frigging brought her into this world and she can't spare me a few minutes of her time. Cheeky mare.'

'You might have brought her into this world, but you did fuck all else for her,' Danny snapped.

For some reason this made Glenda grin. 'Same old Danny, eh? Won't lift a finger to protect yourself, but leap to your sister's defence?'

Danny clenched his fists as the anger started bubbling inside him. 'What do you want, Mum?'

She tilted her head and looked at him for a few seconds. 'I just wanted to see my kids. Is that too much to ask? I'm getting on a bit now, Danny. I don't want to spend my old age all alone. I can't get by the way I used to.'

Danny shook his head in disbelief. 'At least you're honest, Mum. I'll give you that.'

'What?' she said, appearing genuinely confused by his statement.

'You came back here for you. It's nothing to do with me or Stacey. You want looking after. And by that you mean money. You wouldn't care who bunged you a few quid every week as long as someone did though, would you?'

She sat back against the chair and took a long drag of her cigarette. 'You should watch your mouth, Danny. I didn't raise you to speak to your mother like that,' she hissed.

He was about to remind her that she didn't raise him at all but thought better of it. There was no point getting into an argument with her. She never backed down because, in her mind, she was always right.

'Isn't that what you want? Money?' he challenged her.

'Well, I'm not going to lie. I don't have a pot to piss in, Danny. This Universal Credit is doing me right in. I should be on bloody disability benefit. I can't work,' she said with a shake of her head. 'I don't understand how they expect people to live on it.' She sniffed.

'Plenty of people manage,' he said, reminded of his childhood, when they'd had to scrape by on whatever pennies were left after her and Steve's needs were taken care of.

'It's not just money though. I wanted to see you too. Especially you. You were always my favourite. My Danny Boy.' She smiled at him and he wondered whether it was intended to evoke some positive memories from him. In fact it had entirely the opposite effect.

He stood up and laughed. 'You're fucking deluded,' he spat. This woman was rotten to the core, but she was still his mother. He would send her a few hundred quid each month to make sure she had enough to cover her bills, but beyond that, he wanted nothing to do with her. He was about to tell her that when she looked up at him. Her face had changed completely. Whereas before there had been some softness to it, now it was twisted up in anger.

'Who do you think you are, speaking to me like that? Showing up in your fancy car and your fancy clothes, pretending to be something you're not. You think you're better than me now, *Son*?'

She stood up and walked over to him, jabbing a bony finger in his chest as she sneered. 'Don't ever forget I know who you really are, Daniel. Do you think your new friends would even give you the time of day if they knew what you were? They would drop you faster than a flaming bag of dog shit if I told them. They would be disgusted, and quite rightly too. I'm disgusted by you, and I'm your mother!' she screeched.

Danny flinched and stepped back from her. He wasn't a stranger to her hatred, but he hadn't been the direct target of it for over a decade.

She started laughing then and suddenly he felt like a little boy again. She had taunted him all his life. He was filled with rage and shame. He felt the tightness in his chest. Suddenly, all he wanted was to be out of that room. He brushed past her and headed for the stairs.

'I'll be in touch, Danny Boy,' she shouted after him. 'I have a lifestyle to maintain.' She started cackling again as he ran down the stairs and out into the fresh air. As soon as his feet touched the pavement, he bent double and heaved the contents of his stomach onto the concrete, thankful that he hadn't eaten breakfast.

Wiping his mouth with the back of his hand, Danny straightened up and walked to his car. His mother's words echoed in his ears. Not only the ones she had just spoken, but all her years of accusations and torment. He was the reason his and Stacey's lives had been ruined, and his mother's too, according to her. He was the reason Stacey had grown up without a father. She was right too. When people found out what he really was, they would never look at him the same way again. All they would see was a monster. Jake would never trust him around his daughter Isla. Grace and Michael wouldn't let him near Belle and Oscar. They would be disgusted by him too. Maybe his mother was right. If she couldn't even love him, then who could?

Danny rested his head against his cool steering wheel as he waited for the nausea to pass. He realised he had no choice but to give in to his mother's demands. At least all she seemed to want was money – for now.

Chapter Eight

Danny had been home and changed his clothes after his visit to his mother. He'd scrubbed himself in the shower for half an hour trying to get the stench of her flat off his skin, but it was as though it was embedded in his nose. Now he was sitting in his office at Cartel Securities waiting for Luke when their secretary, Carla, popped her head through the door.

'There's a woman on the phone demanding to speak to you, Danny. She claims she's your mother.'

Danny rolled his eyes. 'Tell her I'm in a meeting.'

'Of course,' she said, and left the room.

As Danny flicked through the staff rotas on his desk, the phone rang again. He could hear Carla speaking to the caller and he went back to his paperwork. Then phone rang again. And again. Each time Carla answered and spoke briefly.

After the fourth ring, Carla came back into his office. 'She says it's urgent, and she won't stop calling until she speaks to you. I'm happy to keep fobbing her off if that's what you want though?'

Danny ran a hand over his jaw and sighed. 'Put her through.'

Carla smiled at him as she slipped back out of the office and closed the door.

A few seconds later, the call came through to the landline and Danny answered.

'At last. I've been phoning for twenty minutes,' she slurred and he wondered whether she was high, pissed – or both.

'Well, I'm busy. What the hell do you want?'

'I'm behind with my rent and I thought you could help me out? You wouldn't want to see your poor old mum out on the streets now, would you?'

'You're a fucking disgrace,' Danny hissed.

'Now, now, Danny. You don't want me to tell all your new friends your dirty little secret now, do you? All I need is a few hundred quid. That's nothing to you. Don't think I didn't notice that fancy watch and flash motor you showed up at my flat in.'

Danny swallowed. He wouldn't put it past her to try and ruin this new life he'd built for himself. She'd always been a bitter, jealous woman, but he'd hoped that time would have mellowed her. It seemed it had only made her worse.

'Will five hundred cover it?' he snapped.

'For now. But then next month I'll only be in the same position again, I expect. I told you, this universal credit is a joke, you know?' She was slurring even more now. 'How they expect people to live on it is beyond me.'

'I'll arrange to send you five hundred a month,' he snarled. 'But that's it. And if you want to keep it that way, then you'd better keep your mouth shut. Because if anyone gets even a sniff of who my dad is...'

'I won't breathe a word.' She started to cackle. 'Now, how do I get my money, Son?'

He shuddered. She hadn't been his mother for a very long time. 'I'll have someone drop it off within the hour. He'll post it through your door. Don't speak to him.'

'Ashamed of me?'

'Yes!' he growled.

'Cheek.' She sniffed. 'You should have more respect for your mother.'

Danny shook his head and put the phone down. He hoped this would be the last he heard of Glenda for a while, but he had a sinking feeling that it wouldn't.

Danny was sat deep in thought when Luke walked into their office. He looked up and plastered a smile on his face to disguise the anxiety that was sitting like a ball in the pit of his stomach. He blinked in surprise when he saw his sister walking in too.

'Hiya, Stace. What are you doing here?' he said as he stood up, walked over to her and gave her a hug. His conversation with their mother had him rattled and although he was usually pleased to see Stacey, at that particular moment he would have preferred some time on his own. He needed to figure out who he could trust enough to deliver Glenda's money and not ask any questions. He wondered why Stacey was there to see him and how he would get rid of her without being rude or raising her suspicions.

'I wanted to talk to you,' she said with a smile.

'Actually, we both want to talk to you,' Luke added.

Danny frowned at them both. What could they both need to speak to him about? He swallowed. Surely his mother hadn't told them anything. It had only been ten minutes since he'd spoken with her.

'What?' he asked, trying to sound calm.

'Shall we all sit down?' Stacey suggested.

'I'm fine where I am, thanks,' Danny said as he looked between his sister and his best mate and noted the way they looked at each other too. 'What's going on?' He had a sudden feeling that this wasn't about him at all.

Luke cleared his throat. 'Me and Stacey are seeing each other,' he said.

Danny scowled at him. 'What?'

Stacey put a hand on his arm. 'Danny,' she said softly. 'Let us explain.'

He turned to her. 'How long has this been going on?'

'About two months,' she replied.

'Two months! You've been sneaking around behind my back for two months and neither of you thought to tell me?'

'We haven't been sneaking around,' Luke insisted.

'Well, you've been doing God knows what with my sister for two months and I'm only just finding out about it now. If you weren't sneaking around, what else would you call it? Is she the hotel woman?'

Stacey blushed at the question and Danny got his answer.

'For fuck's sake,' he hissed as he sat down and ran a hand over his face. How the hell hadn't he noticed this was going on? But then of course he wouldn't have. Because he'd been sneaking around with Jake for the past two months as well. He'd been too wrapped up in his own love life to notice that the two people he loved and trusted most in the whole world had been lying to him. But hadn't he been doing the same to them too?

'We weren't sneaking around, Danny,' Stacey said as she sat in a chair beside him. 'And we didn't mean for this to happen. But it did. And as soon as we knew it was something serious, we were waiting for the right moment to tell you.'

Danny looked up at Luke.

'I love her, mate,' Luke said with a shrug.

Danny felt the breath leaving his lungs. For some reason, he felt like he was losing both Stacey and Luke.

But then Stacey smiled broadly at Luke and the look on her face made something soften inside Danny. His little sister had been through more heartache in her life than anyone should endure, and she deserved to be happy. Luke was a good guy. He was trustworthy and he treated women with respect. But if something went wrong between them, then would Danny be forced to choose? And how could he choose between his sister and the man who was his brother in every sense of the word?

'We know what we're doing, Danny,' Stacey said as she placed her hand over his. 'And we really want you to be happy for us.'

Danny smiled at her but then he turned to Luke and frowned. 'If you hurt her...' he said, not needing to finish the sentence. The threat was implicit.

'I wouldn't dare,' Luke said as he held his hands up in surrender.

Danny shook his head. This day was getting steadily worse.

He needed a drink.

He needed Jake.

But first, he would deliver his mother's money himself. He didn't need anyone asking questions about why he was paying off the old dragon. The truth was, he would have bunged her a few quid every month anyway, without her resorting to blackmail. But now that she was threatening to tell the world who he really was, he couldn't let anyone he knew have anything to do with her. He stood up and fastened the buttons on his jacket.

'Where are you going? I thought we were going to do the rounds?' Luke asked.

Danny frowned. He'd forgotten about that. He and Luke usually did a check on all their venues together once a week. They'd missed the previous week because Danny had been busy with Jake, and obviously Luke hadn't been overly bothered because he'd had Stacey to keep him occupied. But they couldn't afford to let things slip just because they were both thinking with their dicks instead of their heads.

'I just need to sort something first,' he said. 'I'll only be an hour.'

'Shall I come with you?' Luke offered.

'Nah. Take Stacey home and I'll meet you at The Blue Rooms in an hour.'

'I can come with you. We can drop Stacey off on the way,' Luke said.

'Really. It's fine,' Danny snapped, his tone harsher than he'd intended it to be.

'If you're pissed off with us—' Luke started to say.

'It's not that,' Danny interrupted him. 'I just have something to do. I'll see you in an hour.' He turned to Stacey and kissed her on the cheek. 'See you later, sis,' he said and then he walked out of the office and left them to it.

Chapter Nine

Danny stood at the door to his mother's flat, kicking at the stone step in frustration as he waited for her to answer. There was no way he was going inside this time. The girl from the nail salon who had waved and winked at him earlier was looking at him again through the window and he turned his head and edged closer to the doorway in a futile attempt to shield himself from view. He made a mental note not to visit his mother during daylight hours again. The last thing he wanted was to draw attention to himself and have someone find out he was paying Glenda off.

A few seconds later, the door opened and Glenda leaned against the frame, the gap-toothed smile once more stretched across her face.

'I knew you'd come back, my Danny Boy,' she slurred.

Danny took the wad of notes from his pocket and held them aloft.

Glenda made a grab for them and he jerked his hand

back. 'There's five hundred quid here. You'll get the same on the first of every month, but on the understanding that you stay away from me and Stacey.'

She blinked at him and he noticed her pupils were heavily dilated, meaning she was already off her head on crack. He sighed as he realised that would be where most of his money was going to go. But if it got her off his back, then it was money well spent as far as he was concerned.

'Fine,' she slurred as she made another grab for the money. This time he handed it over.

'You not coming in?' she cackled.

'Fuck off!' he spat and then he turned on his heel and made his way back to his car. He was opening the door when he heard a female voice calling from behind him.

'That's twice I've seen you and your flash motor here today.'

He spun around to see the girl from the nail salon standing in the shop doorway. She was wearing a miniskirt and six-inch heels. Her long blonde hair was styled in the traditional Scouse 'curly blow' and she had tits the size of watermelons. A few months earlier, she would have been just his type. 'What's it to you?' he snarled.

She grinned at him. 'We don't get a lot of your sort round here, that's all.'

'My sort?'

'Yeah. Loaded and good-looking.' She grinned at him. 'Will you be coming back any time soon? Because I know a really nice Chinese up the road.'

He had to give it to her, she wasn't shy in going after what she wanted. He admired that in people. 'You're about two months too late, girl,' he said with a laugh and a shake of his head as he climbed into his car, leaving her standing there staring after him.

Yes, he would definitely make sure not to visit Glenda during the day again.

Danny gripped the steering wheel as he drove back towards the city centre to Jake's club. He hoped that the money he'd just given his mother would buy him some time. He couldn't have her telling anyone who he really was. He'd had no choice but to pay her off, at least until she disappeared again.

He felt a strange feeling of dread settling over him and he couldn't shake it. Even the thought of seeing Jake shortly, which usually made him feel like a horny, lovestruck teenager, wasn't helping.

He swallowed hard as he looked in the rear-view mirror, half expecting to see Glenda running down the street after him with a crackpipe in one hand and a whisky bottle in the other, shouting that she already needed more money. As much as he tried to convince himself otherwise, he knew that his mother's return to Liverpool was only going to bring him a world of grief.

Chapter Ten

Luke sat across the desk from Jake in his office in The Blue Rooms. Jake had taken two cans of Coke from the fridge and handed one to Luke, who took it gratefully. He still wasn't sure whether Danny's reaction to the news about him and Stacey was good or bad. He'd seemed annoyed at first, but then he'd seemed distracted too. Luke had expected at least a punch to the face.

'Where's Danny? I thought he was with you?' Jake asked as he sat down.

'He said he had something to do. He should be here soon.'

'Oh? What did he have to do that didn't involve you?' Jake frowned.

Luke shook his head. 'No idea. But I just gave him some news that I imagine he didn't want to hear. So don't be surprised if he's in a bad mood when he gets here.'

'What news?'

'That I've been seeing Stacey for the past two months,'

Luke said as he looked down at the can in his hands.

'Fucking hell! You dirty dog, Luke,' Jake said, but when Luke looked up, Jake was grinning.

'Piss off. I feel bad enough.'

'Why? You're both adults,' Jake said with a shrug.

'I know that. But she's his little sister. And I feel like shit that we've been lying to him.'

'Well, it's not exactly lying, is it? More like withholding the truth?' Jake said with a grin.

Luke laughed and took a swig of his Coke. 'That's exactly what Stacey said.'

A moment later, Danny walked into the room. He looked on edge and Luke wondered if there was something bothering him other than him and Stacey.

'All right, Danny?' Jake said.

'Yeah,' Danny grunted.

Luke felt the sudden tension in the room and was sure he saw a scowl flicker across Jake's face but then Danny spoke. 'Come on, Luke, we should get going.'

Luke looked at Jake and rolled his eyes before standing up. 'See you later, Jake.'

'Yeah,' Jake said as Luke followed Danny out of the room.

Luke and Danny were driving through Liverpool city centre on their way to their first venue. Danny had hardly spoken two words since they'd got into the car five minutes earlier.

'Did you do what you needed to do?' Luke asked.

'Yeah.'

'Anything I need to know about?'

'No.'

Luke shook his head. 'Well, you're a fucking barrel of laughs tonight, mate.'

'What?'

'Is this about me and Stacey?'

Danny sighed. 'No.'

'I'm sorry we didn't tell you sooner, mate. I hated keeping it from you.'

'So why did you?' Danny snapped.

'Because we didn't know what it was at first. We just wanted to keep it to ourselves until we knew that it was something worth telling you about. Surely you can understand that?'

'Just make sure you look after her,' Danny said before turning back to the window and leaning his forehead on the glass.

'You know I will, mate. But I need you to be okay with this.'

'I'm fine.'

'Well, obviously, you're not. So, if it's not me and Stacey, what's going on with you? Is there something going on I need to know about? Where did you go before?'

'Just forget it, Luke. Everything's fine.'

Luke shook his head and carried on driving. 'Just know that there's nothing you can't talk to me about, Danny.'

'That's rich coming from the fella who's been sneaking about with my sister for the past two months,' Danny snorted but it broke the tension.

'Yeah. Well, do as I say, not as I do,' Luke said with a grin. 'Now are you going to cheer up? Because I don't fancy driving round all night with you when you're being a miserable bastard.'

Danny sighed. 'I'll cheer up if you promise me we can grab a kebab on the way home.'

'Sounds like a plan,' Luke agreed.

A few hours later, Danny walked into Jake's office at The Blue Rooms. It was almost closing time and Jake was drinking a bottle of Budweiser.

'Where's Luke?' Jake asked.

'I dropped him off home. I have no doubt my sister was there waiting for him,' he said and shuddered at the thought.

'How do you feel about the two of them then?'

'It's a bit fucking weird, isn't it? My best mate and my sister. But Luke is a thousand steps up from her last boyfriend, so I suppose I can't complain. And I can't exactly judge them lying to me about it, can I? When I've been sneaking about with you?'

Jake stood up and walked across the room to where Danny was standing. 'Where did you go earlier?'

Danny felt his heart start pounding in his chest. 'When?'

'Before you came here. Luke said you had something to do. But he didn't know what it was.'

'Does it matter where I was?' Danny said. The way Jake was looking at him made him nervous.

'It does when you're looking so fucking shifty about it. You're hiding something from me, and I want to know what it is. Where were you?'

Danny stared at him. What could he say that wouldn't make Jake suspicious? He decided on the truth – at least half of it. 'I went to see my mum,' he eventually said. 'Is that okay with you, Boss?'

Jake ignored the sarcastic comment. 'Again? But you only saw her this morning. Why?'

'She needed some money. She couldn't pay her rent. So I dropped some off to her. I didn't tell Luke because I don't want Stacey to know. I just wanted to give her a few quid and get her out of our lives.'

'And you think she'll stay out of your lives? Especially now that she knows you'll give her money whenever she asks?'

Danny shrugged. 'No. But what was I supposed to do, Jake? She's my mum, for fuck's sake.'

'I know,' Jake said as he put a hand on the back of Danny's neck. 'If you want to give your mum money, it's no one's business but yours. But you're deluded if you think giving her a few quid is going to get her out of your life.'

Danny stared into Jake's bright blue eyes and wished that he could tell him everything. He hated lying to him. 'I don't know what else to do though. I can't see her on the street, can I?' he said with a shrug.

'Okay. I get why you don't want Stacey and Luke to know, but you don't have to keep stuff like that from me. You don't have to keep anything from me.'

Danny looked at him. If only that were true.

Chapter Eleven

The following morning, Jake and Connor were tucking into one of Maria's famous fry-ups in her café on the Dock Road when two teenagers pulled up chairs at either side of their table and sat down. Jake looked up at Connor and raised an eyebrow and Connor shrugged in amusement as he took a bite of his toast.

'Who the fuck are you and why are you interrupting my breakfast?' Jake asked as he looked at the two intruders. They couldn't have been older than seventeen or eighteen at most. One of them still had his teenage pimples peppered across his chin and forehead, and the other was clearly trying to grow a beard but hadn't quite been able to. Instead he had a patchy scruff of bum-fluff sprawled over his chin.

'I'm Jerrod, and this is my brother Devlin,' the spotty one said.

'Ay-ight,' Bum-fluff said with a nod as he stretched his legs and shoved a hand down the front of his trousers.

Jake rolled his eyes. 'Do you mind, I'm trying to eat my

fucking breakfast!' he snapped. 'So do yourselves a favour, and fuck off!'

'We've got a business proposition for you,' Jerrod said as he scowled across the table at his brother, who immediately removed his hand from his balls and sat up a little straighter in his chair.

Connor raised his eyebrows and grinned at Jake but continued eating his breakfast in silence.

'I seriously fucking doubt that. Do you even know what a business proposition is?' Jake said as he looked the pair of them up and down.

Jerrod glared at him and leant forward in his seat. Jake was sure he saw the outline of a gun in the kid's pocket and he fought the urge to slam Jerrod's head into the table. Who did these little gob-shites think they were, coming into their favourite café with a gun and sitting at their table like they knew them? But they were kids, and the café was busy. He put his elbows on the table and leaned towards Jerrod. 'Well, we don't do business in here. So, if you really do have anything worthwhile to say, make an appointment like everyone else.'

'How do we do that?' Devlin asked with a scowl.

'If you two clowns can't figure that out for yourselves, then you're really not worth doing business with. Now I won't tell you again, fuck off!' Jake snarled.

'Come on, Dev,' Jerrod said as he flicked his long hair out of his eyes. 'We'll be in touch, Mr Conlon.'

Then, as quickly as they'd arrived, the two teenagers left the café.

'What the fuck was that?' Jake said and Connor started to laugh.

'Fuck knows, mate. This place is going down the nick.'

'I think the mouthy one had a gun on him, Con,' Jake said incredulously.

'Ah, we were that young once,' Connor reminded him.

'Yeah, but we were cool,' Jake said with a grin. 'And we didn't try and do business with people who were way out of our league while they were trying to eat their bacon and eggs. Can you imagine if we'd pulled shit like that?'

'You got to admire their balls, though,' Connor said, still laughing. 'Just pulling up a chair each and sitting down. Your face was a fucking picture, mate.'

'Admire their balls? I think we've got different ideas of what that means, Con. You call it balls, I call it stupidity.'

'Well, if they've got anything about them, they'll turn up at the club.'

'I'll ask Danny and Luke to do a bit of digging. Who knows what stupid shit these kids are capable of?'

'Well, I know I did stupid shit when I was their age,' Connor said. 'If it wasn't for your mum, I'd have had my arse handed to me more than once.'

Jake could only agree. In fact, when he was nineteen, Connor and his twin brother, Paul, had tried to shoot Jake's father, Nathan Conlon. It wasn't something either of them acknowledged or ever spoke about. There wasn't much love lost between Jake and his dad, but he was still his dad. Connor and Paul had done it for Grace. She hadn't asked them to, but they'd wanted to help her out and prove their loyalty. Still, no matter what stupid stuff he and the twins had ever pulled, they'd never had the brass neck to do what Jerrod and his brother had just done. They'd never been that stupid or arrogant. Had they?

'Probably a good idea to find out who the little pricks are though,' Connor added as he checked his watch. 'We need to meet Gary Mac in an hour. Shall we call in and see Danny and Luke on the way back?'

Jake nodded. Any excuse to see Danny was a good one as far as he was concerned.

It had been two days since Jake and Connor's breakfast had been rudely interrupted by Jerrod and Devlin. Sure enough the two youths had turned up at The Blue Rooms yesterday looking to arrange a business meeting with them. The club manager had contacted Jake and Connor and they'd agreed to sit down and hear what the little ferret-faces had to say last night.

Jake sat behind the desk in his office while Connor lay on the small sofa scrolling through his mobile phone. He looked up to see Danny and Luke walking in.

'Hello, gents,' Jake said.

Connor sat up and put his phone in his jacket pocket.

'What did you find out about the Chuckle brothers then?' Connor asked.

Luke and Danny sat on the chairs near Jake's desk and looked at each other.

'Well?' Jake asked.

'Jerrod and Devlin King,' Luke replied. 'Jerrod's

nineteen and Devlin is almost eighteen. You already know they're brothers, but they are also the leaders of their own crew—'

'What crew?' Jake interrupted.

'They call themselves the Bridewell Blades,' Luke said with a shake of his head as Danny rolled his eyes.

'What?' Connor asked before starting to laugh.

'Bridewell Bell-ends more like,' Jake added.

'They live on the Bridewell Estate in Kirkdale. They basically rule the place through bullying and intimidation. The whole community is terrified of them. The local Chinese takeaway and the corner shop both ended up going out of business because this crew terrorised them. They run a dog-fighting ring too. They steal dogs to use as bait and use their own to help them patrol *their streets*.'

'Twats,' Jake snarled as he thought about the dogs he'd had as a kid, and his mum and Michael's rescue dog, Bruce.

'That's not the worst of it. They let one of the local crackheads run up a two hundred quid debt, and when he couldn't pay up, they tortured him for a laugh and burned his house down, with everything he owned in it. For two hundred quid!' Luke said.

Jake stared at them.

'They sound fucking feral,' Connor snapped from the corner of the room. 'Why haven't we heard about this crew before?'

'Well, in their world, they're huge fish in a tiny pond, but they don't usually venture far from their estate, never mind Kirkdale. They get their drugs from one of your suppliers, but they are about sixteen links in the chain below you two,' Luke said.

'But they're an organised outfit,' Danny interrupted him. 'Don't underestimate them just because they're kids.'

'They're definitely up and coming,' Luke agreed. 'Since Jerrod and Devlin moved in twelve months ago, they've taken over that whole estate and all of the supply for the area. They've built themselves a crew of at least two dozen and all of them are fiercely loyal to the brothers, because they're all coining it in since Jerrod stepped in and appointed himself leader.'

Jake twirled a pen in his hand as he looked at Luke and Danny. They'd certainly done their homework. 'Well, we may as well see what they have to say for themselves, eh, Con?' he asked as he turned to look at Connor.

'Can't hurt.'

'Want us to stick around?' Danny asked.

Jake shook his head. 'Nah. I'm sure we can handle them. But thanks for doing the background checks.'

Luke stood up. 'Shall we go then, Danny? I need to speak to Murf about those new lads he took on.'

Danny stood up too.

'Actually, Danny, could I have a word?' Jake asked. 'I'll get one of the lads to drop you off if you don't want to hang around, Luke?'

Luke looked at Danny who nodded. 'Right, I'll catch up with you later then. Let me know how your meeting with the Bridewell Bell-ends goes,' Luke said with a grin.

Luke walked out of the room.

Jake turned to Connor. 'Didn't you need to pick Jazz and Paul up about now?'

Connor checked his watch. 'Shit. Yeah,' he said as he jumped up. 'I'll be back in two hours before those muppets are due in.'

'Good. Hope everything's okay,' Jake said knowing that Connor and Jazz were taking Paul for his immunisations.

'Yeah. See you later, mate. Later, Danny,' Connor said as he gave Danny a pat on the shoulder on his way out.

'Shut that door after you, Con,' Jake shouted and Connor closed it behind him.

Danny leaned back in his chair. 'So, what did you want to see me about?' he said, trying to suppress a grin.

'What do you think?' Jake replied as he stood up and walked around to the other side of the desk.

'Are we going to your place?'

'If we have to. But we don't have much time,' Jake replied. He was happy to stay in his office, but Danny was too jumpy about doing anything in there in case anyone walked in on them. Not that they would. People didn't just walk into Jake's office without knocking, but he couldn't convince Danny of that.

'What am I supposed to tell Luke later when he asks me?' Danny asked.

Jake shrugged. 'I'm sure you'll think of something. You always do,' he said as he perched on the desk directly in front of Danny.

'Hmm,' he grinned. 'But it's getting harder to think of reasons why you want to speak to me.'

'Then maybe you should tell him what we really do when we're alone together?' Jake suggested.

Danny narrowed his eyes at him as Jake leaned towards him for a kiss. Their lips had barely touched when they were interrupted by a knock at the door.

'For fuck's sake,' Jake hissed before raising his head. 'What?' he shouted.

'I need to speak to Danny, Boss,' he heard his club manager, Richie, shout. 'Apparently, there's not enough door staff on for tonight.'

Jake rolled his eyes. 'You'd better sort that then, hadn't you?'

Danny stood up. 'Sorry. I'll come to yours after work instead?' he suggested.

'Yeah. See you later,' Jake said and watched as Danny walked out. He sat back in his chair and sighed. He was gagging for it and he'd have to wait for at least eight hours to get his hands on Danny again.

Chapter Twelve

A few hours later, Jerrod and Devlin King were ushered into Jake's office. He sat back in his chair, Connor beside him, and they gave each other a quick glance. They had already agreed that Jake would do most of the talking. He and Connor were always on the same page and they spoke for each other. It made him smile inwardly as he thought about their rock-solid partnership. They'd had their share of troubles in the past, but no one would ever come between them now. Jake felt a brief twinge of guilt and realised that he'd have to tell Connor about him and Danny sooner rather than later.

'Hello again, lads. Have a seat,' Jake said to the two teenagers as he indicated the two empty chairs. They strolled further into the room, full of cockiness and swagger, and sat down.

'I see you found us then?' Jake asked.

'Yeah,' said Jerrod, as though it was a huge achievement.

'Yeah? Was pretty fucking easy, wasn't it? So, don't ever

interrupt us while we're eating our breakfasts again,' Jake snarled.

Jerrod and his brother frowned in confusion at the change in his tone, and Jake suspected they weren't used to being spoken to with anything but fear or reverence. These kids had a lot to learn about the way their world really worked.

Connor sat in stony silence while Jake went on. 'So what did you want to speak to us about then?'

Jerrod shuffled forward in his seat while Devlin continued to slouch in his, glaring at Jake and Connor like a stroppy teenager who'd had his Xbox taken away. At least he was refraining from sticking his hand down his pants, although Jake got the feeling he was itching to.

'We came to speak to you about a partnership,' Jerrod said with a grin.

Jake heard Connor chuckle softly beside him but he ignored it and went on. Connor was right. These kids did have balls, he'd give them that. 'A partnership? With us? You two?' Jake asked with a raised eyebrow.

'Yeah,' Devlin snarled.

Jerrod, who Jake had already decided was infinitely smarter and more diplomatic than his idiot little brother, spoke again. 'Hear us out. I know we might seem like a small outfit compared to you—'

'Well, that's a fucking understatement,' Connor interrupted.

Jerrod narrowed his eyes at Connor but went on, undeterred. 'But we have built an operation up from the ground in a little over twelve months. We control all of the drugs on the Bridewell, and we've taken over the Poets as well.'

The Poets were a large group of streets of terraced houses named after famous poets, near to the huge Bridewell estate. Jake was sure they'd been named by someone with a huge sense of irony, given that the area was one of the most rundown places in Liverpool.

'Sounds like you're doing okay for yourselves,' Jake replied. 'So what do you need us for?' He leaned forward and rested his elbows on his desk, his fingers steepled under his chin.

'Well, if you supply directly to us, we cut out the middleman and we are able to get your product into more hands and with a bigger profit margin.'

'Won't be more profit for us though, will it? You'd expect me to sell it to you for the same price I sell to my dealers?'

'We can give you a cut of everything we make,' said Jerrod.

Jake narrowed his eyes. 'Fifty per cent?'

Jerrod opened his mouth. 'I was thinking more like ten.'

'Ten per cent?' Jake said with a laugh. 'For our name and our protection, you'd give us a shitty ten per cent? Are you fucking with me?'

Jerrod shifted in his seat. 'Well, we can negotiate your cut,' he suggested. 'But together, we can take over the whole of Kirkdale. We can make sure that yours is the only product that gets anywhere near the customers.'

Jake sat back and looked across at Connor, who nodded at him.

Jake sucked air between his teeth. 'I'm not sure you two

understand the business model we have. We are already the primary suppliers for the whole of Merseyside. You increasing your output doesn't affect us one bit. Now, you had something with the profit-sharing thing, I'll admit. But ten per cent is a fucking insult and you're lucky I don't kick the pair of you in the nuts for even suggesting it.'

'I said—' Jerrod interrupted and Jake held up a hand to stop him talking.

'Don't ever fucking interrupt me when I'm speaking,' Jake snarled. 'The truth is, lads, that even if you were giving us one hundred per cent of your profit, we wouldn't go into business with you. You see, unlike you two, we do our homework, and what you're selling just doesn't interest us.'

Jerrod and Devlin looked at Jake and Connor in confusion and Jake shook his head. 'What I'm saying is, we don't like the way you do business. And we would rather jack it all in before we agreed to have our names associated with your fucking motley crew of bullies and fucktards.'

'So you're saying no then?' Devlin snarled as he sat up straight in his chair.

Connor started to laugh as he shook his head.

Jake stood up and was pleased to see the two boys flinch. At least they weren't completely stupid. 'We're saying, fuck no!' he growled. 'So, I suggest you two get the fuck out of here before I let Connor take over negotiations. And I think you'll find he's not quite as polite as me. Now fuck off!'

Jake turned to Connor as Jerrod and Devlin skulked out of his office. 'Can you believe the fucking cheek of those two?' he asked.

Connor shook his head. 'Pair of wankers. We should have given them a good fucking kicking.'

Jake shrugged. 'There's always time for that. See what they do next. If they slope off and don't bother us again, then we'll leave them be. But if they don't, then we'll handle things your way.'

'You think they're going to come back?' Connor asked with a frown.

'I honestly don't know, mate. I know they're a pair of scum-suckers, but they've got balls. Whether we agree with their methods, they have risen through the ranks pretty quickly.'

'No idea how. They're thick as pig shit,' Connor said.

'Yeah. But maybe that makes them even more dangerous, Con?'

'How's that?'

'Because they've got where they are through sheer fucking stupidity and brutality. They don't give a shit who they come up against or what they have to do to them to get ahead. They have no idea how to play this game so they're writing their own rules – and no one else knows what they are. Give me someone who's smart enough to understand the game any day.'

'Hmm, you might be right,' Connor said as he stood up and walked over to the fridge in Jake's office. 'Anyway, is there something going on with you?'

'What do you mean?' Jake asked before nodding as Connor held up a bottle of Budweiser.

'You're getting all philosophical and calm and shit,' Connor replied as he handed him a beer.

'Philosophical and calm and shit?'

Connor laughed. 'You know what I mean. And you had a dopey grin on your face when I walked in before.'

Jake shook his head. 'No, I didn't.'

'You fucking did. Have you met someone?' Connor asked with a smile. 'Is that it?'

Jake took a swig of his beer but he didn't answer.

'Who is he then? He is a he, right?'

'Of course he's a he,' Jake snapped.

Connor flashed his eyebrows and Jake realised that had been a trap and he'd completely fallen for it. 'You knob,' he said as he put the bottle on his desk.

'He'd want you to be happy, you know?' Connor said, his tone serious all of a sudden.

Jake knew Connor was referring to his twin brother Paul. The only man Jake had ever loved – at least, he had been the only one up until now. 'I know,' Jake said. 'But it's complicated.'

'Is he married?' Connor asked.

'No.'

'In the closet?'

'Well, he thought he was straight until very recently,' Jake said with a sigh as he took another swig of his lager.

'Someone I know?' Connor asked.

Jake looked at him but he didn't reply.

'What? You know you can trust me, mate,' Connor said and Jake felt that twinge of guilt again.

'It's Danny,' Jake said, realising that he couldn't keep it from him any longer.

'Danny? As in Danny Alexander?'

'Yep.'

'Fucking hell,' Connor said as he let out a long breath. 'You certainly have a type, don't you?'

'Well, I told you it was complicated,' Jake said with a half-smile. 'No one else knows yet. It's still new. I would have told you…'

'Don't worry about it. I won't say a word, mate. To be honest, I'm kind of relieved.'

'Why?'

'The amount of time you were spending with him, I thought he was your new best mate,' Connor said as his face broke into a grin.

'Sod off, you daft bastard,' Jake said as he started to laugh. Telling Connor had made him feel much better. Now all he had to do was let Danny know what he'd done.

Chapter Thirteen

Jerrod King floored the accelerator of the old VW Golf as he sped down the Dock Road and away from Jake Conlon's night club. He felt the anger coursing through him. He hadn't been disrespected like that in a long time and it stung. Who the fuck did Jake Conlon and Connor Carter think they were? Just because they dressed in fancy fucking suits didn't make them any better than him and his crew. He and Devlin had worked their way up from nothing to running their own firm. Unlike Jake and Connor, who'd had their empire handed to them on a plate. His hands gripped the steering wheel as he replayed the conversation over and over in his head. How fucking *dare* they treat him and his brother with such contempt? He glanced over at Devlin, who was staring out of the window in silence.

'What's up with your face?' Jerrod snapped.

Devlin turned to him. 'What do you think?' he snapped back. 'That pair of arrogant cunts thinking they own this fucking city. Refusing to work with us. Those fucking psychos refusing to work with us!'

'I know, bro. They're a pair of cunts all right. But don't worry about it. We've got plenty of other irons in the fire. And one day soon, Jake Conlon and Connor Carter are going to be cleaning the shit off our shoes and wishing they'd taken us up on our offer when they had the chance.'

A grin spread across Devlin's face. 'Too right, bro.'

Jerrod turned his attention back to the road. He and Devlin might not have the manpower that the Carters did, but they had made their way to the top by doing whatever was necessary to get there. They had taken on plenty of people who were bigger than them and who had thought they were better than them, and they had won every single time. Jerrod didn't see why this time would be any different. He and Devlin had something in their arsenal that Jake and Conor didn't – there was *no* line they weren't prepared to cross to take down their enemies, and Jake and Connor had just made themselves new enemy number one.

People thought Jerrod was stupid because of the way he dressed and the way he talked. But just because he didn't go to school and do any fancy exams didn't mean he was thick. He was prepared to play the long game and bide his time to ensure he brought Carter and Conlon down.

Jake strolled through The Blue Rooms. The music thumped in his ears and he recognised the song as one of Danny's favourites, which made him smile. He squeezed himself through the throng of customers. Some of them pressed up against him as he passed – both men and women. All smiles and tanned, toned skin. He didn't react, moving past them as quickly as he could. There had been a time when he would have taken his pick of the crowd back into his office for some light relief. His club was full to the rafters four nights a week with young, hot, barely dressed bodies. It was a veritable meat market and he had indulged on many occasions – never encouraging a repeat performance, of course. He'd never needed to either. He was a rich, successful club owner, and he looked like he belonged on the cover of *Esquire*. He was the complete package. However, none of them interested him any longer.

He felt his phone vibrate against his chest. Reaching into the inside pocket of his jacket he took it out and smiled as he saw the text from Danny, signalling he was outside in the car. Jake made his way to the entrance.

'Night, lads,' he said to the bouncers as he passed.

'Night, Boss,' they chorused.

Seeing Danny's car parked over the road, Jake jogged across and climbed in.

'Busy night?' Jake asked, refraining from leaning over and giving Danny a kiss in view of their bouncers.

'Not bad. All's quiet. How about you? How was your meeting?' Danny asked as he pulled the car away from the kerb.

'As expected. Pair of cocky little fuckers, I'll give them that. But we sent them packing.'

'Good. I have a bad feeling about the Bridewell Bell-ends.'

'Hmm. Me too. Connor stayed around for a few hours after they left. We had a few beers. It was good to catch up with him. He's been so busy with Jazz and the baby lately, I don't see him as much as I used to.'

'How's he doing?'

'He's good. It's nice to see him so happy.'

Danny continued driving through the streets towards Jake's apartment.

'He asked me if I was seeing anyone,' Jake said.

Danny turned to him. 'Oh? What did you say?'

Jake took a deep breath. There was no point in trying to lie to him. He'd have to tell Danny what he'd done. It was only fair. 'I told him I was. And I told him it was you.'

Danny almost crashed the car. 'What? Jake!' he snapped. 'I thought we agreed…'

'What was I supposed to say, Dan? He asked me outright. Me and Connor don't keep things from each other. We certainly don't fucking lie to each other's faces.'

'I know that.' Danny shook his head. 'I just…'

'Just what?' Jake snapped. He was being unfair. Outing Danny to Connor was a big deal, even if he felt like he'd had no other choice.

Danny didn't answer. He gripped the steering wheel tightly. Jake put a hand on his thigh. 'I'm sorry, Dan. But he asked me, and I couldn't lie to him. He knows the score. He won't tell anyone. You can trust him.'

'I know that,' said Danny. 'It just feels like now it's out there, it's only a matter of time before everyone knows.'

Jake sat back in his seat and sighed. A part of him hoped that was true. He would like nothing more than to tell the whole world that Danny Alexander was his significant other. But the other part of him worried that Danny was still far from admitting the truth about being gay, and even less ready to admit that the two of them were in a relationship. Jake was technically Danny's boss, and he knew that them being open as a couple would be a strange dynamic for Danny to handle. They were both typical alpha males, and he knew that inevitable questions, if not asked, would certainly be whispered. Which one of them was the boss when it came to what really mattered? And while the truth was they were equal partners, and Jake didn't give a shit what anyone else thought, he knew that Danny did.

Far too much.

Chapter Fourteen

DI Leigh Moss shrugged off her coat as she walked into the hallway of John Brennan's house. The aroma of roast lamb filled the air, making her stomach growl.

'You're late, Detective,' he shouted from the kitchen.

Leigh kicked off her shoes, leaving them in the corner, and walked along the hallway to the kitchen to find John taking roast potatoes out of the oven.

'I'm sorry. We've got a new case and I had to brief the team,' she replied. 'I'm glad you waited for me though. That smells delicious.'

John smiled. 'Well, don't get used to home cooked dinners every night when you come home from work. This is the only thing I'm any good at cooking. This and cheese toasties.'

Leigh laughed. Neither of them particularly enjoyed being in the kitchen, but John could cook basic meals and the truth was she was becoming used to his home-cooked food. The fact that he'd referred to her coming home hadn't escaped her notice either. This wasn't her home. It was John's house. She still had her own house in Crosby, although she rarely seemed to spend much time there lately. But him calling this place her home just sounded so natural, and it made her feel content in a way that she had never experienced before.

'I love your cooking,' she said to him as she walked over and kissed him on the cheek.

'Then pull up a chair and I'll dish out,' he replied.

Leigh sipped her wine as she looked across the table at John, who had just finished eating.

'That was gorgeous. Thank you,' she said with a smile.

'My pleasure,' he replied as he took a swig of his beer. 'Your turn to do the dishes though.'

Leigh nodded absent-mindedly. Her new case was preying on her mind. They'd had numerous Crimestoppers reports in the past few months about the goings-on at the Bridewell estate. A new gang had moved in and taken over the estate more than a year earlier. Headed by the King brothers, they were a particularly vicious and ruthless crew. In Leigh's previous role as the OCG task force Inspector, they had been up and coming and she had been aware of their numerous exploits. But since her move to the Phoenix team, Merseyside's specialist unit dealing with sex crimes, they hadn't been on her radar at all – until a few weeks ago, when reports about the gang using young teenage girls in some kind of sick, twisted initiation ceremony had started coming in. They'd been monitoring the situation but with no one willing to go on record for fear of reprisals, their hands had been tied.

Earlier that day, a sixteen-year-old girl had been dumped at Aintree hospital with some of the most horrific injuries Leigh had ever seen. Feeling she had nothing left to lose, the girl had been brave enough to name several of her attackers as members of the Bridewell Blades crew. They had set up an investigation team and arrested two of the suspects already. Leigh hoped that other victims would feel able to come forward once they saw arrests being made. She never talked about work with John. Given his chosen profession as the right-hand man of Grace Carter, the head of the biggest crime family in the North West, they had both agreed that was the best way forward. But sometimes she really wanted to.

'Rough day?' he asked her, his eyes narrowed in concern.

'You could say that,' Leigh replied with a sigh as she thought about young Kacey Jones. Suddenly, tears sprang to her eyes.

John stood quickly and walked around the table to her. 'Hey, what's going on?' he asked softly as he crouched down and put an arm around her shoulders.

Leigh turned to him and buried her face in his neck, inhaling his clean, fresh scent that she'd come to love. 'Sometimes I wish I could do more to help people, you know?' she sniffed as she lifted her head.

John rubbed the tears from her cheek with the pad of his thumb. 'Yes, I know.'

'Take no notice of me. It's been a long day,' Leigh replied, feeling foolish for ruining a perfectly pleasant evening.

John smiled at her and kissed her forehead. 'Why don't you take your wine into the living room and I'll clear the dishes,' he said.

Leigh shook her head. 'No. A deal's a deal. You cooked, after all.'

'Leigh. Please go and relax. This will only take me a few minutes.'

'If you're sure?' she said. She wasn't used to being looked after, but John did it so well.

'I am,' he insisted.

———

A few minutes later, John walked into the room carrying the rest of the bottle of wine. He topped up Leigh's glass and placed the bottle on the table.

'You okay?' he asked.

'Yeah,' she said with a faint smile. 'Some things just get to you though.'

John sat on the sofa beside her. He put his arm around her shoulder and pulled her close but she could feel the tension in his body. She looked at him and saw his brows knitted into a frown.

'What's up?' she asked.

'I need to talk to you, Leigh,' he said as he pulled away from her and turned so he was facing her.

Leigh felt her stomach somersault. This couldn't be

good, could it?' 'Okay. What about?' She put her glass on the table. She wanted to be in full control of her senses for whatever was about to happen next. She rarely saw John looking so serious.

'I know you've been talking about leaving the police,' he started.

'Yes.'

'But I can't let you do that for me, Leigh,' he said with a sigh.

'Who said it would be for you?'

'Well, isn't it? I know how much our relationship places you in a difficult position. I see the stress it puts you under—'

'I'm fine,' she interrupted.

'No, you're not. You've come home tonight upset about whatever case you're working on, and you can't tell me anything about it because we agreed that we would never discuss your job – and that's because of what I do and who I work for. Can you honestly say you would be thinking about leaving the force if it weren't for me?'

Leigh shrugged. She didn't know the answer. She had thought about leaving for a while now. When she was with John, he was all that mattered to her. She imagined a life with him that didn't involve her being a police inspector. But when she was working, and trying to help people like Kacey Jones, she felt like she was where she belonged too. How could she belong equally in both lives? She had to choose one or the other because keeping a foot in both camps was becoming harder and harder each day. Although she had the feeling that John was about to choose for her.

'It's true, Leigh, and you know it is,' John said softly. 'I can't let you give up your career because of who I am. You care about it too much. You care about the people you help too much.'

She sniffed. She wasn't about to cry again. 'I care about you too.'

'I know that. I care about you too, Leigh. That's why I've been thinking about this for a few days now. And you coming here upset has only confirmed that I'm making the right decision.'

'What decision?' she asked.

John took a deep breath and Leigh prepared herself for the worst.

Chapter Fifteen

Michael and Sean Carter stepped out of the doorway of the offices of Cartel Securities and into the bright sunshine. They were dressed almost identically in dark navy three-piece suits and pale blue shirts. The only significant difference was their ties – one navy and one bright purple. Apart from a slight difference in height, they were so similar they could pass for twins rather than brothers.

I leaned back against the glass of the bus shelter and watched them talking and laughing as they walked towards Michael Carter's car. I wished I could hear their conversation. What were they laughing at? Was it something personal or business-related? Or were they reminiscing about something from their past, as brothers often did? I frowned. Most likely they were laughing about the latest poor bastard they'd done over.

Anger surged through my veins as I watched them and I clenched my fists inside my jacket pockets. How dare they walk around this city like they didn't have a care in the world? I bet they never even had a single sleepless night despite all the hurt and pain they had caused people over the years. People just like me. I bet they never even gave people like me a second thought.

'Has the 82 been yet, love?' a woman's voice said behind me.

I turned and frowned at the distraction. 'I don't know,' I snapped at her. She walked closer towards me, pulling a shopping trolley behind her until she came to a stop right beside me. Then she stood squinting at the timetable through thick glasses.

'Okay. Keep your hair on,' she said with a comical raise of her eyebrows.

I turned back to the Carter brothers who were now safely ensconced in Michael's Aston Martin.

'Flashy fucker!' I hissed under my breath. Everything about Michael Carter and his whole fucking family was offensive. I would have thought that given his family's chosen profession as purveyors of misery, they would keep a low profile. But no. They swanned around the city in their flash cars and their designer swagger thinking they were fucking untouchable. Well, not for much longer. Their day of reckoning was coming and it was coming soon. I curled my fingers around the handle of the gun inside the pocket of my leather bomber jacket.

Tick Tock, Michael.

Tick Tock.

Chapter Sixteen

Grace looked up from her laptop as John Brennan walked into her office. She'd been going through some accounts and her eyes were beginning to sting from staring at the numbers on the screen for too long. She was glad of the distraction.

'Hello, stranger,' she said with a smile. Since he'd started seeing Leigh Moss, she'd made a conscious effort to find him less problematic jobs than the ones he would usually do for her.

'Boss,' he said with a nod and a grin as he sat down opposite her.

'To what do I owe this pleasure?' she asked him.

Suddenly his smile faltered and he closed his eyes briefly before answering. 'I need to talk to you.'

Grace swallowed. In the history of the spoken word, had those words ever led to a pleasant conversation? She doubted it. She sat forward in her chair. 'Okay. What about?'

John leaned forward too, his eyes scanning her face for a moment before he spoke. 'I want out, Grace,' he said quietly.

She sat back and blinked at him. She'd heard him all right, but she didn't understand. 'What?'

'I want out,' he said, louder this time. 'I can't do this anymore.'

'But John, you can't,' she stammered. 'I can't do this without you.'

He smiled at her. 'Well, that's quite the compliment, but we both know it's not true.'

Grace frowned. 'Okay. But I don't want to do this without you, John. You're...'

'I'm what, Grace?' he asked as he stared at her.

Grace closed her eyes. She didn't know how to put into words what he was to her. He was more than an employee. More than a good friend. He was her confidante. Her sounding board. Someone she trusted with her life.

'For the past five years I've given you everything, Grace. You have always been my priority. I've put your needs ahead of everyone else's, even my own. And don't get me wrong, I've been happy to do that for you...'

'But not anymore?' she said with a heavy heart as she realised that what he said was true, and that she could no longer ask him to do that. It wasn't fair to him, or to Leigh.

'I care about you, Grace. Nothing will ever change that. My loyalty to you has never been in doubt, and it never will be. But I can't keep doing this. I'm in love with Leigh. I want to make a go of it. She makes me want to be a better man.'

'But what are you going to do?' Grace asked. 'You've been in this game since you were a teenager.'

John shrugged. 'I'm not exactly sure yet. But I've got plenty of savings. I'm thinking about my options.'

'If this is just about you going legit, let me find you a job with the restaurants, or even in Cartel Securities,' Grace offered in a last-ditch attempt to keep him from deserting her.

He shook his head. 'You know that would never work. If I work for your company, then I work for you, and if I work for you, then nothing changes, Grace. Do you honestly think I'd be able to sit back and do nothing if I knew that you were in any kind of trouble? It will be hard enough to do that even if I make a clean break.'

'But John,' she said again, as she blinked back the tears, 'what will I do without you?' She knew she was being completely selfish. John had given her his undivided loyalty and if he wanted out then he had earned his right to leave. But that didn't make letting him go any easier.

'Please don't ask me to stay, Grace. Because you know I won't say no to you,' he said, his voice thick with emotion now too.

Grace stared at him. She trusted him and she loved working with him. Losing him was going to hit her hard. But how could she deny him a chance of happiness?

Finally, she nodded. 'Of course, if you really want out, John, then you're free to do as you choose. But then you always have been.'

'Thank you,' he said with a sigh. 'It's been an absolute honour working by your side for all this time.'

Grace stood up and walked around the desk. 'The honour has been all mine, John,' she said. He stood up and wrapped her in a hug.

Grace pressed her head against his broad chest and blinked back the tears. This felt like the end of something bigger than her and John. With Michael making noises about stepping back, and Luke and Danny doing such a good job with Cartel Securities, it almost felt like there was about to be a changing of the guard. She wasn't exactly sure how she felt about that. She'd been on top for so long, she didn't know if she knew how not to be. In her heart, she'd known she'd have to let go at some point, but it had always seemed like some distant pipe dream. Something to do one day – but not now.

Grace stepped back and John released her from the embrace. 'Bye, Grace,' he said with his trademark smile.

'Bye, big fella,' she said, smiling back, and then she watched him walk out of her office.

She sat down again. She looked around the room and her eyes scanned the framed pictures on the wall, lingering on a photograph of the opening of Sophia's Kitchen. It was a picture of her, Michael, Sean, Sophia, her in-laws Pat and Sue, Jake, Connor and, of course, John – standing beside her, like he'd done unwaveringly for the past six years. He was so much more than an employee. And now he'd left her.

She knew it was the right thing for him to do.

But she couldn't help wondering if this was the beginning of the end. Perhaps it was? And perhaps that was a good thing?

Chapter Seventeen

Jake leaned back in his chair and smiled at the now familiar sight of Danny Alexander walking through his office door. He closed it behind him and sat opposite Jake.

'What can I do for you?' Danny asked with a grin. Usually Jake's late-afternoon phone calls were a blatant ploy to get Danny alone for an hour, and they would meet at Jake's flat, as Danny was twitchy about taking things too far in Jake's office, where he worried that anyone could barge in.

'Actually, I really do have something I wanted to talk to you about,' Jake replied.

'Oh?' Danny sat forward. 'What's going on?'

'I've been thinking about getting a new club manager.'

'Really? What about Richie?'

The current club manager, Richie, was okay, but he'd been doing the job for two years and he was becoming complacent – and that made him sloppy. 'He's not exactly dynamic, is he?' Jake raised an eyebrow.

Danny laughed. 'Dynamic is not a word I'd use to describe him – no. But are you just going to let him go?'

'I've got another job in mind for him,' Jake said. 'As a driver. If he doesn't want it, then he can leave. But that's up to him.'

'So, who's going to be your new manager?' Danny asked with a frown. 'And why do you want to talk to me about it?'

'Well, it kind of involves you,' Jake said.

'I'm not doing it,' Danny snapped.

Jake threw his head back and laughed out loud. 'I'm not asking you, you plum. Why the fuck would I ask you to do that?'

Danny shrugged. 'Well, who then?'

'Stacey,' Jake said with a smile.

'As in my little sister Stacey?' Danny asked.

'The one and only.'

'But why? She's never managed a club before. She's never managed anywhere before. And she's my fucking sister, Jake. I don't want her working here.'

Jake scowled at him. 'Why the fuck not?'

'Would you want Belle working here?' he countered.

'Well, she's only fucking six, so no,' Jake shot back. 'But if she was a grown woman and she wanted to, then of course I would. Where else would she be safer than where her brother is?'

Danny sat in silence, his jaw clenched in anger.

Jake sighed and decided on a change of tactic. The truth

was, he didn't need Danny's permission to offer Stacey the job, and he would do it regardless, but it would make his life a whole lot easier if Danny was on side. 'Did you know that Siobhan used to manage this place for me?' he asked.

'No,' Danny replied.

'Yeah. Before we split up, obviously. But she did a brilliant job. The club has never run as smoothly as it did when she was in charge. Do you know why?'

'Why?'

'Because women, for the most part, aren't driven by their egos and they think with their brains instead of their dicks. Richie spends most of his nights deciding which bird he's going to take home and bang rather than actually managing the club. I always thought I might ask Siobhan to come back and take over again one day, but I think that might be a bit too awkward. Especially with her and Connor's history,' Jake added, recalling the massive fallout Connor and Siobhan's one-night stand had caused in the family.

'So your choices are limited to your ex-wife or my sister?' Danny asked.

'Of course not,' Jake growled, beginning to tire of Danny's constant questioning. 'Do you really have to argue with every fucking thing I say?'

Danny sucked his top lip, no doubt trying to stop himself from responding and proving Jake's point. Jake stared at him and was reminded of him doing that very same thing earlier that morning while Jake had been sucking on something else. Despite being annoyed, he closed his eyes and smiled to himself at the memory.

Everything about Danny Alexander drove him crazy, and he loved it.

'Look, Dan, you've seen how well she's done at my mum's restaurant. She worked her way up to shift manager in a matter of months. She's ambitious but not arrogant. She's on the ball. She's brilliant with customers. She knows her way around the finances and she can handle people when they're creating a fucking nuisance. She's basically a female version of you – so why wouldn't I want her working for me?'

'What if something happened to her?'

'Why would it? This is a nightclub, not a fucking crack den. Has anything ever happened to our bar staff? To our dancers? To Richie? Who, let's face it, probably deserves a slap in the face. You work here. Luke works here. I work here. Everyone in this place works for you or me – where else would she be any safer?'

'Have you asked Luke about this?' Danny said.

'No. It's nothing to do with him. He's her boyfriend, not her fucking keeper. The only reason I'm talking to you about it is because we're...' He trailed off. He didn't know how to finish that sentence.

'We're what?' Danny asked.

'I don't know, Dan. What are we?' he asked with a sigh. 'You spend every single night in my bed but you won't tell anyone about us.'

'You know I'm not ready for that yet,' Danny said, his voice suddenly full of emotion. 'I will. Just not yet.'

Jake shook his head. 'Whatever. I'm asking Stacey if she

wants the job. Get on board with it, or don't. But I'm pretty sure she's going to bite my hand off.'

Danny stood up. 'Is that all you needed me for then, Boss?' he asked.

Jake ran his tongue over his lower lip. Even though Danny had done it to piss him off, he loved it when he called him Boss. It made his dick twitch. 'No,' he said with a grin. 'But if you want to leave, be my guest.'

Danny stood rooted to the spot. Jake Conlon knew how to push every single button he had. A part of him would like to see the look on Jake's face if he walked out of the office, but he couldn't. He was drawn to him like he possessed some kind of magnetic field. He couldn't stay away from him and could barely go a few minutes without thinking about him. Jake had turned his whole world upside down and Danny was still trying to come to terms with the fact that after all his years chasing every woman with a pulse, the one person whom he couldn't get enough of happened to be a man. Jake Conlon had him by the balls and the worst thing was, the bastard knew it all too well.

Danny knew all about Jake's previous reputation. If Danny had been a player, then Jake had been far worse. He had rarely bothered to learn any of his former conquests' first names, never mind giving them any chance of a repeat performance. Yet he and Danny had been almost inseparable for over two months. What was that about? Danny sometimes wondered if it was because Jake felt just as strongly about him. But how could that be true? He was Jake Conlon. Men and women threw themselves at him –

literally in some cases. He was in a whole other league to Danny.

So instead of walking out of there, he stayed right where he was. Just as Jake had known he would. 'Do you know how fucking annoying you are?' he asked.

Jake grinned back at him, showing his perfect white teeth. 'I try my best.'

Chapter Eighteen

As Belle and Oscar had slept over at their grandparents' the night before, Grace and Michael were enjoying a morning in bed together when the sound of Grace's mobile phone disturbed them. Michael lifted his head from Grace's neck and cursed under his breath as he reached across to get it for her.

'Tell whoever it is that we're very busy and they should fuck off,' he said with a grin.

Grace glanced at the phone and saw Faye Donovan's name flashing on the screen. She sighed, pushed Michael off her and sat up against the pillows before she answered the call. Whatever the reason for her solicitor calling her at eight o'clock on a Thursday morning, it couldn't have been a good one.

'Hi, Faye,' Grace answered, while Michael watched her.

'Morning, Grace,' Faye replied. 'I have some news to share, and you're not going to like it.'

Grace took a deep breath as she felt her pulse quicken. What the hell had happened now? 'What is it?' she asked with all the calm she could muster.

'Craig and Ged Johnson appeared in court again this morning. They've changed their pleas to Not Guilty.'

Grace sat up straighter, lifting the covers from her and Michael as she did. Craig and Ged Johnson had caused her family no end of trouble. She had finally figured out a way to be shot of them a few months earlier when she had set them up to kidnap DS Nick Bryce and made sure they'd be caught red-handed, which they had been. Not only had Craig and Ged been arrested for kidnap and wounding, but their eldest brother, Bradley, had confessed to the murder of their younger brother, Billy, a crime that Jake and Connor had actually committed and been in prison for at the time.

During their subsequent police interview, Craig and Ged had confessed to everything they were charged with. They had been assured Grace's protection while they were inside, and, from what she knew, they had it, so why were they suddenly changing their plea? It made no sense. 'What? But why?' she asked.

'I don't know. They appeared this morning and the court clerk let me know about two minutes ago. I have no involvement in the case now so I wasn't party to any discussions, but the clerk knows I have an interest in it. Want me to see what else I can dig up?'

'Yes, please, Faye. But what about Bradley? Is he still pleading guilty to Billy's murder?' she asked. As annoying as it was about Craig and Ged, it was far more dangerous to have Bradley changing his mind about their arrangement.

He had basically agreed to take the fall for his brother's murder in exchange for his life and Grace's protection while he was in prison. Bradley Johnson had pissed off more people than Donald Trump and he knew he was a sitting duck without someone prepared to look out for him.

'No. I checked with his legal team. He's due for sentencing next month,' Faye answered.

'Good. If you find out any more on Craig and Ged, let me know as soon as, will you?'

'Yes, of course. I'll see what I can find out. Bye, Grace.'

'Bye, Faye,' Grace said, ending the call. She turned to look at Michael, who was waiting patiently for her to fill him in on what was going on.

'Craig and Ged Johnson changed their pleas to Not Guilty this morning.'

He frowned at her. 'What? But they were banged to rights.'

Grace shrugged. 'They still have a right to a trial. It seems they fancy their chances for some reason.'

Michael shook his head. 'But they know we're not going to be happy about this. Why would they risk that? They think we're on their side?'

'Maybe that's just it. They've realised that we're not. They must know that John is still working for me. Perhaps they've realised that it was a set-up all along?'

Michael lay back against the pillows. 'Will the Johnson brothers ever stop being a pain in our arses?'

Grace laughed. 'Probably not. But don't worry. One way or another, we'll deal with them.'

Michael looked up at her. 'Shall we let the boys know?'

'Yeah. Shall we get them round here and we can plan what to do next.' Jake and Connor would want to know about the latest developments and how it was going to affect them all.

Michael raised an eyebrow. 'Well, wonders will never cease, Mrs Carter.'

'What do you mean?'

'Well, usually you come up with the plan, and then you tell the rest of us what it is,' he said with a laugh.

She leaned down towards him. 'Well, maybe I'm fed up of always making the plans,' she said as she kissed him. 'Perhaps it's time for the boys to start thinking of solutions for themselves.'

'I couldn't agree more,' he said as he pushed her up and rolled on top of her. 'It's about time me and you had some time off, isn't it?' Then he kissed her, and they continued where they had left off before Faye's phone call had interrupted them.

An hour later, Grace and Michael were sitting at the breakfast bar in their kitchen with Jake and Connor. They all cradled mugs of tea and the boys were enjoying bacon sandwiches as Grace told them about her phone call from Faye. Jake and Connor shared her and Michael's surprise at the recent development and wondered why on earth the two brothers thought they could suddenly convince a jury that they hadn't kidnapped and assaulted Nick Bryce.

'What about Bradley?' Jake asked. 'Has he changed his plea?'

Grace shook her head. 'No. He's still pleading guilty to Billy's murder. He's due for sentencing next month.'

'So why have Craig and Ged changed their minds?' Connor asked as he took a bite of his sandwich.

'I don't know for sure. It could be they're just chancing their arm, or it could be that they're thinking about implicating John,' Grace answered. 'They must have realised by now that he's still working for me. It was him who talked them into kidnapping Nick Bryce, after all, and he made them believe it was all on behalf of Alastair McGrath.'

'Ged and Bradley are fuck-nuggets,' Jake said. 'They haven't got a clue what day it is, never mind anything else.'

'Yes, but Craig isn't,' Grace reminded them. 'He must be wondering why John Brennan is still working for me and with all of his limbs attached. He's either realised that John set them up and was actually working for me all along, or he may even think that John has managed to double-cross us all. Either way, they might be intending to pin the blame on John.'

'We need to deal with this now!' Jake snapped.

'Take them out?' Connor suggested.

Grace was about to reply with all of the reasons why that was an awful idea when Jake spoke up. 'No. That would look well dodgy, especially if Craig has already mentioned John's involvement to his brief or the police. Besides, with his brothers gone, Bradley might have a change of heart and change his plea to not guilty too. He might think he's next and get twitchy, or just for good old-fashioned revenge. But a word in Craig and Ged's ear, and a reminder of what happens to them in prison when they don't have our protection, should do the trick. Who have we got in Walton right now?'

Connor took a swig of his tea as he thought about his response.

Grace looked across at Michael and he smiled at her and gave her a wink before picking up his own mug. Grace smiled too; she knew exactly what he was thinking.

'Gary Mac's lad is in there,' Connor suggested. 'He could organise something, no problem.'

Jake shook his head. 'He's been recalled though, hasn't he? He'll need to keep his head down. We need him out again. If there's a sniff of him being involved it will go on his security report.'

Connor nodded in agreement.

'We've got a few lads from Cartel in there on remand. Want me to speak to Luke and Danny about getting word to them?' Michael asked.

'Sounds good. I'm seeing Danny later, I'll have a word with him,' Jake offered.

'Sound,' Connor added as he finished off his sandwich.

Grace couldn't help smiling at her two boys. They had come such a long way in the past twelve months, but they still didn't quite think outside the box. There were other and more discreet ways of ensuring co-operation. 'As well as that, it wouldn't hurt to have Faye Donovan pay Craig a visit and offer him our own kind of plea deal,' she suggested. 'Then we'd have all bases covered.'

'Sounds like a plan then,' Michael said. 'Anyone fancy another brew?'

Jake looked at his watch before replying. 'Yeah, I'll have another,' he said with a smile.

'Yeah, go on,' Connor added.

'I'll make it, love,' Grace said as she stood up. She walked over to the sink and filled the kettle. As she waited for it to boil she watched the three men fall into an easy conversation about the football. How different things had been just eighteen months earlier. She had wondered how they would ever recover from the murder of Connor's twin, Paul. And although the pain of his loss was never far away, it made her happy to see that they were stronger than ever.

Grace looked at Jake. The change in him was astounding. In the few months immediately after Paul's death, she had worried that she was going to lose Jake too. He had gone completely off the rails. Drinking and taking drugs to blot out the pain as well as embarking on a violent rampage across the city, which had ended up with him and Connor being arrested and charged with murder. Since he'd come out of prison, he'd been a changed man. He'd stopped drinking whisky for breakfast, and she hadn't seen him drunk for months. He didn't do drugs at all now, as far as she was aware. He'd also stepped up for his daughter, Isla, too, and she stayed with him two nights a week at his flat. But something else had changed in recent weeks. He seemed happier than she had ever seen him. He always had a smile on his face. Just as she was starting to wonder what that could be about, the kettle finished boiling and she turned her attention back to making four cups of tea.

Later that evening, when she had finished putting Belle and Oscar to bed, Grace walked into the kitchen to find Michael preparing dinner. After Jake and Connor had left, she and Michael had both been at work all day before picking the kids up from their grandparents. Then Belle and Oscar's bedtime routines had taken over and they hadn't had much chance to talk any further about the earlier revelations.

'Hey, you. What are we having tonight?' Grace asked as she walked over the kitchen counter. She never tired of her husband's incredible skills in the kitchen. She counted herself a lucky woman.

'Chicken and stuffed peppers,' he said as he gave her a quick kiss on the cheek.

'Smells delicious,' she said. Her afternoon meeting had finished late and she'd only eaten a cereal bar that she'd picked up from the petrol station for lunch. 'I'm starving.'

'Then sit yourself down and I'll dish it out,' he said as he gave her a playful smack on her behind.

Grace poured two glasses of sparkling water and then sat at the table.

Michael brought over two plates of food and sat opposite her.

'It was nice to involve the boys in the decisions about the Johnson idiots today,' Michael said.

'It was. They had some good ideas.'

'Jake surprised me.'

'Did he? Why?'

He smiled at her. 'It was almost like listening to you.'

Grace smiled back at him. She had noticed herself how much more measured and thoughtful Jake was about things lately. She was starting to think that all of her and Michael's guidance was starting to rub off on him after all.

Chapter Nineteen

Jake walked through The Blue Rooms to his office at the back of the club. The door was open and he was pleased to see Danny Alexander was already there waiting for him, leaning against the desk. Jake stepped inside and closed the door behind him.

'You been waiting long?' he asked.

Danny looked up from his phone and smiled. 'Only a few minutes.'

Jake walked towards him until they were only standing a couple of inches apart. 'I'm glad you came on your own. Where's Luke?'

Danny slipped his phone inside his jacket pocket. 'He's going through the books with Michael.'

'That will keep him busy for a few hours then,' Jake said with a grin.

'He's expecting me back in a few hours though. We've got to sort out some new contracts.'

Jake grabbed hold of Danny's suit jacket by the lapels. 'A

few hours is all we need,' he said as he pulled Danny towards him for a kiss.

'Not in here,' Danny said as he shifted uncomfortably.

Jake glanced behind him. 'The door is closed.'

'But someone might come in.'

'It's locked,' Jake said as his hands slipped underneath Danny's jacket and onto his back, and he planted kisses along his neck.

Danny groaned in pleasure before placing his hands on Jake's chest and pushing him back. 'Not here,' he said as he took a deep breath. 'What if Luke or your mum or someone dropped by? I'm not sure I could lie to their faces. I'd rather people didn't know...'

Jake took a step back and frowned. He and Danny had been seeing each other for almost three months now. Jake could hardly stop thinking about him. He hadn't been in any committed relationship since Paul – and even that had been nothing like this. As much as he'd loved Paul, their relationship had been doomed to failure and they could never have made a success of it, least of all because they had become step-brothers while they were on one of their many breaks.

Jake and Danny had spent almost every night together during those three months, and large parts of their working day too. They had done it all under the guise of sorting out security for the club, but sooner or later they were going to have to tell people what was really going on between them. There were only so many fake problems Jake could invent to get Danny there on his own.

Although Connor knew the truth, Jake hated lying to

everyone else. He had kept his sexuality a secret for years, only finding the courage to tell people after Paul had been killed. He often wondered how differently his life might have turned out if he'd been brave enough to be open about himself and Paul from the outset. So, while he understood exactly where Danny was coming from, he also resented being forced back into the closet and having to lie to his family.

'What is it you don't want people to know, Dan?' he snapped. 'That you like men as much as women?'

Danny didn't answer and looked down at his feet. They'd had this conversation dozens of times in the past few weeks, and Jake was becoming increasingly frustrated by it. 'I said I'd give you some time to figure out what you wanted. To see whether this was just a phase. How much longer do you need?'

'I don't know, Jake. Can't you see this from my point of view?'

'Of course I do. I've been where you are. But what are you waiting for, Dan? If this isn't what you want, then tell me now and we can both fucking move on.'

Danny looked up at him then and Jake saw the hurt flash across his face. He didn't care. He was hurting too, and he needed Danny to face up to who he really was. He didn't want to go on pretending that they were just good mates.

'You know that's not what I want, Jake,' he said. 'But this is my whole fucking life we're talking about here. Until a few months ago, I didn't even know I was bi.'

'You're right, Danny. It is your life, so you'd better figure out what you want to do with it, because I'm not hanging around waiting for you to grow a pair of bollocks and admit that what you want is me.'

Jake turned around and walked towards the door.

'Jake? Where are you going?' Danny asked.

'To spend some time with someone who's not ashamed to be seen with me,' Jake snapped as he pulled open the door and walked out. That had been a low blow and he knew it, but maybe it would make Danny think about their future and whether they had one together. As far as Jake was concerned, life was too short to worry about what other people thought of you. He'd spent far too much time worrying about that himself, and all he'd ended up with was a whole bucket of misery and a marriage to a woman he didn't love, at least not in that way. He knew he was pushing Danny for a decision, but he also knew it was a decision that would make them both a whole lot happier in the long run.

Jake climbed into his car and realised that he'd forgotten to ask Danny about which of their bouncers were on remand in Walton.

'Shit!' he snapped as he punched the steering wheel. He'd phone Luke and ask him instead. He started the engine and pulled out of the car park. Jake wondered if Luke suspected anything was going on between him and Danny. Luke and Danny were as close as brothers and rarely kept any secrets from each other.

Jake liked Luke, or Uncle Luke as it now transpired he was. That had been a shock, to say the least, and Jake had wondered how Luke would fit into the whole family dynamic, but he needn't have been worried. Discovering his parentage and the fact that he was the half-brother of the most powerful woman in the North West didn't seem to have changed Luke at all. He continued to graft his arse off at Cartel Securities and he didn't expect any special treatment from anyone because of who he was. Jake respected him for that, and he had grown closer to Luke over the past few months too. He wondered how Luke would take the news that he and Danny were seeing each other – if indeed they ever got the chance to tell him. Maybe Danny would decide that it was too much hassle to come out of the closet? What would Jake do then? He didn't have a clue, because he could hardly stop thinking about Danny Alexander and his perfectly chiselled abs.

Chapter Twenty

J ake was getting a glass of water before heading back to bed when he heard the banging on his front door and frowned. No one had buzzed the intercom and the security in his building was usually tight. He glanced at his phone on the coffee table as he passed and saw six missed calls from Danny. He'd put it on silent earlier and forgotten to switch the sound back on. The next knock was louder and he glanced towards his bedroom and cursed under his breath. He opened the door slightly and saw Danny standing there.

'How did you get past the doorman?' Jake snapped.

'I told him I forgot my key. He thinks I live here with you. Can I come in?'

Jake glanced behind him down the hallway towards the bedroom again.

'Now's not a great time,' he said.

The hurt flashed across Danny's face. 'Have you got someone in there with you?' he asked.

Jake nodded and was about to speak when they were interrupted by a shout. 'Daddy! Where's my water?'

'Coming, baby,' Jake shouted back.

Danny sighed with relief and took a step back. 'I'm sorry, I didn't realise you had Isla with you tonight. But you weren't answering your phone.'

'I've been trying to get her to go to sleep for the past hour and a half, that's why,' Jake said.

Danny looked down at the floor. 'I'll go then,' he said quietly.

'Yeah. I'll speak to you tomorrow,' Jake replied.

Danny started to walk away, but before Jake closed the door, Danny turned around. 'I'm not ashamed to be seen with you, Jake,' he said, the words sounding like they caught in his throat.

Jake stared at him. This man drove him crazy. He opened the door wider. 'You can come in if you don't mind waiting for me to get Isla back to sleep?' he offered.

Danny smiled at him. 'Okay.'

It took another forty-five minutes for Jake to finally settle his daughter. When he was sure she was sound asleep, he moved her to her own bed in her own bedroom. He didn't usually let her fall asleep in his room, but she had insisted on watching *Frozen* for the one millionth time and he and didn't allow a TV in her room – but perhaps it was time to rethink that particular rule.

Danny was sitting on the sofa watching *Top Gear* with a

can of Coke in his hand when Jake walked into the living room. He muted the television as Jake sat down beside him.

'She finally asleep then?' Danny asked.

'Yeah,' Jake replied with a sigh. 'I thought she was going to stay awake all night. I'm sure Siobhan filled her with sugar before I picked her up,' he joked. He knew his ex-wife Siobhan would never actually do that. Despite their dysfunctional marriage and their difficult history, they co-parented well.

Danny smiled and the two of them sat on the sofa in awkward silence for a few moments before Danny finally spoke. 'I'm sorry, Jake—'

'I don't want an apology, Dan,' Jake interrupted. 'You need time to figure this shit out. I, of all people, understand that. But I hate lying to my mum and Michael. Not to mention Luke and Stacey. I hate sneaking around and pretending that you're just my mate.'

'I know. I do too,' Danny said with a sigh. 'It won't be for ever though.'

'Well, just promise me you'll think about what it is you really want.'

'You know what I want, Jake,' Danny said as he put a hand on Jake's thigh.

'Do I?' Jake growled, aware that the atmosphere in the room had suddenly changed.

'I thought I'd made it pretty clear,' Danny said.

Jake glanced back at the hallway leading to his daughter's bedroom. The last thing he needed was for Isla to walk in and find him and her uncle Danny in a compromising position. But she was fast asleep. The sofa was facing away from the hallway. He'd hear her before she saw anything. And Danny Alexander sucked cock like he'd been in training for it all his life.

'Why don't you remind me?' Jake said with a flash of his eyebrows.

Danny didn't need asking twice.

Chapter Twenty-One

G race walked into The Blue Rooms and along the corridor to Jake's office. She passed the smaller office on her way, the one that she'd used herself for a while when she'd come back to Liverpool to help Jake out of a sticky situation he hadn't even known he was in. She and Michael had argued and made up many times in that office and the memories tugged the corners of her mouth into a smile. It had only been five years earlier, but in some ways it felt like a lifetime ago. They had all come so far since then. She'd enjoyed working at the club. The place was always full of energy and there was usually some drama or other going on. But she preferred the quieter surroundings of her office in Sophia's Kitchen these days. Maybe Michael was right, and they really were getting too old for life in the fast lane?

She was surprised to see someone inside the small office, as it was very rarely used now. On closer inspection, she saw it was Danny's sister Stacey. She knocked on the door and Stacey turned, her face streaked with dust.

'Hi, Stacey. You don't start until Monday, do you?' she asked, aware that Stacey had accepted the job as manager of The Blue Rooms. It had pained Grace to let one of her best waitresses go, but she had an army of great staff, and if having Stacey managing the club helped Jake, then she didn't mind at all. Grace was impressed with her son's decision-making on the matter, and she thought Stacey would be a great addition to his team.

Stacey wiped her hands on her jeans. 'I know. But I wanted to clear this place up a bit. Jake said I could use it as my office.'

Grace stepped inside. 'This used to be my office,' she said wistfully as she looked around at the piles of boxes and junk the place had been used to store over the past few years.

'I know.' Stacey beamed at her. 'Jake told me you had it really nice in here.'

A few seconds later, Grace heard Jazz's voice behind her. 'Hi, Grace,' she said, walking into the room carrying two mugs of coffee. 'I didn't know you were stopping by. Do you want a drink?'

'No, thanks, Jazz. I just need to see Jake.' She smiled at her soon-to-be daughter-in-law. 'You helping Stacey sort this mess out?'

'Yep,' Jazz said with a laugh. 'I've left Connor at home with the baby, and I'm looking forward to a few hours of any talk that is non-baby related. Stacey has been telling me all about her and Luke,' Jazz said with a grin and a flash of her eyebrows.

'I bet she has. Well, I don't think that's a conversation I

need to hang around for,' Grace said with a laugh. Hearing about her brother's sex life was definitely not something she was interested in. 'I'll leave you two ladies to it, and I'll see you both Sunday.'

'Of course,' Stacey said.

'Actually, Grace, could I have a word?' Jazz said as Grace was leaving the small office.

'Of course. What is it?'

Jazz continued walking, as though she wanted to have the conversation in private, so Grace stepped into the hallway with her.

'Stacey getting the job here has made me think about what I want to do. As soon as Paul's a bit older anyway.'

'Oh, like what?'

'I was wondering if you might have any suggestions? Or any openings in the restaurants? I know you always need staff.'

'Waitressing?' Grace asked in surprise.

Jazz shrugged. 'I'd be happy to start at the bottom and work my way up if I needed to. But eventually I'd like something bigger. Managing this place would have been something I'd have loved to do. But I didn't know Jake was looking for someone, and I doubt Connor would have wanted me to work here. Besides, I think Stacey will be great at it and I don't begrudge her the opportunity.'

'You don't need to start at the bottom, Jazz. That's the beauty of us being a family business. Have a think about what you want to do, and I'll make sure it happens.'

Jazz blinked at her. 'Just like that?'

'You're my daughter-in-law. In less than two months

you'll be a Carter in name as well. You can work anywhere you please. Besides, I think you'd be amazing at whatever you turned your hand to.'

'I don't really have any idea what I'm looking for though,' Jazz said. 'The only job I've ever done before was dancing.'

'Then I'll have a think too. I'm sure we can come up with something between us.'

Jazz smiled. 'Thanks, Grace. I really appreciate it.'

'No problem at all. Now, I'd better find Jake before he dashes off somewhere.'

'Of course. I'll see you Sunday,' Jazz said before walking back into the office to help Stacey.

Grace walked along the corridor to Jake's office. His door was closed and she noticed the newly fitted keycode lock. She'd been telling him for ages he needed a lock for his door, given the business he was in and the fact that he often had tons of cash in the place. She was pleased to see he'd finally listened to her and got one. She raised her hand to knock on the door, pausing for a few seconds as more memories of her past rushed to the surface. This had been Jake's father's office once too. Nathan Conlon had been a vicious, cruel bastard, but she had loved him once. She closed her eyes as she thought about the naïve eighteen-year-old girl she had been when she'd met him. She'd had no idea back then that her life would change beyond all recognition.

She knocked on the door, and as she did, she realised that she had the perfect job for Jazz after all. But would she want it?

'Hang on,' Jake shouted, snapping her from her train of thought.

A moment later, he opened the door and smiled when he saw her. 'Hiya, Mum,' he said as he pulled her into a hug. 'This is a surprise.' He let her go and Grace stepped into his office. Danny was sitting on the small sofa in the corner of the room, looking decidedly sheepish, and she wondered what sort of business dealings she'd interrupted.

'Hi, Danny,' she said.

'Hey, Grace.' He smiled back as he stood up. 'I was just leaving.'

'You don't have to go on my account.'

'I'm not. I have to get back to the office,' Danny said, then he looked at Jake. 'I'll see you later, yeah?'

'Course,' Jake answered.

'Bye, Grace,' Danny said as he walked out of the office. Grace watched Jake stare after him.

No. It couldn't be! *Could it?*

'What did you want to see me about, Mum?' Jake interrupted her thoughts again.

'Oh.' She blinked at him. If what she'd just witnessed really was what she thought, then he obviously wasn't ready to tell her about it. 'I want to buy Michael a new car for his birthday.'

'You going to buy him a Bugatti then?' he said with a grin.

'Don't be daft. But you know what types of cars he likes. I wondered if you could come and look at some with me. I'll take you for a slap-up breakfast too.'

'Yeah. Course I will. When were you thinking?'

'How about next Monday? Just after nine once I've dropped the kids off?'

'It's a date,' he agreed.

'Thanks, Son. So, how is business doing then?' she asked as she took a seat opposite him.

'Great,' Jake said with a smile. 'In fact, it couldn't be better.'

Grace only half listened as Jake talked about the new ideas Stacey already had for the club. She was too distracted thinking about what she might have just walked in on. Danny had looked uncomfortable – almost embarrassed. Jake and Danny spent a lot of time together lately. They seemed to get on well, always happy in each other's company, and it occurred to Grace that Jake had seemed much more relaxed and content in recent months than he'd been in a long time. Was Danny the reason? And if Jake did have feelings for him, were they reciprocated?

Grace liked Danny. If she was going to choose a partner for her son, Danny pretty much ticked all the boxes. He was loyal, smart, ambitious, handsome, funny and, despite what he did for a living, he cared about the people he loved. But he was also well known for being a ladies' man, although she supposed that didn't mean he didn't like men too. She just hoped that Jake knew what he doing, and hadn't got himself involved in another relationship that was doomed to fail.

Chapter Twenty-Two

Craig Johnson was walking along the landing to his cell when he felt the hand on the small of his back.

'Just keep walking, lad,' the voice growled behind him. 'Don't want to cause a fuss in front of the screws, do we?'

Craig recognised the voice of Big H. He was a giant of a man who ruled B wing, and although he didn't work for Grace, Craig had a sinking feeling that he'd made a recent alliance with her. He swallowed and heard the sound of his heartbeat thumping in his ears. They approached a screw walking past and Craig made eye contact, hoping that the screw might ask him what he was doing or stop for a conversation, but all he did was wink at Big H and give him a nod as they passed. Bent fucker!

'No one in here can help you now, lad,' Big H said with a sinister chuckle. As he reached his cell, Craig noted that Ged wasn't there, but there were three other prisoners on his bed instead. Big H pushed him into the room and Craig stumbled inside.

'Where's Ged?' he snapped.

'He's gone for a shower,' one of the men on the bed answered with a grin. 'Might need some help walking later.' At this, the four men in the room started to laugh and Craig lunged for one of them. He was pulled back by Big H who proceeded to wrap a large forearm around Craig's throat.

'You should have kept your gob shut and done as you were told, Craig,' Big H hissed in his ear. 'Consider this a friendly reminder of what happens to people who don't keep their word.'

Craig lurched forward in agony as one of the men from the bed jumped up and punched him in the gut, but he was prevented from moving too far by Big H's continued hold on his throat. He was hit with another punch before Big H threw him to the floor. Soon all four men were kicking and punching him and Craig curled up into a ball, holding his arms over his head to try and protect himself as the blows rained down on him. He felt a sharp kick to his jaw and the metallic taste of blood filling his mouth. He wondered how much more of a beating he could take. Every part of his body screamed in agony and his head was starting to spin. They weren't going to stop until they finished him off. He was going to die on the floor of this filthy cell in Walton nick.

Then as quickly as the assault had started, it stopped. Craig took a deep breath and was about to open his eyes when he felt the warm liquid hit his cheeks and eyes, dripping down his face and onto his lips, some slipping into his open mouth. It was warm and salty. The sound of laughter filled the small cell as he realised they were all pissing on him. He spat the foul liquid from his mouth. Filthy bastards.

The next thing he heard was Big H's voice close to his ear. 'Think carefully about how you want to spend the rest of your time in here,' he growled.

Then he heard the sound of footsteps as the four men left his cell. When he was sure they had gone, Craig rolled onto his back, groaning in pain as he stretched his battered and bruised body. Raising his arm, he wiped the piss from his eyes and face. He winced. The effort made him feel like his chest was being stabbed with a thousand tiny knives. He looked up at the grey stone ceiling, wondering what fate had befallen Ged. This had to be the Carters' doing. He'd known it was risky for him and Ged to change their pleas, but when he'd found out that John Brennan was still swanning around Liverpool as large as life, and still Grace Carter's right-hand man, he'd realised that the lot of them had played him like a fiddle. That had to be the only explanation for it. There was no way that Grace would have allowed John's treachery to go unpunished.

Craig had been furious and when he'd told Ged about his suspicions, the two of them had sat up all night plotting their revenge, each of them fuelling the other's anger. Not only had Grace somehow convinced their eldest brother Bradley to take the fall for Billy's murder – not that the traitorous fucker didn't deserve to go down for life – but she had obviously been pulling the strings in the kidnap of that copper too, and he and Ged were going to go down for it. At least six years each, according to their brief – probably more. Well, if they were going down, they would take the whole fucking lot of them down too.

It was only now, lying in a cell, covered in someone else's piss and his own blood, that Craig realised what a stupid idea that had been. He'd been blinded by his rage, and fuelled by Ged's anger and general stupidity. It had been a spur-of-the-moment decision. He'd been standing in the dock and the words had left his mouth before he could consider the implications of what he was doing. Ged had looked across at him and then he'd changed his plea too, the pair of them deciding that a trial could be their best option to drag John Brennan and the Carters through the mud. And this was the result. Not only did they no longer have Grace Carter's protection, but they had gone and made an enemy of the woman, and in doing that, they'd gone and made an enemy of almost everyone else in Liverpool. If you weren't with Grace Carter then you were against her – and no one in their right mind ever went against her, because this was how you ended up.

Chapter Twenty-Three

Faye Donovan smiled at the prison officer as he showed her to the small interview room in Walton prison. She sat on the chair facing the small corridor and waited for her charge to be brought to her. A few moment later, a man wearing a prison issue grey tracksuit and fluorescent orange vest was escorted into the room. He had a black eye, a gash across his nose and a split lip. The way he held his arm across his broad chest as he walked into the room and winced when he sat down assured her that he had already been paid a visit by some of Grace Carter's men. She smiled to herself – if they were the stick, she was there to offer the carrot.

'You're not my brief,' Craig said coolly as he let his eyes roam over her face and down to her breasts.

'Well, you are a clever boy, aren't you?' Faye replied with a roll of her eyes. 'No, I'm not your brief, Craig – you couldn't afford me. My name is Faye Donovan.'

At the mention of her name, Craig started to scowl. 'You

work for Grace Carter. So what the fuck do you want with me?' he snarled.

'I wanted to speak to you about your recent change of heart,' she said with a smile.

He snorted and then clutched his stomach as the though the effort had pained him. 'What's it to you?'

'I'm not here to play games, Craig. You know who I work for. I want to know why you went back on your word and changed your plea to not guilty.'

'Well, I have a few questions of my own, *Faye*.' He spat her name. 'Such as, why is it that John Brennan is not only walking around with his head still attached to his body, but is still Grace Carter's right-hand man? I can only conclude that the pair of them stitched me up.'

'So what's your game plan then? Plead not guilty and try and pin it on someone else?'

Craig shrugged. 'If this thing goes to trial, then I get to tell the court about John Brennan setting me up, don't I?'

'And you honestly think that will work?'

'What have I got to lose?'

'Well, I'm sure you're pretty attached to your appendage, aren't you?'

'As you can see, I've already been on the receiving end of Grace Carter's threats,' he said as he held out his arms. 'So I think I'll take my chances in court.'

Faye leaned forward and looked into Craig's eyes. 'Whatever you might say in court, the fact of the matter is, you kidnapped Sergeant Bryce. He has positively identified the pair of you. You were caught in the lock-up with him. Your DNA was on his clothes. There is no getting away from that. This is what we refer to as an open and shut case, Craig. So it doesn't matter if you implicate anyone else – you and your brother are still going down for it.'

Craig glared at her. 'I see you're not denying that her and that *fucker* stitched me up though.'

Faye rolled her eyes. 'I don't concern myself with the intricacies of what Grace does, and I don't care one way or another if you were stitched up. I expect you got exactly what was coming to you. But I am here to offer you a deal.'

Craig stared at her, his eyes narrowed. 'What kind of deal?'

'Plead guilty and I will have my firm represent you.'

'You'll represent me?' Craig said, raising his eyebrows.

'My firm will. You know how good we are, Craig. I will make sure we get you the best possible sentence. But you and I both know that six years in here with Grace's protection will be easier to get through than six months without it.'

Craig leaned forward. 'Is that another threat?' he snarled.

Faye smiled at him. Arrogant little pricks like him didn't intimidate her one bit. 'I'm not in the business of making threats. You have twenty-four hours to instruct me as your solicitor and change your plea. After that, you're on your own.'

Chapter Twenty-Four

D I Leigh Moss sat at her desk and sighed as she thought about the mountain of paperwork she had to complete. The admin was a necessary part of the job, but she was much more hands-on than most DIs and so she struggled to keep on top of her workload. She glanced at her watch and realised she was going to be late for dinner again. It was her turn to cook too. Still, John wouldn't mind. He was a night owl and never seemed to care what time she rolled home, as long as she got there eventually. She smiled as she thought about John. She could hardly believe that he had walked away from his life as Grace Carter's right-hand man for her. It didn't change who he was, and her seeing him was never going to be straightforward, but he had sworn to be legit from now on and what more could she ask of him? He couldn't change his past, just as she couldn't change hers. She loved him just as he was, and he loved her, and she had never felt happier in her whole life.

The sound of her mobile ringing snapped her from her

thoughts of John. She wondered if it was him and felt her heart flutter in her chest at the thought of hearing his deep, soothing voice. God, she was acting like a love-struck teenager.

Taking her phone from her pocket, Leigh saw the call was coming from a withheld number. She swiped the screen and answered.

'Hello?' she said.

'Leigh? It's Kelly Ward. From Walton. We met a few months ago.'

Leigh remembered the petite, blonde prison officer she'd met during a trial involving one of her colleagues being sexually assaulted. The two women had got on well and had realised they had come from the same neighbourhood in Manchester, albeit Kelly was a good ten years younger than Leigh. They hadn't remained in contact but both women had a lot of respect for each other.

'Hi, Kelly. It's nice to hear from you. Is everything okay?' Leigh asked.

'Not exactly. I have something to tell you, and it's kind of … delicate.'

'Okay?' Leigh said, the hair on the back of her neck standing on end. The tone of Kelly's voice suggested this was something Leigh wasn't going to want to hear.

'Are you alone? Can you talk?' Kelly asked.

'Yes. I'm in my office,' Leigh replied.

She heard Kelly drawing in a breath and then a pause.

'What is it?' Leigh prompted her, her anxiety about what Kelly was about to reveal getting the better of her.

'Look, I may be way off base here, but I've heard on the grapevine that you're seeing John Brennan,' Kelly said.

Leigh felt like she'd been punched in the gut. She and John were discreet, they didn't advertise their relationship, but then Leigh supposed they didn't exactly hide away in secret. But what on earth did this have to do with Kelly? It was none of her damn business who Leigh went out with.

'What does who I am or I'm not seeing have to do with anything?' Leigh snapped.

'Oh, come on, Leigh, I don't care who you're seeing. That's not why I'm calling. But I heard something about John that I thought you would want to know.'

Leigh leaned back in her chair as her heart started to thud against her ribcage. 'What?'

'That it was him behind Nick Bryce's kidnap. Apparently, he orchestrated it all. No doubt on the Carters' orders.'

Leigh felt like she couldn't breathe, as though all of a sudden all the air had been sucked from the room. 'What?' she gasped. 'Who is your source?'

'You know the Johnsons changed their plea?'

'Yeah. For about five minutes,' Leigh replied.

'Well, they told their brief it was because John was behind the whole thing.' Kelly said.

'How do you know this?'

'You know things get around the wing. It could be a load of bollocks, especially as the Johnsons changed their plea again a few days later. But I just thought you'd want to know what had been said.'

Leigh wasn't sure if she did want to know. 'Thanks,

Kelly,' she said as she ended the call, not even waiting for Kelly to reply. She looked around her office in a daze. Surely this couldn't be true? How could John keep that from her? She knew the type of man he was, but he wasn't cruel. He wasn't a liar. It must have been the Johnsons trying to weasel their way out of the whole thing. That was the only rational explanation. At least it was the only one she was prepared to consider right now, because the alternative was unthinkable. And if was true, what the hell had it all been about? John would have been acting on Grace's orders, so why the hell had she arranged to have Nick Bryce kidnapped?

Suddenly, the paperwork on her desk was the last thing on Leigh's mind. She grabbed her car keys from her desk, picked up her handbag and headed for the door. She had to see John so he could tell her that there wasn't even an ounce of truth in what Kelly had just told him.

———

Leigh let herself into John's house. He'd given her a key a few weeks earlier as she barely stayed at her own place anymore. Little by little, she was leaving more of her things there and, as she walked down the thickly carpeted hallway, she realised that she was beginning to think of this place as home.

She looked up as John came jogging down the stairs in just a pair of shorts and with damp hair, suggesting he'd taken a shower.

'You're early,' he said with a smile. 'Miss me, did you?'

Leigh looked at him and swallowed. She hoped that he was going to tell her that what she was about to ask him was completely crazy. She hoped that he would pull her into his giant arms and tell her she was being ridiculous. Because the thought that John had been involved in Nick's kidnap, and had then kept it from her all this time, was too much to bear.

As she stared at him, she decided she was just going to ask him straight out. She wanted to catch him off guard so he wouldn't have time to think of anything to tell her but the truth.

'Did you have anything to do with Nick's kidnapping?' she asked.

He stopped mid-jog. 'What?'

'I asked you if you had anything to do with Nick's kidnap. You remember him, don't you? My ex-boyfriend? My colleague.'

John rushed down the rest of the stairs and placed a hand on her arm. 'Leigh,' he said.

Leigh's heart felt like it dropped through her stomach and onto the floor. He hadn't denied it. Why hadn't he denied the accusation immediately?

'Well?' she shrieked, feeling the anger and the uncertainty swirling in her chest.

He put his hands on her arms and stared at her, as though searching her face for something.

'John!' she shouted. Why wouldn't he just answer her?

His hands dropped from her arms and he ran one over his stubble. 'Yes,' he answered with a sigh.

Leigh felt like someone had taken a sledgehammer to

the back of her knees. She stumbled backwards, away from him. He reached out to her. 'Don't you dare touch me,' she hissed.

'Please, Leigh. I can explain.'

'Explain?' She went on backing away and bumped up against the oak sideboard in the hall. She rested against it in case her knees gave way. Placing her hands either side of her onto the solid piece of furniture somehow helped to ground her. She gripped the edge of the wood, her fingers clenched around it. 'Well, please do. Because I'd like to know what the hell is going on. How the hell have you let me share your bed knowing what you did to me, to Nick, to my relationship?' she shouted.

'It wasn't personal, Leigh. I didn't even know you then,' he said quietly. 'He was never going to be hurt.'

'Never going to be hurt?' she screeched. 'He had concussion and a broken wrist.'

John shook his head as though that was nothing to him, and Leigh suddenly realised that in John's world that *was* nothing. Jesus, what had she been doing, allowing herself to fall for a man like this?

'I mean he was always going to be okay,' John said.

'Okay? You might want to ask Nick about that, John. Because from what I've heard, he hasn't been the same since you and those Johnson fools kidnapped him and beat him up.'

John stared at the floor and she shook her head in disgust. At least he had the courtesy to look a little ashamed of himself.

'You're a fucking animal,' she spat at him. 'I can't believe

I ever thought you could be anything more,' she snarled. She wanted to hurt him now, like he had hurt her. She wanted to push him until he snapped. He just stood on the spot nodding, as though he agreed with her. That made her even more angry. He was just giving up. He wasn't even trying to justify his actions or making any attempt to excuse his behaviour. Under ordinary circumstances, that would have been a noble character trait, but she wasn't thinking rationally. Why wouldn't he fight for this? Why wouldn't he fight for her? She wanted to rage at him – to pummel his chest with her fists. But she stood glaring at him, waiting for him somehow to make all of this okay. He said nothing and they stood in silence for a few moments as the tension in the air crackled around them.

'Why did even you do it?' she asked.

He looked at her like she'd just asked him the most obvious question in the world – and then she realised that it was. Of course. She shook her head. 'Grace fucking Carter told you to. That's why.'

John shrugged his shoulders.

'That's the reason you do everything. Did she tell you to do this?' She indicated the empty space between them with her hands. 'Me and you? Is this on her orders as well?'

She saw the instant change in his face. 'No! Of course not,' he said with a frown.

She laughed. 'And you expect me to believe that? You expect me to believe anything you tell me ever again?'

'I have never lied about how I feel about you, Leigh. Everything that has happened between us is real.'

'No!' she shouted. 'No. It's not real, because it is all

based on lies, John! All of it. Do you think if Nick hadn't been kidnapped I'd even be here with you? You destroyed my relationship with a perfectly good man. Nick Bryce is ten times the man you are, and if you hadn't fucked him up, then I would be with him now – not you!' She spat the last words out and watched the pain flicker across his face. None of that was true but she didn't care. All she cared about was the fact that John Brennan had ripped her heart from her chest and trampled on it – and she wanted to do the same to him.

John stood in his hallway and watched helplessly as the woman he loved discovered exactly what a monster he was. He got the sense that she wanted him to justify himself – even to lie, perhaps? But how could he? There was no justification for what he'd done. All he could offer her was the truth.

'I did what I was paid to do, Leigh. I'm not going to try and excuse that. It was my job. I didn't ask questions. That's why I left. I don't do that anymore because I don't want to be that man anymore. And that's because of you.'

She snorted in response.

'I love you, Leigh. I'm sorry that I hid this from you—'

'But you're not sorry for what you did to Nick?'

'It was my job.'

'So, no then?' she snapped.

'I'm sorry that it hurt you. I'm sorry that what I did ruined your relationship. I hadn't realised that. But what I did to Nick – that is the man I am, Leigh. But you knew that about me.' He didn't ask her why she was prepared to overlook all the other men he had kidnapped or beaten up or even killed, because he didn't want to remind her any more than he already had of the type of man she was in love with.

He watched as her shoulders drooped and wondered if there was any hope to be gleaned from it.

'I do know that, John. But this is different. Every minute you kept that secret, you weren't being honest with me. I can't forgive that.'

John chewed on his lower lip. He wanted to walk over to her and wrap her in his arms and tell her that they could make it work, but he knew it was futile. She had made up her mind and he supposed he couldn't blame her. He had worried that his involvement in Nick's kidnapping would eventually come out and be their undoing. Grace had even warned him about it. She'd advised him to pin all of the blame on her and claim he had no choice, but he wasn't prepared to do that. He might have been working under Grace Carter's orders, but he never did anything he didn't feel comfortable with. And kidnapping Nick Bryce had been something he'd been more than happy to do at the time.

Leigh took her keys out of her pocket and started to unthread his house key from the ring that held them together. He watched in silence as she placed it on the wooden sideboard.

Then she turned to him with her eyes full of tears. 'Bye, John.'

He watched as she walked out of the front door. As soon as it closed behind her he sat on the bottom stair and took a deep breath. He'd never experienced this before. He had never felt so helpless in all his life. Leigh Moss had just torn out his heart and thrown it away and there wasn't a single thing he could do about it.

Chapter Twenty-Five

Grace dialled Luke's number and waited for him to answer. She hadn't seen much of him since their visit to Glenda a few weeks before. She'd spoken to Stacey, who said that he was still struggling to process what Glenda had done, and the fact that his mum had known all about his half-sister but had never told him.

'Hi, Grace,' Luke answered after a few rings.

'Hiya. Are you free?'

'I can be, why?' he asked.

'I wondered if you fancied coming for a drive with me?'

'Okay? Where to?'

Grace paused for a few seconds. 'The past?' she finally said.

'Sounds intriguing,' Luke said with a laugh.

'Shall I pick you up in half an hour then?' she asked.

'Yeah. See you then,' Luke replied.

• • •

Luke was waiting for her when Grace pulled up outside his house. He jogged down the path and climbed into the passenger seat.

'So, where is this mysterious place you're taking me?' he asked.

'Wait and see,' she said with a grin.

Fifteen minutes later she pulled the car over into a side street off Smithdown Road and turned off the engine.

Luke frowned at her and looked around the street.

'Come on,' Grace said with a smile.

They stepped out of the car and Grace led the way to an empty plot of land a few hundred yards around the corner. It was fenced off with huge security signs warning trespassers to keep out. Grace pulled a key from her pocket and opened the padlock on the steel gates while Luke looked on in bewilderment.

'Coming in?' she asked him.

'Have you bought this place, Grace?' he asked.

'Not exactly,' she said as she stepped inside the gate.

Luke closed it behind him and stepped inside the large plot. He looked around appreciatively. 'This is a great space. You could build anything you want on here, Grace.'

Grace smiled. 'You certainly could. But I'm not building anything on it.'

He frowned at her.

'In fact, you could say this is the place that built me,' she said as she looked around. 'At least what once stood here did. This was The Rose and Crown a long time ago.'

'Of course it was. I remember it now. I used to drive past it all the time, but I didn't recognise it like this.'

'It was a beautiful pub. Dad helped to design it, you know? But after the fire, it had to be knocked down. The structure was completely knackered. Nothing could be salvaged.'

'Are you thinking of rebuilding?' Luke asked as he wandered around the plot.

'No. You know what they say, Luke. You can't go home again,' she said with a faint smile.

'So, why are we here?'

'I'm thinking of selling it. I've had so many offers for this land over the years, but I never had the heart to accept any.'

'But you do now?'

'This is my past. It has no place in my future. But I thought I should show you the place before I sold it. This is your legacy too, Luke.'

He shook his head. 'No. This was yours and your dad's place.'

'Our dad's,' she reminded him. 'He was a great dad, you know? He would have spoiled you rotten. It's not his fault he never got to share any of your life with you.'

'I know.'

Grace sat on a small pile of bricks and Luke sat on the ground nearby. 'You know, back when I lived here, I would have killed to have a little brother. I used to dream about my dad meeting someone else and having kids,' she said with a shake of her head as long-forgotten memories came flooding back.

'I wish she'd told you – both of us,' Luke said.

'She had her reasons and I'm sure she believed she was

doing right by the both of us. From what you've told me about her, I can't imagine your mum was a vindictive person. It sounded like it was a secret that tormented her towards the end.'

'I know,' he said with a sigh. 'But it's shit that we only just found out about each other.'

'It is,' she agreed. 'But would either of us be the people we are today if we'd known about each other? Maybe I would never have fallen for Nathan if you and your mum had been in my life? Maybe you would have lived here and never met Danny and Stacey?'

He shrugged. 'Maybe?'

'As awful as some things are to live through, I've always thought that everything that happens in life leads us to exactly where we're supposed to be.'

'That's a nice philosophy to have, Grace. Although I'm not sure everyone would agree with it.'

She smiled. 'Well, it doesn't work for everyone.'

He frowned at her. 'I have a feeling there's a lesson here for me somewhere. This feels like more than a walk down memory lane.'

Grace started to laugh. 'Not a lesson, no. Just wanted you to see a part of your history before someone converts it into student apartments.'

He looked around. 'Haven't you ever thought about rebuilding?'

'Yes. Plenty of times, but like I said, this is my past. You could rebuild though. It's yours if you want it?'

He shook his head. 'No. I couldn't.'

'Why not? This place is as much yours as it is mine.'

'No. It wouldn't feel right. And you're right. This is the past. Maybe it's time to let it go?'

'Well, I have until the end of the week to sign the papers, so if you change your mind, it's all yours.'

'It's a definite no. But I do appreciate the offer.'

'Well, anything for my little brother,' she said as she stood up and ruffled his hair.

'I'm not sure I'll ever get used to you calling me that,' he said with a genuine smile.

'Well, you'd better. I have twenty-eight years of embarrassing you to make up for.' She held out her hand and helped him up. 'Take a last look around then, little bro, because we're about to make a shitload of money from this piece of land.'

He brushed the dust from his trousers as he stood. 'How much are you selling it for?' he asked.

'It's a surprise. You'll find out when I give you your half.'

'No.' He shook his head. 'This isn't mine, Grace. It's yours. I don't want half.'

'Our dad bought this plot for twelve grand in 1974. It's worth over fifty times that now,' she said as she started to walk back towards the gate.

'He left me and my mum money though. He made sure I had a good life. This is your inheritance, not mine.'

Grace held up her hand. 'It's not up for discussion, Luke. Come on, I'll let you buy me some lunch and then we can call it quits.'

He shook his head in exasperation. 'That would be some lunch,' he said with a grin.

'Well, I am pretty hungry.' She laughed and opened the gate for him. She knew that he wasn't in need of the money from the sale of the land. He earned more than that in a few months, working for Jake and Connor, but it was important to her that he allow her to share this with him. Despite everything that had happened, she believed her father would have wanted it that way.

'Right then. Where do you fancy?' Luke asked as he ducked through the gate and back out onto the street.

'How about that new Thai place on Allerton Road? I fancy something different,' Grace suggested.

'Sounds good to me.' He put his hands into his jacket pockets and Grace linked her arm through his as they walked back towards her car.

Chapter Twenty-Six

DI Leigh Moss looked up at the large whiteboard in the incident room, noting the photographs of the two suspects they had arrested the previous day – Brodie Fox and Dean Wilkinson, two of the newest members of the notorious Bridewell Blades crew. The twenty-four hours they'd originally had to charge had run out, but Leigh had successfully applied for a twenty-four-hour extension. It had been granted, given the serious nature of the charges the two eighteen-year-olds were facing – rape and wounding. The victim, Kacey Jones, had provided their names, but had claimed she didn't recognise any of her other attackers. The police doctor had taken forensic evidence and once they had all of the necessary results back from the lab, Leigh was confident they could make some further arrests. There had been witnesses to the assault and it had happened in a house on the estate that belonged to one of the gang members, but Leigh and her team had been met with a wall of silence when they had visited the estate to undertake enquiries. The Bridewell crew had the whole community running scared.

Leigh had hoped that Kacey's bravery might encourage some of the other victims to come forward, but as yet none had. It was a well-known fact that the Bridewell crew used young women as part of their initiation into the gang and the thought of all the other victims who had endured assaults just like Kacey's made her feel sick.

'Any news from Forensics, Mark?' she asked her sergeant.

'Not yet, Boss. I've asked them to put a rush job on it. But they're backed up down there.'

'Let's hope they get us some more matches and we'll bring in as many of those sick bastards as we can.'

'You think we'll get the King brothers?' Mark asked.

Leigh shook her head. 'I have no doubt they oversaw the whole thing, but if they had been involved, I doubt poor Kacey would have ever made it to A&E. They wouldn't have risked it.'

'You're probably right.'

'Where are we with a charge with Fox and Wilkinson anyway?'

'Still waiting on CPS, Boss. We should have a decision by the end of the day, tomorrow morning at the latest.'

'What the hell are they waiting for? We have DNA evidence. The victim has injuries consistent with her statement.'

'I know. But Fox and Wilkinson deny everything. They say it was all consensual. They claim she is well known across the estate for "liking it rough" and their brief has provided a host of names who will apparently attest to that fact.'

'I bet they will. But, regardless of that, we have the evidence to charge.'

'Kacey has form for shoplifting and assault herself—'

'Don't even say it, Mark,' Leigh snapped, aware of the direction this conversation was heading in.

He shrugged. 'It's not me, Boss, you know that. I want to see these fuckers rot as much as you do. But CPS are questioning whether she's a credible witness.'

'A credible witness? Well, we'll see about that,' she said as she slammed the folder in her hand onto the desk in front of her and stormed out of the room.

'Credible witness'! Leigh hated that term with a passion. It should be banned from legal terminology as far as she was concerned, particularly any case involving sexual assault and rape. All too often victims of such offences didn't come forward. They were too ashamed, or too afraid because of the way they were treated by the Criminal Justice system. And bullshit terms like 'credible witness' didn't help matters. Things had certainly improved in recent years, and Leigh's Phoenix team had been set up as a direct response to such concerns, but there was still far more to be done.

She crossed the office to the back stairwell on her way to the CPS office. John had been right, she couldn't give up this job. The people she helped meant too much to her. The thought of John came out of the blue. It was natural to her as breathing. She often thought about him during her working day – something he'd done or said would often make her smile or see things from a new perspective. She supposed she would have to stop doing that now. It had been two days since she had told him it was over and the pain of his betrayal was still raw. She had completely let her guard down with him. Despite who he was, she had stupidly believed they might have some sort of future together. Although she hadn't said the words out loud to him, she had fallen in love with him, and she had believed that he loved her too. So how could he have kept that from her? How could he have looked her in the eye day after day, knowing what he had done?

She felt a renewed anger, mixed with a deep sadness. John was in her past, and after she'd discovered that he was connected to Nick's kidnap, it was exactly where he belonged. She took a deep breath as she pushed open the heavy glass door on the second floor. It was for the best anyway. She and John were completely incompatible. Better she found out now before she got in even deeper than she already was. Her work was her one true love after all. Maybe that was all she'd ever have?

Maybe that was all she deserved?

Chapter Twenty-Seven

G race picked up the menu and glanced over it as she thought about what to choose for lunch.

'What are you two having?' she asked Michael and Sean.

'Steak,' they replied in unison.

She shook her head. 'You're so predictable,' she said with a laugh.

'At least it doesn't take us half an hour to decide what to have,' Sean grinned as he poured himself a glass of iced water from the jug on the table.

'Well, I like to try different things. Your daughter puts a lot of thought into these dishes,' she replied. Sean's eldest daughter Steph was the head chef at Antonelli's and she oversaw the menus for all of their restaurants.

'She cooks an amazing steak too,' Sean replied. 'Try it?'

Grace closed the menu. 'Fine. I'll have a steak too. Isn't Sophia working today?'

'No. Steph asked me to change the rota so they had less

shifts together,' he said with a knowing smile. Sean's wife, Sophia, also worked at Antonelli's with their daughter – behind the bar mostly. She didn't need to, and often tried to interfere in Steph's kitchen, but she liked to keep herself busy and Sean was always willing to indulge his wife in any way he could.

Michael signalled the waitress over and sat back in his chair, his arm draped around Grace's shoulders. 'What's this new venture of yours then?' he asked Sean.

'I was talking to my contact in the council and he told me that the nightclub next to Sophia's is about to go into administration. I think we should buy it.'

Grace had heard that too several weeks earlier from the owner of said nightclub but she kept that to herself.

'You want to expand Sophia's?' Michael asked.

Sean shook his head. 'No. Let's keep it as a nightclub. Rebrand and reopen.'

'But then we'll be in competition with ourselves,' Grace said with a raised eyebrow.

'Not really. Our late-night customers are a different clientele. And those people who start off their night at Sophia's but move on elsewhere will have somewhere to go right next door.'

'A nightclub though, Bro?' Michael said as he shook his head and smiled. 'I think we're about twenty years too old to start running nightclubs. Let's leave that to Jake and Connor.'

Sean remained undeterred. 'You don't have to be that involved if you don't want to. I'll oversee it.'

'But Sean, we've only just opened Oscar's,' Grace said, reminding him of their new restaurant and bar in Chester. 'I thought we'd agreed we were going to relax for a bit before we decided on our next venture.'

'I don't want to relax, Grace,' he snapped.

Grace heard Michael sigh beside her. Sean had been acting strangely lately. He was restless and he was looking to take risks that he didn't need to take.

Sean looked at Michael. 'You keep saying we're too old for shit, Michael, but you're only forty-seven, for fuck's sake.'

'Yeah. Maybe we're not old. But I'm far too long in the tooth to be getting into the fucking nightclub game, Sean. I want to sit back and enjoy what we've built before we move onto out next thing. And I'm sorry, mate, but I don't want our next thing to be a nightclub.'

'Look, you two say you want to relax, but the reality is you don't. You're still in the thick of it and don't pretend otherwise.'

'Is that what this is really about?' Grace asked him. 'You want back in? Are you completely mental?'

'We're only watching out for Connor and Jake, mate. Or else we'd be out of it too,' Michael added.

Sean frowned. 'If we're not opening a nightclub, then I want back into the other side of the family business.'

'I think I'd prefer the nightclub,' Grace said and Michael laughed.

'Sean, I would love to have you back on board with me. You know that. But Sophia will kill you. And me da will kill you as well if he ever finds out. Do you know how proud he is of you being completely legit?'

'Dad will be fine. He can hardly say anything, can he? He was still splitting heads open in his sixties. Besides, neither him nor Sophia need to know.'

Grace shook her head. 'I'm not lying to her.'

'You don't have to. Just don't tell her – that's completely different,' Sean replied.

'I think you'll find it's not, Sean,' Grace said.

'I'm just asking to be involved in the action sometimes,' he countered.

'I'm not even involved in the action, Sean.' Michael's voice was serious now. 'I leave that to the lads. Trust me, mate. You're well out of it.'

Just then their waitress came over to take their orders and their conversation turned to talk of their respective children as well as plans for Michael's upcoming birthday. Grace was relieved that Sean had forgotten about his crazy ideas, for now at least. But she knew him well enough to know that this wouldn't be the end of it. For some reason, Sean had been getting increasingly restless lately. There was a time when he had been determined to leave that life behind him, and he'd made a bloody good job of doing so. So why the hell he wanted back in was beyond her.

Grace loved Sean. Even before she and Michael had got together, the two of them had been good friends. He'd always been there when she needed him, and she liked to think he thought the same of her. But as much as she loved him, she also knew he was as stubborn as an ox. If he wanted back into the family business, then she wasn't sure she could talk him out of it. He was willing to throw away everything he'd worked for, and for what? She couldn't understand him lately. All she could think was that he missed working by Michael's side. But if Michael had his way, he'd be leaving the family business himself as soon as he could.

Michael pushed open the heavy glass doors of Antonelli's and walked outside, holding it open for Sean. Grace had stayed behind for an afternoon of cocktails with Steph after she'd finished her shift and he had promised to collect her later after he'd dropped off their youngest children for their sleepover with Jazz and Connor.

As they walked along the road to Michael's car, Sean put an arm around his shoulder. 'You're not seriously going to freeze me out if I want back in, are you?'

Michael sighed. 'I think you're off your head, mate. I've told you, as soon as Grace gives me the nod, I'll be out of here like a shot. The thought of just managing the restaurants and the wine bar is like a dream come true. I don't understand why you want to get involved in all the dodgy shit again.'

'Are you saying no?' Sean replied with a scowl.

Michael looked at him. The truth was he loved working with Sean, even if he did think he was mental. But how could he refuse him? 'You can be as involved as you want, mate. But it's your funeral if Sophia or the arl fella find out.'

'Well, we'd better make sure they don't find out then,' Sean said as he pulled him tighter.

'I'm telling Grace,' Michael added.

'Of course. She'll be fine though. She loves me.' He winked.

'Yeah, and that's the problem, you divvy.'

Chapter Twenty-Eight

I sat in the coffee shop window, sipping my latte and watching the Carter brothers as they walked down the street towards Michael's car. I watched as one put an arm around the other. They walked and talked– as though they didn't have a care in the world. They didn't give a shit about who they hurt or the people they stepped on to get to the top. They just took.

I stared intently as they stopped beside the car. They were deep in conversation and one of them started to laugh.

Prick!

Anyone who didn't know them would just think they were a couple of brothers sharing a nice moment. The fact that Michael Carter got to share any moments with his brother stuck in my throat. I felt like running out of the café and over the road to warn all the passers-by that these men were monsters. I wanted to tell the whole world who Michael Carter really was and what he had taken from me. But I wasn't stupid. I knew that was tantamount to suicide. Instead, I would continue to bide my time. Waiting for the right moment when Michael would be alone. When he wouldn't have his brother or his sons around him.

The brothers climbed into the Aston Martin and I watched as it pulled away from the kerb. It irritated me that they had left so soon. I'd been sitting in the café for two hours waiting for them to come out of the restaurant – and all I'd got for my efforts was a few minutes of watching Michael and his brother chatting like a pair of old women.

I drained my latte and placed the cup on the table. If only I could follow them now – see where they were going next. But it was too risky. The old red Fiesta I was reduced to driving around was too conspicuous. And Michael Carter was not a stupid man.

But soon he would be a dead one.

Tick Tock, Michael.

Tick Tock.

Chapter Twenty-Nine

Jake rolled over and picked up his mobile phone as the sound of it vibrating on his bedside table roused him from his sleep. He saw his mum's name flashing on the screen and swiped to answer the call.

'All right, Mum,' he said sleepily.

'Morning, son. I'm on my way up. Are you ready?'

'What?'

'You forgot, didn't you?' she said with a laugh.

'Oh fuck! The car. Sorry, Mum,' he said as he sat up in bed and glanced at a sleeping Danny. 'I'll just get a quick shower and then we can go. You can buy me breakfast on the way.'

'Sounds like a deal. I'll be there in a minute. I'll make myself a coffee while I wait.'

'See you in a minute,' he said before ending the call. He nudged Danny awake.

'What?' Danny mumbled.

'Didn't you hear that? My mum is on her way up here.

She'll be here in about forty-five seconds,' he said as he got out of bed and started pulling on some shorts.

'Fuck!' Danny said as he sprang out of bed and started scrabbling around the floor for his clothes. 'What's she doing here?' he snapped.

'Well, she's my fucking mother, so she doesn't really need an excuse to visit me,' Jake snapped back.

Danny pulled on his boxers. 'I'm sorry. I just meant … well, she doesn't usually just turn up?'

'She's buying Michael a new car for his birthday and I promised her I'd go and look at some with her. I completely forgot it was this morning.'

'What am I going to do?' Danny said.

Jake stopped and looked at him. 'Well, we can lie and tell her you slept on the couch – but remember this is my mum we're talking about, and she has the best bullshit detector of anyone I've ever known. Or we can tell her the truth?'

Danny swallowed. 'That I slept in here with you?'

'She won't tell anyone else if that's what you're worried about. Well, except for Michael. But he won't tell anyone either. It's up to you,' Jake said as he pulled a T-shirt over his head. A knock at the door stopped their conversation from going any further.

Jake walked out of the bedroom and Danny followed close behind him. He walked into the kitchen as Jake opened the front door.

'Morning, Mum,' Jake said as he pulled her into a hug.

'Morning, Son. I'm not interrupting anything, am I?' she asked with a raise of her eyebrows.

'Danny's in the kitchen,' Jake replied. 'He's making coffee.'

Grace followed her son into the kitchen to see Danny Alexander standing there in shorts and T-shirt. He'd obviously spent the night. Perhaps he'd slept on the sofa? But she recalled the way Jake had looked at him the other day, and the tension in the air suggested that there was much more between Danny and her son than either of them had let on.

Jake lifted a bottle of water from the fridge and took a long drink. 'I'm going for a shower. I won't be long,' he said with a smile before disappearing.

'Coffee, Grace?' Danny asked as he held up the kettle full of boiling water.

'Oh, yes, please, I'd love one,' she replied.

She watched as Danny manoeuvred around the kitchen making them both a drink. It was clear he was familiar with the place and he seemed very comfortable in his surroundings. A few moments later, he placed two mugs of coffee on the kitchen table and sat down opposite her.

'Thanks,' Grace said with a smile. 'So, I know this is none of my business really, but are you and Jake seeing each other?'

Danny blinked at her for a few seconds, obviously considering his answer. 'Yep,' he replied eventually, his cheeks flushing a light shade of pink.

'Good,' Grace replied.

'Good?'

'Yes. Why wouldn't it be?'

'I thought you might think I was taking advantage of him.'

Grace laughed. If anything, she'd been wondering if it was the other way around – not that she'd admit that to Danny. She had heard of Danny's reputation as a bit of a player. If the rumours were true, he used to have a different woman for every night of the week. But she'd never had any inkling that he enjoyed the company of men too. And now he was in a relationship of some sort with Jake. Grace adored her son and she always believed the best of him, but he was just like his father in many respects, full of charisma and charm and making sure he got what he wanted by any means necessary. He had a way of making people bend to his will and thinking it was their own doing.

'Of course I don't think that, Danny,' she said instead. 'Why would I?'

He shrugged. 'It's just, you brought me and Luke in to work for you, and now I'm seeing your son. I didn't plan this, Grace.'

'Danny,' Grace said as she put a reassuring hand on his arm, 'Jake is a grown man. I worry about him every day in so many ways, for many different reasons, but him being taken advantage of is not something that concerns me at all.'

Danny smiled and shook his head. 'No, I suppose not.'

'It's nice to see him so happy. I was wondering if it had anything to do with him having someone in his life. I didn't realise you were bisexual though.'

Danny started to laugh. 'Neither did I until I met Jake.'

———————————

Jake was driving Grace to Maria's café. She had promised him one of Maria's famous fry-ups before they headed to the car dealership to choose Michael's birthday present. Danny had got dressed and left Jake's flat just before they did. Grace had excused herself to use the bathroom to allow them to say goodbye without her standing around watching them.

'So, how long have you and Danny been seeing each other then?' she asked.

Jake started to laugh loudly.

'What?'

'You've been itching to ask me that since Danny left, haven't you? I'm surprised you managed to wait so long. It must be, what, all of fifteen minutes?'

'Well? Are you going to put me out of my misery then? Tell me what I need to know.'

'Such as?' He turned to her as he stopped at some traffic lights.

'How long have you two been seeing each other? Do I need to buy a hat?' It was Grace's turn to laugh now.

'A couple of months. That's all. Don't be getting ideas, Mum.'

'Well, you must be serious if he's sleeping over. And if you told me.'

'Well, I didn't actually tell you. Danny did, and that was probably only because you interrogated him.'

'I did not interrogate him,' Grace said and when Jake started laughing again she knew he was teasing her.

'Yes, it's serious,' Jake said quietly. 'But Danny...' He shook his head. 'I don't know. He wants to keep things quiet, and I get where he's coming from, Mum, but I don't want to hide who we are anymore.'

'Well, he told me. And I swear I didn't interrogate him. So that's something.'

'It's a start,' Jake said with a sigh.

'Give him time, Son. I got the feeling this is all a bit new to him.'

'What? Being into men?'

'Well, yes, there's that, but I actually meant being in a relationship. He's never been big on them, has he?'

'No. But then neither have I,' Jake said with a shrug.

Grace suppressed a smile. She had a feeling that her son was completely in love with Danny, and it made her happier than she could have imagined. Jake could be intense; he'd always been that way since he was a kid. When he really wanted something he went after it at full pelt. She was sure that Danny just needed some time to come to terms with their relationship before they declared it to the world.

'It's really nice to see you so happy anyway, Son,' Grace said.

Jake turned to her and smiled. 'Thanks, Mum.'

Chapter Thirty

G race pulled the car into her driveway. The gates were open and she assumed Michael had just nipped out somewhere. She was surprised to see Leigh Moss's distinctive red BMW on the drive. Grace hadn't seen Leigh or John since John had visited her a few days earlier and given her his notice. Although Grace missed John, and she and Leigh got on well, they were never going to be the best of friends. Perhaps in another life they might have been, but they were just too different.

Grace stepped out of her car and watched as Leigh climbed out of hers.

'Everything okay, Leigh?' Grace asked.

'Can we talk inside?' Leigh snapped.

Grace frowned at the other woman. Something was obviously bothering her. Her face resembled a bulldog chewing a wasp, but Grace wondered what the hell that had to do with her. Whatever it was, she didn't particularly feel like arguing with a Detective Inspector on her driveway so she invited Leigh inside and they made their way into the kitchen.

'I was just going to make a coffee. Do you fancy one?' Grace asked.

'No. This won't take long,' Leigh said sternly.

Grace leaned against the counter and folded her arms across her chest. 'Then what is it, Leigh? Spit it out.'

'Did you order John to kidnap Nick Bryce?'

Grace stared at her, trying to read Leigh's face. Was she there as DI Moss? John's girlfriend? Or Nick Bryce's ex-girlfriend? Or perhaps all three? She needed to know how much Leigh knew. She would never incriminate herself in front of a copper – she wasn't that stupid. But if she could, she would try and divert any responsibility from John.

'Why would you think that?' Grace asked.

'Hmm, let me see now, because it makes sense, doesn't it? I've been thinking about it non-stop for the past three days. You knew I'd come to you for help.'

'How could I know that? You hated me. Remember?'

Leigh frowned at her. 'I don't know how you knew. I haven't figured out your entire game plan. But I know you were behind it.'

'Have you spoken to John about this?'

Leigh snorted.

'Well?'

'Yes, I've spoken to John,' she hissed. 'He didn't deny it. He was just doing his job, apparently. Not that he would ever name you, of course. You have some kind of hold over him that I can't quite fathom.'

Grace was saved from responding when Michael walked

into the room. 'What the hell is going on?' he asked. 'I could hear you two at it from the hallway.'

'Leigh thinks that John was behind Nick Bryce's kidnap,' Grace said with a knowing look at her husband. He read her face and flashed an eyebrow at her as he walked to her side.

'Don't you dare fucking patronise me, Grace Carter. I'm not one of your minions you can manipulate. I *know* you did it.' She turned to Michael then. 'Do you have any idea why your wife has such a hold over John Brennan? I'd keep my eye on the two of them if I were you.'

Grace looked at Michael and saw the change in his face. 'I don't care if you're a copper, but you'd better get out of my house right now,' he snarled.

'Or what?' Leigh challenged him.

'Or I will fucking carry you out of here myself,' he growled.

Grace placed a hand on Michael's arm. 'It's okay,' she said softly.

Leigh grinned. 'You always do what she tells you?' she laughed and Grace saw a glimpse of the Leigh she had known over twenty years earlier – bitter and vengeful.

'Not exactly,' Grace replied. 'But fortunately for you, my husband isn't into manhandling women. My first one was, but of course you know all about that, don't you? He manhandled you plenty of times, didn't he?'

Leigh scowled at her.

Grace took a few steps towards her. 'Never forget that I know who you really are, Leigh. You don't get to come into *my* house and judge me and *my* decisions. I do what I do to protect the people I love and care about, and yes, that includes John Brennan. If you had an ounce of loyalty in your body, you would know what I mean by that. Don't you dare lecture me on morality when you know nothing about it. Now, you heard Michael, get the hell out of our house.'

Leigh glared at the two of them, her cheeks flushed pink and her fists clenched at her sides. Then without another word, she stormed out of the kitchen and out of the house.

'Are you okay?' Michael asked once they'd heard the sound of the front door slamming shut.

'I'm fine. Poor John though. He'll be devastated. I don't think Leigh is going to back down. I was worried she'd find out somehow,' Grace replied with a sigh.

Michael slipped his arms around her waist and planted a kiss on her forehead. 'John will take care of it. You worry about everyone too much.'

Grace leaned into him, placing her head on his muscular chest and inhaling the smell of his aftershave. He was probably right, but she couldn't help feeling guilty about John and Leigh. At the time, she'd done what she needed to, as she always did, and there wasn't a doubt in her mind that she would do the same again. Although no one could have predicted how things would play out with John and Leigh, she still felt some responsibility for their current situation.

Chapter Thirty-One

Jerrod King sat on the bonnet of the burned-out car. He was surrounded by most of his crew, who all watched him anxiously waiting for his decision. The wasteland at the end of his street was their new headquarters for the time being, although he had his eye on the pub down the road which had just been reopened. Jerrod was too suspicious to talk in any of their houses now. The busies were sniffing around the lot of them because of that slag Kacey Jones. They'd only been having a bit of fun with her and now she'd gone and blabbed to the filth about their little initiation ceremonies.

Bitch!

It wasn't like they hadn't looked after her afterwards. She'd been taken to the hospital to get herself stitched up, and if she'd just kept her filthy gob shut, she could have been one of their birds. Instead, two of his best men had been arrested for rape and wounding, and the rest of the crew were on pins in case they got pulled in too. A least half a dozen of them had been involved, including Jerrod himself. Fortunately, he wasn't stupid enough to leave DNA behind and Kacey had been hardly able to see by the time he'd got to her. He was a good leader, always letting his boys have their fun first – except with his own special birds anyway. They should have killed the bitch. If he ever saw her ugly face again, he would put a bullet in it.

'Do you think Foxy and Wilks will talk?' one of his crew, Jeff, asked.

Jerrod shook his head. 'Nah. Not a chance.' Brodie Fox and Dean Wilkinson knew the score. If you ever got lifted for anything, you did *not* grass on the rest of the crew. You took the fall and you did your time. Then when you got out, you'd have the respect of the whole crew. The alternative was that you'd meet a very painful end.

'What if they offer him a plea deal or something?' Jeff went on as he stood fidgeting with the zip on his North Face coat.

'They won't fucking talk, I told ya,' Jerrod snapped. Then he beckoned one of the girls, Natalie, to his side. She looked at the floor and then walked over to him. They all liked to pretend they were shy but they loved it really. He grabbed hold of her and pulled her towards him. 'You were friends with Kacey, weren't you?'

'Yeah,' she mumbled.

'You wouldn't speak to the filth though, would you?' he snarled.

She shook her head furiously. 'No, Jerrod.'

He knew the police had already spoken to her and she had been a good girl and kept her mouth shut. He ran a fingertip down her cheek and down her collarbone and she shuddered. 'Suck my cock,' he said to her with a grin.

'What? Here?' She looked around at the rest of the crew, who were watching them intently.

'You suck mine, or you suck everyone's,' Jerrod said with a shrug. Then he put his hand on top of her head and forced her to her knees. She pulled at his tracksuit bottoms and got to work while he carried on talking.

'Anyway, we're here to talk about those fucking pricks Conlon and Carter.'

He watched the nodding of heads around him and listened to the mumblings of assent.

'We ain't gonna stand for them treating us like we're shit on their shoes. Just because they drive their fucking flash cars and wear their poncey suits, doesn't make them no better than us, does it?'

'No,' they chorused.

'What are we gonna do?' someone shouted from the back.

'Fuck! Hang on,' he groaned as he put his hands on the back of Natalie's head. 'She's good at this, lads.' His crew cheered him on and he felt his pulse quicken. He was a fucking god to these lads!

'We're going to go in there and fuck them up!' he shouted and was met with a roar of approval. He had no idea how and when it would happen, but it would. For now, he leaned his head back and enjoyed the feeling of Natalie's warm mouth wrapped around him.

Chapter Thirty-Two

D anny walked out of the door of his mother's flat and sucked in a lungful of clean air. The smell of the place made him want to vomit every single time he went there. It was becoming a frequent occurrence now. She would phone the office demanding to speak to him, and then she would demand money, and he would inevitably give in to her just to get her off his back for a few days.

He climbed into his car and started the engine. The knot of anxiety in the pit of his stomach wasn't easing at all. He hated lying, but he felt like he was constantly lying to everyone lately. Well, at least that was about to change a little, although the thought of the afternoon ahead made him feel like throwing up again.

Half an hour later, Danny knocked on the door of Luke's house and waited for him to answer. He'd spoken to Stacey earlier and confirmed she was there too. As difficult as it was sometimes to see his little sister and his best mate together, on this occasion he was relieved to find that she was at Luke's house with him. That would mean he could have this conversation with the two of them at the same time.

Danny wiped his brow as a few beads of perspiration trickled down his forehead. He wasn't sure if he was sweating due to the heat of the midday sun or because he was about to tell his best mate and his sister, the two people that knew him best in the whole world, not only that he was bisexual, but that he'd been seeing Jake Conlon for the past three months.

It was Stacey who opened the door. 'Hi, Dan,' she said with a smile. 'Come in. I've just put the kettle on.'

She opened the door and he stepped inside the hallway. She opened her arms for a hug but Danny was too nervous to notice and he walked straight past her.

'Oh, you're not still bothered about me and Luke, are you, Dan? I told you I was here this morning. You shouldn't have come round if you didn't want to see me here,' Stacey said as she followed him down the hallway towards the kitchen.

Danny turned to her. 'What?' he said with a shake of his head. 'What are you on about?'

She stared at him and obviously saw the worry in his face. 'What's up, Danny?' she asked, her voice going up a few octaves, the way it always did when she was excited or worried.

'Where's Luke?' he said as he pulled at the collar of his shirt.

'He's upstairs. He's just getting dressed. Why? What's wrong?'

'Luke!' Danny shouted up the stairs. 'Hurry up and get your arse down here, mate.' Then he turned to Stacey and saw the concern on her face. 'Everything's okay. I just need to speak to you both before we go to Grace and Michael's.'

Danny continued down the hallway into Luke's kitchen and Stacey followed close behind. A few seconds later, Luke strolled into the room, pulling his T-shirt over his head.

'What's up, mate?' he asked.

Danny sat down at the kitchen table and Luke and Stacey followed suit.

He looked at the two of them and wondered how on earth he was going to tell them his news.

'Danny,' Stacey said again, 'you're scaring me.'

'Yeah, spit it out, Dan,' Luke added.

Danny took a deep breath. It was now or never, he supposed. 'I've been seeing someone,' he said.

Stacey jumped up and gave him a playful punch on the arm. 'Jesus Christ. I thought you were dying or something. You bloody idiot!'

'Sorry,' Danny said sheepishly.

'Well, that's good news, isn't it?' Stacey asked in surprise. 'I mean, it's unexpected coming from you, but it's good. Right?'

'Yeah. So, apart from the fact that you rarely make it past a second date with someone, why the big build-up?' Luke said with a frown. 'What else is going on, Dan?'

Danny swallowed. Luke knew him far too well. 'I've been seeing someone for a couple of months.' He looked up at the two expectant faces and wondered what their reaction to what he was about to tell them was going to be, and whether it would change their relationships in any way. It probably wouldn't matter much at all to Stacey – but Luke? In that moment, as he sat in his best mate's kitchen, almost overcome with anxiety, Danny honestly didn't know. 'It's Jake,' he said.

Stacey sat back in her chair and blinked.

It was Luke who spoke first. 'Jake Conlon?' he asked, his eyes wide with shock.

'Yeah.'

'I didn't even know you were gay,' Stacey said. 'Did you?' she asked Luke.

Luke shook his head.

'Did you?' He looked at Danny.

'I'm bisexual. At least I think I am. I've never...' Danny stammered, not knowing quite how to find the words. 'Not until Jake anyway.'

'But you like Jake?' Luke asked.

'Yeah,' Danny replied.

'Are you two serious?' Stacey asked.

'Well, I've told you two and we're about to tell the rest of his family this afternoon, so I guess so,' he said with a shrug.

'You guess so?' Stacey said with a roll of her eyes. 'Are you happy, Dan?' she asked softly.

He looked at his little sister and realised that she didn't care whether he was gay, bi or anything in between. 'Yeah, Stace. I really am.'

She smiled at him and reached out to squeeze his hand. 'Good.' Then she stood up and gave him a kiss on the cheek. 'That's all that matters to me. And if you were going to start sleeping with dudes, then at least you've picked yourself one who's hot and loaded. Well done, bruv,' she said with a laugh. 'I'm going to finish getting ready.'

She walked out of the room. Danny was grateful that she'd allowed him a few minutes alone with Luke.

'Well, you're a dark horse, aren't you?' Luke said as he ran a hand over his face and let out a low whistle. 'You and Jake?'

'I'm sorry I didn't tell you, mate. But, well, it's been complicated. I know I look like a hypocrite after the way I reacted to you and Stacey…'

'Well, that was different. She is your sister, and I was surprised you let me off so lightly, if I'm honest. But now I know why.' He cocked an eyebrow.

'I wanted to tell you, but I could hardly believe it myself. I still can't. I was convinced it was just a phase and I just needed to get it out of my system. But I can't. I've never felt like this about anyone.' Danny shook his head and sighed.

'Well, I wish you'd told me, mate. If only because I could have talked some sense into you. But I suppose I understand why you didn't.'

'Talked some sense into me?' Danny frowned.

Luke nodded. 'If I know you, which I do, this will have been eating you up for the past few months. You're always worried about what people will think of you, when it's really no one's fucking business what, or who, you do.'

'You're okay with this then? With me and Jake?' Danny asked.

Luke frowned at him. 'Of course I am, Danny. As long as

you're happy, I don't care who you sleep with. Is that why you didn't tell me?'

Danny shrugged. 'Partly.'

Luke pushed back his chair and walked around to the other side of the table. He motioned Danny to stand up and when he did, Luke wrapped him in a bear hug. 'I'm not going to lie and tell you I'm not as surprised as fuck about you and Jake, but I love you, mate. You're my brother.'

'Love you too, mate.'

Danny shifted from one foot to the other as he stood on the doorstep of Grace and Michael Carter's house. Despite being with Luke and Stacey, he felt very much alone. He was overwhelmingly anxious about the reception he was going to get on the other side of that door. Every Sunday, the whole of the Carter family got together at Grace and Michael's house for dinner. It was tradition and it was rarely missed by any member of the family. Luke was included in that number now too, and Stacey, as his partner, was also invited along. Danny had been there plenty of times before, but always as Jake, Connor and Luke's mate. He'd never been there as Jake's significant other.

By now, everyone inside the house would be aware of his and Jake's relationship. The plan had been for Jake to tell them while he was telling Stacey and Danny. Jake, however, hadn't been anxious at all. He'd told Danny that no one would care, at least not in any negative sense. Jake confidently claimed that everyone would be happy for them, and Danny wished he could believe him.

'You all right, mate?' Luke said as he put a hand on Danny's shoulder.

Danny ran a hand through his hair. 'I feel like I'm meeting the parents,' he said with a smile.

'Well, you are, aren't you? Not something you're used to, is it?' Stacey started to laugh. 'Your previous dates would have been lucky to get a phone call, never mind meeting the parents.'

Danny frowned at her. Now wasn't the time to be making jokes about his previous sex life. Before he could respond, the front door opened.

'Afternoon,' Michael Carter said before turning quickly to pick up his youngest son, Oscar, as he made a beeline for the door.

'Where are you going, little man?' Michael said with a chuckle.

'Uncle Luke!' Oscar shouted as he tried to wriggle from Michael's grip.

Michael rolled his eyes and handed the squirming toddler to Luke, who took him and hoisted him over his shoulder.

'Hey, little grouch,' Luke said as he stepped into the house.

'Hi, Michael,' Stacey said and gave him a brief hug and a peck on the cheek. Danny watched them both walk inside and felt a pang of something – jealousy perhaps? They both looked so comfortable here – as though they belonged. As though they were already part of the family.

He became aware that he was still standing rooted to the spot when Michael spoke. 'You coming in then, Danny, or what?'

Danny looked up at him. Michael was smiling and holding the door open for him. Just like he usually did. There was nothing different about his demeanour. Nothing in his face to suggest that their relationship had changed in any way. Perhaps Jake hadn't told them?

'Sorry,' Danny said with a smile. 'I was in a world of my own.'

He stepped inside the house and followed Michael into the kitchen.

'Danny!' Belle squealed when she saw him. Dropping her teddy bear onto the floor, she ran over and jumped into his arms.

'Hey, Bella,' Danny said as she gave him a sloppy kiss on his cheek.

Grace smiled and walked over to him. 'Hi, Danny,' she said, giving him her usual hug. She'd known about him and Jake for almost a week now and she hadn't changed towards him at all.

Everyone else carried on as normal, giving him a nod or a smile as they usually would. Sophia and Steph were setting the table. Sean was stirring the gravy. Pat and Sue sat together at the table with baby Paul. Sean and Sophia's other daughters, Nicola and Beth, were sitting at the breakfast bar, glued to Nicola's mobile phone and giggling at something. There was no indication at all that they knew about his secret and he breathed a sigh of relief. Maybe Jake hadn't had a chance to tell them yet? Perhaps, Danny would suggest they waited a little longer until Luke and Stacey had come to terms with it? As he was thinking that, Jake walked over to him, he ruffled Belle's hair and held out his arms. 'I thought you were going to show me your new swing?' he said to her.

She grinned at him. 'Oh yeah,' she said and she hopped from Danny to Jake.

Jake put his hand on the back of Danny's neck and stepped closer to him. Danny's body responded to the warmth of Jake's touch and he felt the colour rising in his cheeks.

'You okay?' Jake asked him.

Danny knew he was referring to his visit to his mother earlier that morning as well as his chat with Stacey and Luke. 'Yeah,' he replied.

'You coming outside with us?' Jake asked.

'Yeah,' Danny mumbled, thankful for an excuse to be outside in the fresh air. He wanted to speak to Jake about the possibility of keeping their relationship under wraps a little while longer. As they were walking out through the patio doors, Belle said, in what Danny thought had to be the loudest voice of any six-year-old in the history of children, 'Are you really Jake's boyfriend, Danny?'

Danny felt his heart lurch into his chest. He imagined that he would turn around and everyone in the room would be staring at him open-mouthed. He looked at Belle, and then at Jake. They both looked at him, waiting for his answer. He swallowed. This was the second time in an hour he'd had to take this leap.

'Yeah,' he said to Belle and she smiled at him, revealing her missing front tooth.

'Good. Can I call you Uncle Danny then?' she asked.

'He's not your uncle,' Jake said as he started to walk outside.

'Well, what is he then?' she asked in her childlike innocence. Jake and Belle stepped further away from him and he didn't hear what Jake said next. He was fixed to the spot again. He turned around quickly, to see the reaction on everybody's faces, but when he did, they were all still as they had been a moment earlier. No one was staring at him at all. They couldn't have failed to hear Belle's question and his answer, but they hadn't taken any notice. Maybe Jake had been right after all. Maybe they didn't care if he was gay or straight or bi?

With an overwhelming sense of relief Danny turned back to the garden and smiled as he walked outside to join Jake and Belle.

———

Danny sat outside in Grace and Michael's large garden at the patio table with a bottle of Budweiser. Grace and Michael were putting the kids to bed. Jazz was feeding Paul, and Jake and Connor were clearing up the last of the dinner dishes. Everyone else had gone home and Danny was enjoying the peace and quiet. He had never had a family, growing up. There had only ever been him and Stacey – and Luke, of course. Jake had grown up as an only child and there had just been him and his mum until he was an adult himself. But since Grace had married Michael four years earlier, Jake had had a huge, and very loud, extended family.

Danny felt a mix of emotions. He'd had a lovely afternoon. His and Jake's relationship hadn't been discussed at all, although it had been clear that they all knew about it. No one had batted an eyelid when Jake had put his hand on Danny's leg during dinner or when he'd put his arm around him. He should have been happy. And in many ways he was, but it was tinged with something else. Danny Alexander knew that happiness never lasted, and sooner or later he would do something to fuck everything up.

He put his empty bottle down beside him and heard footsteps approaching from behind. He turned to see Michael walking towards him carrying two bottles of Budweiser. He took a seat beside him and passed him one of the bottles.

'Peace at last, eh?' Michael said with a flash of his eyebrows.

Danny laughed in response.

'They're a rowdy lot. But you get used to them,' Michael said as he took a swig of his beer.

Danny closed his eyes. That was what he was afraid of. If he allowed himself to feel a part of this incredible family, it would only hurt all the more when it was inevitably taken from him.

The two men sat quietly for a while and Danny noticed how easy it was to just sit there in Michael's company enjoying a beer and not feeling the need to fill the silence.

The sound of Jake and Connor's laughter drifted out from the kitchen and Michael turned to look towards the house.

'It's nice to hear my boys laughing again,' he said softly.

Danny nodded. He hadn't known Paul Carter, but he knew that his murder had devastated the entire family, and that Michael, Jake and Connor felt his loss more keenly than they would ever admit. 'It must be,' he replied.

'For a while there, me and Grace were really worried about Jake, you know? When Paul died, he completely lost it. Connor had Jazz and the baby, and I had Grace and the kids, but Jake… Well, we all lost Paul in different ways, but I suppose in some way Jake felt like he lost more than any of us.'

Danny took a swig of his lager. He knew how much Jake had loved Paul. He thought about it often and wondered how he was ever going to measure up to him. It was hard to compete with a ghost. Was Michael about to tell him that for certain? That he would never measure up to his son – the only man Jake would ever really love?

'You make him happy, Danny, and I can't thank you enough for that. I was made up when Grace told me about the two of you. We realised why he's been so different this past couple of months. And that's down to you.'

Danny looked down at his beer bottle. Michael had taken him completely by surprise and he felt a wave of emotion rush over him. He pushed it down, not knowing how to deal with it. 'I'm not sure I can take all the credit,' he said as he looked up again.

Michael stared at him, his eyes narrowed. 'You have a

real issue accepting a compliment, don't you? I've noticed that about you.'

Danny tried to look away but Michael's gaze held him in place. Who would have thought one of Liverpool's most ruthless gangsters would be so bloody insightful?

'There's nothing wrong with a bit of humility, Danny, but you need to learn to take credit where it's due, son.'

Danny swallowed. Connor was a lucky fucker growing up with a dad like Michael Carter. 'Then thanks, I suppose,' he said with a sheepish grin.

Seemingly satisfied with that response, Michael sat back in his chair. 'Paul would have liked you,' he said quietly.

Danny felt the tears spring to his eyes. He knew that was the biggest compliment this man could pay him.

Danny took off his clothes as he watched Jake pull back the covers and climb into bed. They were in one of the spare bedrooms in Grace and Michael's house. They referred to it as a spare room but it was full of Jake's stuff and he stayed there often. Connor and Jazz had a similar spare room along the hallway. Jake usually stayed over on a Sunday after the wine and beer had flowed all afternoon and into the evening. He'd done it less in the past couple of months, since he and Danny had been seeing each other, preferring to go home instead.

This was the first night Danny had stayed over with Jake. He slipped underneath the covers and Jake immediately rolled on top of him, sealing his mouth with a kiss.

'So, how do you think today went?' Jake said when they came up for air.

'Okay,' Danny replied.

'It's nice to be able to kiss you in public now,' Jake said with a grin.

Danny smiled back. 'I'm glad everyone knows,' he said truthfully. They had taken it so well that he was starting to wonder what he'd been so worried about.

'Good,' Jake growled as his hands started to slide down Danny's body.

'Not here,' Danny said as he pushed his hands away.

'Why not? This is our room,' Jake said, undeterred.

'Someone might hear us.'

'Well, be quiet then.'

'It just doesn't feel right. What if someone comes in?'

'Like who, Dan? This is our room. No one will come in. Do you think Connor and Jazz aren't doing exactly the same thing down the hallway? If you were seeing some bird and you were in her mum's house, you wouldn't think twice about fucking her, would you? I'm pretty sure everyone in this house already knows we're way past the holding hands phase!'

Danny swallowed. 'I know that.'

'You just want to go to sleep then?' Jake said.

'No,' Danny breathed as he put his hand on the back of Jake's neck.

'Good,' Jake said as he trailed kisses down Danny's chest and slipped beneath the covers.

Chapter Thirty-Three

Danny looked up from his desk as Carla, the receptionist, popped her head through the door.

'That strange woman is on the phone for you again, Boss,' she said with a roll of her eyes.

'For fuck's sake,' Danny hissed. 'Put her through.'

'Will do,' she replied before slipping out of the door.

Danny waited for the call to be put through, thankful that Luke had gone to the butty shop over the road to pick them up some dinner. As soon as the phone rang he snatched it from the desk.

'What?' he snarled.

'That is no way to greet your mother, Danny boy,' Glenda slurred down the line.

'What the fuck do you want?'

'I need more money. '

'I gave you another ton two days ago. Are you fucking kidding me?'

'I told you, I can't live on this universal credit, and my rent is due.'

'Your rent was due two weeks ago, ma. Pull the fucking other one. You'll get your five hundred quid in two weeks' time, like I told you.'

'But what am I supposed to do in the meantime?'

'I don't give a rat's arse!'

'But, Danny,' she wailed. 'I swear I haven't got a penny. I owe money left, right and centre. And if I don't pay up – well, you know what will happen, Son. Or should I just tell them to come and get the money from you?'

He sucked in a breath. That fucking witch! The local crack dealers finding out she was his mother was the last thing he needed, and he wouldn't put it past her to start bandying his name around to get whatever she wanted.

'You mention my name to anyone and you won't see another penny from me,' he warned her through gritted teeth.

'I just need a few quid to tide me over, Danny. Another hundred will do.'

Danny heard Luke's voice out in the hallway and knew he had to end the conversation quickly. 'Fine. I'll drop it off tonight. Don't ever call me at work again,' he barked before putting the phone down just as Luke walked back into the office.

———

A few hours later, Danny sat in Stacey's office at The Blue Rooms, sipping his coffee. He fidgeted in his seat as his earlier conversation with their mother played over in his head. Stacey would give him an earful if she found out he was giving Glenda money. She hated the woman, rightly so, and refused to have anything to do with her. But Danny's relationship with her was much more complicated than his younger sister's had ever been. Besides that, he couldn't risk Glenda telling anyone the truth about who he really was, especially Stacey.

'You okay, Danny?' she asked him.

'Yeah. Course I am. You've got this place looking really nice, Stace,' he said as he looked around, trying to change the subject.

She smiled proudly. 'Thanks. I can't believe I have my own office. I can't thank Jake enough for giving me this opportunity. You didn't have anything to do with it, by the way, did you?'

Danny shook his head. 'Nope. I was as shocked as you were.'

'Hmm.' She eyed him suspiciously over the rim of her coffee mug. 'Hey, I just thought, if I'm the manager of this club, and you technically work here, does that mean I'm your boss?' She squealed with laughter.

'No,' he snapped.

'So, who is your boss then?' she asked.

He shrugged. 'Well, me and Luke are our own bosses to a degree. But I suppose we work for Jake and the rest of the Carters.'

'So, Jake is your boss then?' she giggled. 'That must get interesting?'

He shook his head. 'Stop it.'

'He was looking for you earlier, by the way, before he went out.'

Danny nodded. He'd been held up at another meeting and Jake had left by the time he got to The Blue Rooms. But he'd catch up with him later. It gave him a chance to spend some time with Stacey anyway.

She sat back in her chair with a huge smile on her face and Danny watched her. Despite everything she'd been through, she was kind and compassionate and happy. How the hell had that happened?

Stacey must have caught him staring at her. 'What?' she said as she looked down at her top. 'Have I got a foam moustache or something?'

'Why aren't you fucked up like me, Stace?' he asked.

'You're not fucked up,' she said with a sigh. 'You just find it hard to trust people. That's not surprising, is it? And it's not the worst thing in the world either.'

'Yeah, but you're not like that, are you? You see the best in everyone. You believe in happy ever afters.'

'Don't I deserve a happy ever after?' She eyed him suspiciously again.

'More than anyone else in the world.' He smiled at her. 'But why can't I believe in them? How did we end up so different?'

'Well, that's easy, isn't it?' she said as she dabbed her mouth with a napkin. 'I had you.'

He raised an eyebrow at her. 'What?'

'You always looked after me. You protected me from Mum, and Steve. You made sure I never went without. You always made sure I was loved and cared for. I've always known that I deserve more.'

'Even when you were with that prick Simon?' Danny asked, recalling Stacey's ex-boyfriend, Simon Smith. He was currently in prison awaiting trial for his part in a murder and a sex trafficking ring, and he was an odious piece of shit. Stacey had met him when she was just eighteen, and he had well and truly sunk his claws into her, isolating her from her friends and family and generally treating her like shit. Danny had only found out the true extent of what had been going on when Simon had tried to put Stacey on the game. He and Luke had been devastated when they'd found out. They'd gone to Manchester and brought Stacey straight home but Simon had gone on his toes before they'd had a chance to deal with him.

'Yes, even when I was with him. No matter how bad things got with him, I knew deep down that I deserved better and that I was worth more. You instilled that in me. I wish someone had done the same for you. I wish someone in your life had protected you the way you looked after me. I wish you would let someone in enough so they could show you how amazing you really are,' she said as she squeezed his hand. 'Maybe you should let Jake try?'

Danny swallowed. He wished he could, but it wasn't that easy.

Chapter Thirty-Four

John Brennan turned off the engine of his BMW X5 and looked out of the window at the house he had just pulled up outside. He shouldn't be here. It was risky. Leigh might not even be home, although her distinctive red car was parked outside. Even if she was in, she was likely to tell him to go to hell. But he had to at least try and talk to her. He couldn't leave things the way they had ended. He had been prepared to give up his whole way of life for her, and surely that counted for something?

He climbed out of his car and walked up the path, with a feeling of dread settling into the pit of his stomach. He'd been in plenty of dangerous situations in the past, too many of them to even count, but he didn't think he'd ever felt as nervous as he did right now.

Taking a deep breath, he knocked on the door and waited for an answer. A few seconds later, Leigh opened the door and his heart lurched into his throat.

'What the hell are you doing here?' she hissed as she popped her head out and looked up and down the street.

'I need to speak to you, Leigh.'

'We've said all we need to say, John,' she said with a scowl.

'You might have, but I haven't. We can't leave things like this,' he insisted, wishing he hadn't let her leave so easily the other night. He should have fought for her then, but he had been completely floored.

'I'm not interested in anything you have to say. Now, please leave before someone sees you,' she snapped as she started to close the door.

John put his large hand against it, preventing her from closing it on him. 'For fuck's sake, Leigh. Just let me talk to you. Five minutes is all I'm asking.'

'I said: I am not interested in anything you have to say. Now, piss off!'

'Leigh,' he pleaded. 'At least hear me out. You owe me that much.'

'I owe you nothing, John!' she spat and the venom in her voice caused him to take a step back. He knew that she had a ruthless side to her – he supposed she had to in her line of work – but before now he had never seen it for himself.

'You know what, you're right,' he snarled. 'I thought we had something, Leigh. And I know I fucked up, but so have you, and I have never held that against you. You think you're so much better than everyone else, don't you? But you're the same selfish, self-centred woman you were twenty years ago when you went after another woman's husband. You haven't changed a bit.'

Leigh blinked at him and he saw the tears spring to her eyes. He knew that he'd hurt her, but fuck it, she had hurt him too. He was feeling so angry, he worried that if he kept on talking he'd end up saying something that he could never take back.

'This isn't over, Leigh,' he said instead before turning around and walking back towards his car with his heart hammering in his chest.

———

Leigh Moss climbed into her car and checked her mascara in the rear-view mirror. She cursed under her breath as she noticed it was smudged again. She had barely been able to stop snivelling since John had left half an hour earlier.

She had opened the door expecting a parcel that she was waiting on, and had almost passed out with shock to see him standing on her doorstep instead, looking as handsome and as smelling as good as he always did. What was it about him that always made her want to throw herself into his arms? But she hadn't, of course. Because she was still beyond pissed off with him for ruining everything they had. So she had wanted to hurt him too, and she had. She had seen it in his face.

She swallowed down another sob as she recalled what he said just before he left, about how she was the same woman he had known all those years ago. That was such a shameful time in her life, when she had worked as a stripper in Nathan Conlon's nightclub and had shamelessly carried on a torrid affair with him despite knowing he had been married to Grace at the time. It was what Grace had said to her a few days ago too, and the accusation stung.

But she wasn't that woman any longer. She had worked hard to change her life and become a better person. She *was* a better person, despite what John and Grace thought. So why did what they thought of her hurt so much?

Leigh started the car and pulled away from the kerb. She thought about young Kacey Jones and all that poor girl had been through at the hands of the Bridewell Blades crew, and how brave she was to come forward and be willing to face her attackers in court. Leigh and her team had pulled in as many of the crew as they could for questioning, but it wasn't looking likely that charges against most of them would stick. It made her so angry that she could taste it in her throat. She knew that there were at least half a dozen of them involved in Kacey's assault, but it was looking likely that only two would be charged. And worst of all, she couldn't tie a single damn thing to the King brothers, who she knew were the orchestrators of the whole thing.

The King brothers were a whole new breed. They had no morals or principles at all, and certainly no boundaries that they weren't prepared to cross to get what they wanted. But even worse than that, they were cruel for cruelty's sake. Their degrading and disgusting initiation ceremonies for new gang members, involving the exploitation and abuse of young girls like Kacey, were well known, but with the girls and local community being too terrified to ever come forward, there wasn't a lot Leigh and her team could do but wait and watch for the inevitable mistakes they would make one day.

Kacey Jones was just the beginning. Leigh would make sure of that. She blinked back the tears and made a silent promise that she would make it her life's work to bring the Bridewell Blades to justice – every last one of them.

By any means necessary.

Chapter Thirty-Five

Michael sat in his old chair behind his old desk at Cartel Securities and looked at his brother Sean sat opposite him.

'Come on, you miss this, don't you?' Sean said to him with a grin.

Michael shook his head. 'I honestly don't, mate. Not anymore. I'm happy for Luke and Danny to deal with all the day-to-day shit,' he replied.

'Where are they today anyway?'

'They don't work in the office on Mondays.'

'Why haven't you asked them to handle the collections from Jimmy Kelly?' Sean asked.

Jimmy Kelly had worked with the Carters for years and had always been a loyal and trusted employee. He and his two nephews were some of their principal suppliers in the north of the city. But Jimmy was old-school. He got twitchy around new people and he preferred to deal with Michael, Jake or Connor wherever possible.

'You know Jimmy. He gets nervous around new faces. I agreed to help out for a few months while Connor's taking a bit more time with Jazz and Paul. Besides, Luke and Danny deal with the security, they don't really get involved in the other side of the business unless extra muscle is needed.'

Sean nodded his understanding. 'So it's just a money collection then?'

'Yeah. We meet them at the designated drop-off point and they'll hand over the cash.'

'Sounds simple enough,' Sean replied. 'We got time for a coffee before drop-off time?'

Michael checked his watch. He'd agreed to meet Jimmy at two o'clock and it was only five past one. 'Yeah, go on. As long as you're making them?'

'Coming right up,' Sean replied as he stood up and left the room.

Michael looked around the office that once belonged to him but was now Danny and Luke's workspace. He smiled as he remembered some of the good times he'd spent in here. Despite wanting to step back from it all, it had been a wrench to leave the place. But he genuinely didn't miss it any longer. He was feeling ready for a much slower pace of life and he could sense it was on the horizon. Paul was four months old now and it was about time Connor started taking over his responsibilities again. Michael had been happy to support his son in spending more time with his family. But now it was time for Michael to spend some more time with his own.

Chapter Thirty-Six

I watched as Jimmy Kelly and his nephew walked out of the Lady Muck beauty salon and climbed into their car.

Finally, my patience had paid off. Michael Carter thought he was smart – always meeting Jimmy on different days and times and at different venues. But I was smarter – and I'd figured out the pattern. That was how I knew that Jimmy and his nephew were on their way to meet Carter right now. It was too dangerous to follow Michael Carter around. I might have been recognised by him or one of his minions. But Jimmy Kelly had no idea who I was.

So I'd been following Jimmy for months instead. And today, my hard work and persistence was about to pay dividends. In a few hours' time, Michael Carter would be wiped from the face of the earth. And the last thing he would see before he took his last breath would be my face.

. . .

I parked my car on the road a few hundred yards behind Jimmy Kelly and watched as he and his nephew walked up Longmoor Lane. They were so bloody cocky. Walking up the road holding a holdall full of cash and thinking they were untouchable. I followed behind them, and watched as they walked into the Social Club. I could see Michael Carter's new Aston Martin outside in the car park.

Flash bastard!

Well, he wouldn't be driving his fancy new motor home, that was for sure.

If these exchanges followed the usual pattern, Carter would be waiting for Jimmy, and he would leave a few minutes after him.

I stood with my back pressed against the wall. From my vantage point, I would see them coming out of the building. Carter would have to walk right past me.

I waited.

Ten minutes after they had entered the building, Jimmy Kelly and his nephew walked back outside, out of the car park and back to their car.

Then a few moments later, Carter walked out, carrying the black holdall full of cash in one hand and holding his phone in the other. He walked across the car park, looking at his phone instead of paying attention to his surroundings. He looked every inch the respectable businessman, instead of the ruthless killer I knew him to be.

I felt my heart beating louder and faster in my ears as Carter approached. I'd planned this for months, but I'd never done anything like this before. My palm was sweaty as it gripped the handle of the gun in my jacket pocket. But this was my only chance. The Carter family had taken everything from me, and now it was my turn to take their beloved hero. I stepped out of the shadows when Carter was a few feet away from me. I had to make sure I was close enough to get a good, clean shot, but not close enough for Carter to make a grab for the gun and overpower me. I wasn't stupid enough to think that I had a chance in hell of taking him on if he got within arm's reach of me.

I pulled the gun from my pocket and pointed it at him. He didn't even notice me at first. Arrogant bastard! I couldn't stop my hand from trembling as I pointed the gun straight at him.

'Carter,' I snarled.

He looked up. Straight at me. I swallowed. My blood started to thunder in my ears. I felt dizzy. Bile burned the back of my throat. I'd made a mistake. But it was too late now. I was pointing a gun directly at him. If I didn't shoot him, he'd take the gun from me and shoot me in the head without a second thought.

'You? What the fuck?' Carter snarled at me.

I had no time to think. I had to act before I bottled it. 'This is for Billy,' I said as I squeezed the trigger.

The bullet went straight through Carter's chest. I watched as his white shirt began to turn a deep red before he dropped to the floor. He lay motionless as the life drained from him and as much as I wanted to stand by and watch him take his last breaths, I had to get out of there.

I stood over him and watched as his eyelids flickered. He opened his mouth as though he wanted to speak, but no words came out. The adrenaline coursed around my body. I picked up the holdall and pulled it over my shoulder. Then I ran out of the car park and over to my car without looking back.

Chapter Thirty-Seven

G race was in Antonelli's finishing a late lunch with Jake and Danny when her phone rang. She answered it to her mother-in-law, Sue.

'Hi, Sue.'

'Grace,' Sue said as she choked back a sob. The tone of her voice immediately made the hairs on Grace's arms stand on end.

'What is it?' she asked, aware of the desperation in her voice. She looked up at Jake and Danny, who had stopped eating and stared at her.

'It's Michael, Grace. He's been shot,' she gasped the last two words as though it had been painful to get them out.

Grace felt like the world stopped around her. She wanted to ask where Michael was and if he was okay but her mouth wouldn't form the words. It wouldn't form any words. She held the phone to her ear and stayed stock still, as though if she didn't acknowledge what Sue had just said, then it wouldn't be real.

'They've taken him to Fazakerley Hospital. But you need to get there as soon as you can. They don't think he's going to make it.'

Grace ended the call and her body started to move on auto-pilot. She refused to feel anything about what Sue had just said – because she couldn't. She couldn't possibly contemplate the thought of losing him because she didn't know what she would do without him. Michael couldn't die on her. Life couldn't possibly be that cruel, could it? But of course it could, and it was. Grace Carter knew that as well as anyone.

Grace swallowed down the emotion that threatened to pour out of her and picked up her handbag.

'Mum! What's wrong?' Jake asked.

'We need to get to Fazakerley Hospital. Michael's been shot,' she said in a calm voice that didn't sound like it was coming from her mouth. 'Danny, could you pick the kids up from school and nursery for me please?'

'Of course, Grace,' Danny said as he stood up.

'Fucking hell,' Jake said through gritted teeth. 'Is he okay?'

Grace shook her head. 'I don't know.'

'Come on. I'll drive you,' Jake said and they hurried out of the restaurant, leaving Danny to settle the bill.

Grace was quiet throughout the drive to the hospital. She looked out of the window at the Liverpool scenery as Jake sped through the streets as fast as he could. Thoughts of Michael filled her head. His laugh. His hands, which always seemed to be warm no matter what the weather. She felt the tears threaten to overwhelm her and tried to think about something else. But instead she thought about how he'd been wanting out of this game for a while now, and she had convinced him that the time hadn't been right. How she regretted that now. How much would she come to regret it in the future?

———

After what felt like forever, Jake dropped Grace off at the hospital entrance and went to park the car. She ran through the double doors and towards the A&E department, pushing past a drunk who stumbled into her. She made her way to the reception and started to speak to the receptionist, who held up her hand dismissively as she wrote on a piece of paper. Grace resisted the urge to start banging on the glass and spoke anyway. 'I'm looking for my husband. They brought him in here. Michael Carter?'

Grace felt a warm hand on her shoulder.

'Grace.'

She closed her eyes. That voice. Her mind must be playing tricks with her. Of course it was, because she was losing her mind. It couldn't be.

She spun around and came face to face with him and her heart almost burst out of her chest. Suddenly, the room started to spin and her blood thundered in her ears. She reached out to touch his face, but then the room lost its focus and she was falling.

Then everything went black.

———————

'Grace. Grace? Can you hear me?' Grace heard the soft female voice asking her. She opened her eyes and blinked in the bright overhead light.

'There you are.' She looked up into the smiling face of a young woman who was standing over her. 'You gave us a fright there.'

'Where am I?' she stammered as she looked around the room. She was in a hospital cubicle.

'You're in the hospital. You fainted in our reception area,' the woman replied. Grace assumed she was a nurse.

Grace's head started to throb. The last thing she'd remembered was standing in the reception. 'I was looking for my husband.'

'Yes. He's here.'

'The man in reception with me...' Grace started to say but then she stopped. Had she seen his face before or after she'd fainted? Had she imagined it?

'Tell him he can come in now,' said a doctor who was also in the cubicle.

Grace looked up to see Jake walk in through the curtain. 'Mum!' he said as he approached the bed. 'Are you okay? You gave us a proper fright.'

Us? Had Jake seen him too?

'Jake! Did you see…' she started but then the doctor pulled back the curtain fully and he was standing there, as large as life, talking to another doctor who was in scrubs.

'Michael?' she shouted. He turned to look at her and smiled before shaking the doctor's hand. Then he walked into her cubicle and pulled her into his arms. 'Are you okay?' he asked as he stroked her hair.

She felt the relief wash over her like a tsunami as she clung onto him. He was real. He was there. So why had she been told that he wasn't? She pushed him away and stared at him. 'Sue told me you'd been shot,' she said.

'I know. Jake told me.'

'But why?' she asked. What the hell was going on?'

'She thought I had. But it wasn't me. It was Sean,' he said as emotion washed over his face.

'Sean? Is he okay?' she asked, fearing the answer.

'I just spoke to the doctor who operated on him and she said he's stable for now. The next forty-eight hours are critical. He's in a coma while his body has a chance to recover.'

'Bloody hell. Sean?' Grace choked back a sob. 'What happened?' she asked quietly.

Michael kissed the top of her head. 'I'll tell you later,' he whispered then he straightened up. 'The police are waiting to speak to me. Jake, can you stay with your mum while I talk to them?'

Jake nodded but Grace jumped up off the bed. 'I'm fine. I'll come with you.'

The nurse placed a hand on Grace's arm. 'You should

take it easy,' she said. 'The doctor hasn't said you're okay to go yet.'

'But I can leave of my own free will, can't I?' Grace replied.

'Grace,' Michael said with a sigh. 'Can you just do as they say? I've got enough to worry about with Sean. Please just let them check you over properly. I'm only going to the other side of the hospital. I don't have to go to the station.'

Grace wanted to refuse. She hated being told what to do, but she could see the strain on Michael's face and didn't want to make his life any more difficult in that moment. But she didn't want him to leave her side either. Just half an hour earlier, she had thought she was going to lose him for good. The irrational part of her worried that if he left that little cubicle she might never see him again.

She squeezed his hand. 'Okay. I'll stay here. For now.'

He gave her a faint smile. 'Just do as you're told. I'll be back as soon as I can.'

'Who's with Sean?' Grace asked as she suddenly thought about her brother-in-law again.

'My dad's with him. Sophia is on her way. She's only just been told. My dad and Sue thought it was me, so...'

Grace nodded. Her sister-in-law Sophia was going to be devastated, and she was also going to hit the roof. Sean Carter was supposed to be retired from any sort of business dealings that could result in him being shot.

It was almost ten o'clock when Grace, Michael and Jake finally got home from the hospital. Michael's father, Patrick, had stayed there along with Sophia, who, as predicted, had flown into one of her legendary epic rages once she'd found out what happened. She'd refused to even look at Michael or Grace, blaming them for her husband's return to the dangerous lifestyle he'd sworn to leave behind. They both understood that it was her grief talking and her anger was entirely proportionate given that her husband was in a coma clinging to life.

Danny had been an angel and had not only collected Belle and Oscar from school and nursery but given them their tea and put them to bed too. He was sitting on the sofa in the living room with Grace and Michael's boxer dog, Bruce, curled up next to him when they arrived home.

'How is he?' was the first thing he asked, although Jake had kept him updated throughout the day.

'Stable, but he's still not out of the woods,' Michael said with a sigh. Grace had heard him say those words so many times during the course of the evening to every well-wisher who had called to express their shock and offer their best wishes for his recovery.

'Any idea who was behind it?' Danny asked.

Michael shook his head. 'Not yet.'

'We'll find the fucker who's responsible though,' Jake added.

'Yeah. We'll get on it,' Danny agreed.

Michael nodded absent-mindedly and Grace wondered how he had the energy to think about any of that right now.

'Come on, let's get going,' Jake said. 'We can make a start now.'

Danny stood up and Grace hugged them both goodbye. As she was seeing them out of the front door, Michael made his way upstairs. She found him in their bedroom lying on the bed and staring into space. She lay next to him and placed a hand on his chest. She could feel his heart pounding underneath her fingertips and, despite the events of the day, it brought her some comfort. It was heart-breaking to know that Sean was lying in a coma just a few miles away. She adored Sean. He had been one of her best friends for many years before becoming her brother-in-law. But a few hours earlier she had believed that it was Michael lying in that hospital bed and the thought of never lying close to him again was too much to even contemplate.

'How are you feeling?' she asked him.

He placed his hand over hers. 'I can't lose him, Grace,' he said.

'You won't,' she said with a confidence she didn't feel.

'You can't know that,' he said as he turned to her.

He was right, but how could she tell him that? How could she tell him how worried she was that his brother and best friend wasn't going to make it? She had listened to the doctors intently and their prognosis hadn't sounded good. The only thing on Sean's side was that he was so fit and healthy – everything else was against him. By rights, he should have died at the scene. It was sheer luck that the two joggers passing by who had found him happened to be a paramedic and her husband, and that he'd been shot less than half a mile from Fazakerley Hospital. They had taken

Michael's car keys from Sean's pocket and had driven him the short distance to the hospital where he'd been taken straight to theatre.

Grace stared at her husband and her heart broke that she couldn't make things better for him. She wondered if he blamed her. He'd been talking about getting out and she had persuaded him not to.

'I shouldn't have let him go there. Especially not on his own,' Michael said with a sigh and she realised that the only person he was blaming was himself.

'It was a routine pick-up, Michael. Nothing should have gone wrong. How were you to know someone was going to turn up with a gun?'

'He should never have been involved. He's supposed to be out of all of this.'

'Do you honestly think you would have convinced him otherwise?' she asked. 'Sean is one of the most stubborn people I have ever met. There is no way he would have let his little brother tell him what he could or couldn't do, and you know it.'

'What if he doesn't...?'

She placed her hand on his cheek. 'He'll pull through. He's as strong as an ox.'

He slipped a hand round her, pulled her body into his and smoothed her hair from her face. 'Are you okay? I've never seen you faint before.'

'Well, I've never seen a ghost before. I thought it was you who'd been shot, Michael.' She shook her head as the tears threatened to pour out. She needed to be strong. 'I thought you were...' She couldn't say the word.

'My dad was told that his son had been shot. Sean was driving my car. He had no ID on him. They assumed...' he trailed off and shook his head. He pulled her closer to him and buried his head in her neck before letting out a long sigh. 'I love you so much, Grace,' he said, his voice thick with emotion. 'You are never getting rid of me.'

She kissed the top of his head. 'I'm holding you to that, Carter.'

Chapter Thirty-Eight

J ake, Connor, Danny and Luke sat in Danny's car outside Jimmy Kelly's house. They hadn't brought any weapons except for a set of knuckle dusters each.

'That's Alan's car,' Connor said as he indicated the silver Mercedes parked out outside Jimmy's house.

'Jimmy knows the score. He'll be waiting for us to pay him a visit. He'd be stupid not to have Alan and Jay with him,' Jake replied.

Jake and Connor had done business with Jimmy Kelly and his nephews for years. They'd never given them any cause to doubt them before, and Jake didn't believe they were involved in Sean's shooting, but the inescapable fact was that Sean had been shot after a drop with the three men. And as well as Sean being left for dead, the two hundred grand Jimmy had dropped off had been nicked too. Jimmy and his nephews were about to have the shit kicked out of them, whether they were innocent or not.

'Come on then,' Connor said as he opened the car door.

The four men climbed out of the car and walked up the path to Jimmy's house. The door was opened before they'd had a chance to knock.

'Evening, lads,' Jimmy said with a solemn nod of his head.

'Evening, Jimmy,' Connor said. 'Can we come in?'

'Of course,' Jimmy replied as he opened the door wider.

The four men stepped inside Jimmy's three-bed semi and followed him into the living room where Jay and Alan sat waiting. They looked up as the men entered the room and nodded in greeting.

'Have a seat,' Jimmy said, indicating the two armchairs.

Jake and Connor sat down while Danny and Luke remained standing, like a pair of guards on sentry duty. The tension in the small room was palpable.

'Where's Ellen?' Connor asked as he looked at the photographs on the mantel of Jimmy and his wife.

'She's gone to stay with her mum for the night. She's not very well.'

'Good,' Jake said with a nod. 'So, what happened today?'

Alan and Jay sat in silence, eyeing Danny and Luke warily while Jimmy spoke. 'We don't know. We were expecting to see your dad, as usual, and I was a bit shocked to see Sean there instead. But he said Michael had somewhere else to be. We had a bit of a laugh. We gave him the money and then we left. We walked straight to our car. We didn't see anyone suspicious. We'd been home for almost an hour by the time we found out Sean had been shot.'

'So you're telling me you have nothing for us? You don't know who shot Sean, and you don't know who took our money?' Jake snapped.

Jimmy shook his head.

'You seriously expect us to believe that?' Connor snarled.

Jimmy sighed. 'I know that it might look suspicious, but I have known your dad and your uncle Sean since we were younger than you are now. I have a lot of respect for the pair of them. I've always been one hundred per cent straight. I have never given them cause to doubt me.'

'Until today?' Connor interrupted.

'Well, that's your account, Jimmy. But what about you two?' Jake stared at Jay and Alan. 'Two hundred grand is a lot of money.'

'Not if you're dead,' Jay snapped. 'There's no way we'd cross any of you. We can make that in a few months working for you. Why would we risk everything for a couple of hundred grand?'

Jake shrugged. 'Maybe you plan on trying to pick us all off one by one? How the fuck do we know what goes on in your heads?'

Jimmy put his head in his hands.

Jake nodded at Danny and he stepped forward, pulled Alan up from his chair by the throat and smashed him against the wall. Jay went to leap to his cousin's defence, but Jimmy put a hand on his nephew's leg.

'I swear to you boys, we don't know anything. I wish we did. I wish we'd seen someone or something that could help you, but we didn't. Don't you think if we had anything to do with this, we'd be on our toes instead of sitting in my living room, waiting for this visit?'

Alan struggled as Danny's grip tightened and was dealt a blow to the back of his head for his trouble. Jimmy and Jay looked on helplessly.

'He won't stop squeezing unless you give us some information,' Jake said.

'We don't have any information,' Jay pleaded.

'My uncle is lying in a fucking coma. And there's two hundred grand of our money missing, and you expect me to believe you know nothing!' Connor shouted as he jumped up from his chair and punched Jay in the back of the head.

Jimmy stared at Jake, his eyes wide. 'I swear, we would help you if we could. Do you think I like seeing my nephews being beat up?'

Jake stood up and Jimmy flinched. 'Fortunately for you, I believe you, Jimmy.'

Jimmy's shoulders slumped in relief and he sank back against the sofa.

'That being said, Sean had no money on him when he was taken to hospital. How do we even know it was all there? How do we even know you handed it over? We can't have two hundred grand just going missing like that and not send a message that it's completely unacceptable.'

Jimmy nodded. He knew the way the game was played.

'Don't cause too much damage,' Jake said to Danny and Luke. 'We'll wait in the car.' Then he and Connor walked out of Jimmy's living room.

. . .

'You really think Jimmy and his nephews had anything to do with it?' Connor asked as they sat in the car, waiting.

'Nah. Do you?' Jake replied.

Connor shook his head. 'If I did, I'd be in there beating the shit out of them. I was just making sure.'

Jake sighed. 'But who the fuck was it then? Any ideas?'

Connor blew out a breath. 'Not a fucking clue. I think we can agree my dad was the intended target. No one knew Sean would be there instead of him. They'd only decided he was going ten minutes before.'

'So we're looking for someone who wanted your dad dead? None of us have pissed anyone off lately that I'm aware of.'

'Except the Bridewell Bell-ends?'

'Nah. They haven't got the balls or the brains to go after your dad. Seriously?'

Connor shook his head in frustration. 'I don't know, mate. I'm clutching at straws here. It could be someone from years ago for all we know.'

'I haven't got a fucking clue where to start,' Jake said with a sigh.

'Let's wait until tomorrow and see if your mum or my dad can think of anything.'

'Good idea. Here's Luke and Danny now,' Jake said as he saw the two men jogging over the road.

A few moments later, they climbed into the back seat. Jake turned and looked the two of them over. They both appeared unharmed. 'How did that go?' he asked as Connor pulled the car away.

'Fine. A few cuts and bruises. We concentrated on their

faces so they'll look like they've had a good kicking, but they'll be fine,' Danny replied.

'Good. Can't have people thinking we're going soft,' Jake replied.

'What's our next move?' Luke asked as he leaned forward in his seat.

'No idea,' Connor answered. 'Let's call it a night and we'll regroup tomorrow.'

Danny flexed his shoulders and leaned his head back against the headrest, closing his eyes. 'Sounds good to me. I'm fucking shattered. Belle and Oscar had me run ragged. Not to mention Bruce the wonder dog. The three of them were on my back at one point. Give me a punch-up over babysitting those little terrors any day.'

Jake smiled at him. Danny had been a legend all day looking after his little brother and sister so his mum and Michael could stay at the hospital. He knew that Danny adored the kids as much as they loved him. He was the same with Jake's daughter Isla too. Jake couldn't help but wonder what Danny would be like as a father himself. He swallowed the lump in his throat. There had been a time when Jake had thought having a normal family life wasn't possible for men like him. But Danny was changing all that.

Jake turned in his seat and fixed his eyes on the road ahead. Danny Alexander was coming to mean more to him that he'd ever thought possible.

Chapter Thirty-Nine

S cott Johnson lit the Calor gas fire and sat back against the sofa cushions in the old caravan. Despite it being summer, the old heap got cold at night. He glanced at his mobile phone again. He'd sent a text to his brother Craig a few hours ago, telling him he had news. Craig and his other brother, Ged, shared a cell, and they had a mobile phone in there. They had warned Scott not to ring, but he could text if he wanted to speak to them. They usually called twice a week – every Wednesday and Sunday. He couldn't wait until Sunday to tell them his news. He was too excited, the adrenaline still coursing around his body. He'd had to pull over to throw up as soon as he'd driven half a mile down the road. He told himself it was due to the sheer relief of finally going through with his plan, and getting away with it. His brothers were going to be so proud of him. All of his life they had treated him like he was an idiot. They thought he was weak. But he was stronger and cleverer than all of them.

He had picked up his phone to check his social media account when it rang in his hand and he recognised Craig's number. He answered it quickly.

'Everything all right, lad?' Craig asked him.

'Yeah. Better than all right,' Scott said with a laugh.

'Oh? What's happening then? You sound very pleased with yourself.'

'Can anyone overhear you?' Scott asked.

'No. Only me and Ged here. Why?'

'You two will never believe what I did today,' Scott said, his voice trembling with a mixture of excitement and nerves.

'What?' Craig snapped.

Scott bristled instinctively. They always thought the worst of him. Well, he was about to prove himself once and for all. 'Did you hear about what happened on Longmoor Lane today?'

'Yeah. Of course we did. Why?'

'It was me,' Scott said, almost giddy with excitement, waiting for his big brother's approval at long last.

'I think we're talking about different things, lad,' Craig said harshly.

'No. We're not, Bro. Michael Carter. I did it.'

'Michael Carter?' Craig asked and for a second Scott wondered if they really were talking about different things.

'Yeah. He got shot. He's dead.'

Craig let out a long breath. 'Jesus Christ. You are the biggest fuckwit who ever walked this earth.'

'What?' Scott asked. 'I took him out with one shot. I did what no one else had managed to do – ever!'

'You think you killed Michael Carter, do you?' Craig hissed.

Scott heard Ged suddenly in the background. 'What did you say?' Ged shouted.

'I told you, I shot him,' Scott insisted. He had seen him drop to the floor clutching his chest – blood pouring out of him as though it was coming from a tap. There was no way he could have survived.

'You shot Sean fucking Carter, you absolute bell-end!' Craig snarled down the phone. 'And you just shot him. You didn't kill him.'

'But…' Scott stammered.

'Did he see you?' Craig snapped.

Scott thought back to earlier that afternoon. Yes, he'd looked him right in the eyes and told him this was for Billy. 'Yeah,' he said quietly.

'He's in a fucking coma in Fazakerley Hospital, and you'd better pray he dies, you fuckwit, because if he wakes up, you are going to be the most wanted man in Britain. What the fuck were you thinking, Scott?'

Scott's heart was pounding in his chest and he could hardly hear himself think.

'Eh?' Craig demanded.

'I thought that killing Michael would be payback for Billy.'

'But Michael was nothing to do with Billy.'

'Not directly. But I wanted them all to know how it felt to lose someone. I thought if we took him out, the others would know how it feels, Craig.'

He heard Craig sucking in a long breath and could

imagine his older brother trying to keep a lid on his temper. 'Well, all you've fucking done is poked a very, very dangerous bear, and you have made yourself enemy number one to him and his brother. Jesus Christ! Michael Carter is going to skin you alive and skewer you from arse to mouth, you stupid, useless cunt!'

'But, Craig…' Scott started, feeling the tears threatening to overwhelm him. He bit down on his lip, knowing that crying would only make him a bigger fool in his brother's eyes.

'Don't "But, Craig" me. Did you give any thought to me and Ged stuck in here? The only thing we have going for us is Grace and Michael Carter's protection. And when they find out what you did, they're going to come after the lot of us.'

'They won't find out. Nobody saw me,' Scott insisted, trying to convince himself as much as Craig.

'Sean fucking Carter saw you, you twat!'

'But he's in a coma. He won't survive. I saw the blood. No one could come back from that.'

'Well, you'd better hope he fucking doesn't,' Craig barked and then the line went dead.

Scott sank back into the cushions. What the hell had he done? He looked over to the cupboard in the kitchen where he had hidden the gun. He should get rid of it straightaway. Or should he keep it? It was the only protection he had if someone figured out the truth. He chewed on his bottom lip. What the hell was he supposed to do? He wished Craig or Ged were there to tell him. He picked up his phone and dialled Craig's number back. He knew he wasn't supposed to, but they were locked up for the night and it would be safe to call. He knew they were annoyed with him, but they were still his big brothers, and he needed their help.

Scott listened as the phone rang out. After two rings, he was cut off. He tried again and the same thing happened.

'Come on, Craig,' he pleaded out loud and tried a third time. This time it went straight to voicemail. Scott hung up and threw the phone onto the floor. He started to cry. His body was racked with sobs.

Now he really was all alone.

Chapter Forty

Michael Carter jogged over the road to Nudge Richards' scrapyard. He'd spoken to Connor and Jake earlier that morning who had reported on their visit to Jimmy Kelly and his nephews the previous night. They were confident that the Kellys had nothing to do with Sean's shooting and he had to take their word for it. He had no clue who wanted him dead, at least he assumed the bullet had been meant for him. He supposed that he'd made more enemies in his lifetime than most, but he didn't know who was currently looking to kill him. He and Grace had discussed possibilities too and hadn't been able to come up with any viable leads. They'd spoken to their police contacts who had confirmed they had nothing to go on either. The CCTV wasn't working in the car park and the witnesses who had found Sean and saved his life hadn't seen anyone of note.

Grace had encouraged him to sit back and see what

happened next. She believed that whoever it was would make a mistake soon – or someone would talk. But, although he usually listened to his wife's words of wisdom, Michael couldn't sit around and wait for the shooter to make another move. Someone had tried to kill him, and he was terrified that they might come for another member of his family next. God forbid, Grace, or one of their children could be the next target. And he couldn't have any harm coming to any of them.

Michael walked through the yard and over to Nudge Richards' Portakabin. He didn't bother knocking and walked into the small office to find Nudge sitting at his desk staring at a computer screen. He looked up in surprise when Michael barged in, but Michael suspected he'd been awaiting a visit.

Nudge was one of the best fences in the North West. He kept his ear to the ground and he usually had a good knowledge of what was going on in the area – either that, or he knew someone else who did. Nudge was an old friend of Grace's and he was her contact really. She had already reached out to him. He claimed to know nothing but promised to use all his contacts to see what he could find out. But Michael had no time to waste – he needed answers fast.

'Michael?' Nudge said. 'I spoke to Grace this morning. I haven't heard anything yet.'

Michael sat down in the chair opposite. 'You're telling me you've heard nothing, Nudge? Not even a whisper?'

Nudge shook his head. 'I'd tell you if I had, wouldn't I?'

Michael leaned forward. 'Well, I don't fucking know, Nudge. Maybe all those gambling debts of yours have caught up with you?'

Nudge frowned at him. 'I would never—'

Michael slammed his fist down on the desk, making Nudge stop mid-sentence. 'You're telling me that someone shoots my brother in broad daylight and you haven't even heard a sniff about it. Do you expect me to believe that?' he snarled.

Nudge shook his head. 'I swear I haven't heard a thing, Michael. Have I ever given you any reason to doubt me?'

Michael stood up, planted his palms flat on the desk and leaned towards Nudge, who shrank back from him. He felt like punching Nudge in the face and then beating the shit out of him until he was one hundred per cent certain that he was telling the truth. But he couldn't. Grace would tear him a new one if he did. She trusted Nudge and he was right, he'd never given them any reason not to. But Michael was frustrated and angry. The last time he'd felt like this was when Paul had been murdered. He'd felt completely useless then too. Not knowing who had murdered his own son. But Paul's murder had been a professional hit, whereas, fortunately, Sean's shooting had all the markings of an amateur. It was the only reason Sean was still alive – albeit barely.

'If I find out you're lying to me, Nudge, I will torch his entire place to the ground, with you in it.'

Nudge ran a hand over his beard. 'I'm not lying to you,' he said quietly.

Michael stepped back, glaring at Nudge the whole time. He believed that Nudge knew nothing, but that didn't make him feel any less angry. He turned around and walked out of the door, wondering who would be the next person to feel his wrath. Perhaps he could vent some of his pent-up rage on them?

Chapter Forty-One

G race looked up from the paperwork on her desk and saw the familiar figure of John Brennan walking into her office. Despite everything that was going on, she couldn't help but break into a smile when she saw him. She had missed him. Pushing back her chair, she stood up and walked over to him. He wrapped his arms around her and gave her one of his famous bear hugs.

'It's good to see you, John,' she said as she took a step back from him.

'Good to see you too, Grace.'

She walked back to her chair and John took a seat opposite her.

'I'm sorry to hear about Sean. How is he doing?' John asked.

Grace felt the emotion swelling in her chest as she thought about Sean lying in his hospital bed in a coma – never knowing if he would wake up, and if he did, how much of Sean would still be there. She also thought about that awful forty-five minutes when she had thought that it was Michael lying in that bed instead.

She blinked back the tears. 'The doctors say he's stable. He's fit and healthy so there's every chance he will recover,' she said, forcing a smile onto her face and neglecting to add that there was also every chance he wouldn't.

'He's made of iron. He'll be back in here barking orders before you know it.'

Grace hoped that John was right. 'I'm sorry about you and Leigh,' she said, changing the subject.

'You heard then?'

'Yeah.'

'Made me look a fool, eh? Here's me jacking everything in to be with her and as soon as things got a bit rough, she drops me like a hot stone. I feel like a right knob.'

'There's nothing foolish about wanting to follow your heart, John. In fact, I'd say it was brave to walk away from everything you knew to try and grab something better.'

'It's my own bloody fault anyway. We never stood a chance really. It was supposed to be a bit of a laugh. I should have told her about what I did to Nick as soon as I realised it was becoming something more,' he said with a sigh as he ran a hand through his hair.

'Oh, John. You weren't to know she was going to find out. What were you supposed to do? It's not the type of thing you can just tell someone, is it? Those Johnson brothers were supposed to keep their mouths shut.'

'Well, I think we could have predicted that they wouldn't. Pair of lying little pricks. They'd better hope they never come face to face with me again,' he seethed.

'Well, they've changed their pleas back to guilty and they should be sentenced in a few weeks. And one day, they will all get exactly what's coming to them. Believe me.'

'I appreciate you sorting that out for me, Grace. The last thing I needed was to be getting dragged into court.'

'You really don't have to thank me, John. You're my friend, and you were only doing what I asked. If I'd known then that you and Leigh would become something…'

'Well, I really don't think anyone would have predicted that!' he said with a smile.

Grace laughed. That was true. John and Leigh had surprised everyone.

'So, I can come back if you need me to then?' John offered.

Grace stared at him. She hadn't been expecting that. 'I don't think that's a good idea, John.'

He frowned at her. 'Why not?'

'Because things have changed—'

'I've only been gone a few weeks,' he interrupted her. 'Is this some kind of punishment for leaving, Grace? Or some sort of test?'

'Of course it's not,' she said. 'I love working with you, John. I trust you as much as I do my own family. I consider you family. And if I was being selfish, I'd say yes and have you back by my side in a heartbeat.'

'But?'

'But, I think you were right to leave. There aren't many people who get out of this game alive. I think Leigh wasn't the only reason you wanted to leave. If you came back now, you'd never get out, and that would break my heart.'

John stared at her and she wondered if he was angry with her decision. Not that it would change her mind. 'Seems like there have been some changes. But it feels like there's going to be a hell of a lot more soon.'

Grace nodded. 'What happened to Sean has me rattled. Michael is walking around like he's lost a limb. Sophia and the girls are beside themselves. Pat is barely speaking two words to anyone. And the boys are tearing Liverpool apart trying to find out who pulled the trigger. And I can't fix any of it,' she said as a tear rolled down her cheek.

She looked at John and expected him to tell her she was being ridiculous. Offer her some empty words of encouragement or platitudes, but he didn't. He just sat with her and let her be. And that was why she considered him such a good friend.

Chapter Forty-Two

Michael sat at the kitchen table opposite Grace, sipping coffee and frowning.

'There must be something we're missing,' he insisted.

Grace agreed with him but, for the first time in her life, she had no idea what that something was. 'I've pulled in every favour I can think of, Michael. You and the boys have interrogated every single enemy you have. Not to mention some of our friends too,' she said, thinking of Nudge Richards. She had been furious at Michael for threatening Nudge like that, but she knew that he was at his wits' end and being eaten up by his guilt and anger, so she hadn't pushed the matter.

'Maybe we need to go back to the Kellys? They must know something more than they're letting on.'

'Do you really think that's necessary?' she asked. Jimmy Kelly and his nephews had worked for them for years and they had always proven themselves to be loyal. By their own account, they'd left the scene by the time the shooter arrived. The fact that they didn't personally pull the trigger didn't necessarily mean that they weren't involved, but Grace was satisfied that they weren't.

'Don't you?' he scowled. 'I don't see any other leads to follow.'

'Maybe you're right. But Jake and Connor have already dealt with the Kellys. Are you saying you don't trust their judgement? Because that's a pretty big statement to make. If you want to hand over the reins to them, you have to learn to trust them.'

'Well, maybe we shouldn't hand anything over then,' he snapped.

Grace looked at him and he ran a hand through his hair in exasperation. 'I'm sorry,' he said. 'I just don't understand how nobody knows anything at all. We know every fucking criminal from Scotland to Essex and we can't come up with some information?'

Grace was about to respond when Michael's phone started ringing on the table between them. They could both see it was his father Patrick calling. They looked at each other. Was it going to be bad news – or no news at all for the sixth day in a row?

Michael picked it up, his face set in a grimace as he answered. Grace saw the change in him every time he answered his phone lately. He was mentally preparing for the worst.

'Hi, Dad,' he said.

Grace couldn't hear what Patrick said so she watched Michael intently for clues. She saw the tears well in his eyes and his shoulders slump as though all of the air was leaving his body. He looked up at her with the phone still held to his ear. 'He's awake,' he said as he blinked back the tears.

Grace let out the breath she'd been unconsciously holding in. 'Thank God,' she said.

'He what?' Michael asked and started to laugh. 'He must be feeling okay then.'

He looked up at Grace again to relay the message. 'The first thing he said when he woke up was that he was starving,' he said with a roll of his eyes.

Grace smiled as she listened to the rest of the one-sided conversation. She gathered that the first person Sean had asked for was Michael, much to his wife Sophia's annoyance. With Sean lying in a coma, Sophia had directed most of her anger for her husband's situation at Michael. Her eldest daughter, Steph, had ended up almost falling out with her mother over it. But Michael had told Steph not to worry. He was happy to shoulder the blame and give Sophia, whom he ordinarily had a close relationship with, an outlet for her grief. Besides that, he blamed himself too.

'Me and Grace will be there in about an hour,' he finally said. 'Yeah, well, we'll deal with Sophia, don't worry. See you in a bit, Dad.'

Michael put the phone down and Grace walked around to his side of the table. He pulled her onto his lap and wrapped his arms around her, burying his head against her neck. She held him close to her and kissed the top of his head, running her fingers through his hair. He sighed against her and she felt the tension of the past week leaving his body. This wasn't the end of it. Sean's attacker still needed to be found and she hoped that Sean would have the answers they were looking for. But the most important thing was he was alive, and he was going to be okay.

———————

An hour after receiving the call that Sean had woken up, Michael and Grace walked through the corridors of Fazakerley Hospital. Sean remained in ICU and so only two visitors were allowed at his bed at any one time. Sophia and Steph were sitting in the corridor outside, which meant that Patrick and Sue must be in with Sean.

Sophia looked up as they approached and glared at them both. Michael tensed but Grace squeezed his hand. 'Let me talk to Sophia,' she said quietly. 'You go in and see if you can swap places with your dad or Sue, and I'll be in shortly.'

Michael stopped outside the ICU doors and kissed his wife on the cheek. 'Thanks, love,' he said. She always knew exactly what to do, and he was sure she'd have Sophia back on side soon enough.

Michael ignored Sophia's glares and pressed the buzzer to the ward. He gave his name and was buzzed through. He nodded to some of the staff as he passed. They would know who he and his family were, but it always paid to be polite and courteous. These people could throw all of them out if they so chose, and he respected that they were all trying to do a job.

'He's over there,' a young male nurse said as he pointed to a room along the corridor. 'Only two to a bed,' he added.

'Thanks. I'll send one of the others out.'

Michael walked along the corridor until he came to Sean's room. The door was open and he saw his dad and Sue sitting on opposite sides of the bed. And there, sitting up and laughing, was his big brother. Sean glanced up and their eyes met. Michael rushed towards the bed. 'You scared the life out of us, you fucker,' he said as he wrapped his arms around Sean, careful to avoid the machinery he was still hooked up to.

'I scared the shit out of myself, Bro,' Sean said with a smile as he hugged him back.

Michael turned to his dad and smiled. He'd aged ten years in the past week and Michael's heart broke for him. He knew better than anyone the pain of losing a son and he was glad that his father had been spared that heartache. His dad stood up and the two of them shared a long hug too.

'Eh, I didn't get that much of a hug and I'm the one who nearly died,' Sean said from his bed, causing Sue to roll her eyes at the three of them.

'Can I have a word with Michael, Dad?' Sean said and their father nodded to Sue.

'Come on, love. Let's leave these two to it.'

Sue stood up and gave Sean a light kiss on the cheek and then the two of them left the room, closing the door behind them.

'Where's Grace?' Sean asked.

'She's outside talking to Sophia. She'll be in soon.'

Sean closed his eyes. 'God, she's so pissed off, mate. I thought she was going to kill me herself.'

'Yeah, well, who can blame her really? You promised her you were out of the game.'

'I know,' he said with a sigh. 'But it's easier said than done, mate. You know that. I hope she hasn't given you too much grief,' he added quietly.

Michael shook his head. 'Nah. Nothing I couldn't handle.'

'I've told her it was my decision anyway. And I'm sure Grace will smooth things over,' Sean said.

They sat in silence for a few moments, both aware that the next part of their conversation was about to set in motion a chain of events that they would have differing ideas of handling.

'So did you see who it was?' Michael finally asked.

'Yep. I saw him.'

'So who was it?'

'Scott Johnson.'

Michael sat back in his seat. 'Scott Johnson? The Johnsons' weedy little brother who wouldn't know one end of a gun from the other? I thought he'd moved to Leicester?'

'I thought the same. But it was him. He even told me it was for Billy.'

'Billy? You had nothing to do with Billy.'

'Well, I imagine the stupid prick thought I was you,' Sean said with a shrug.

Michael shook his head. It didn't make much sense to him. He'd had nothing to do with Billy's murder either, but he could see how his death would be some sort of revenge. The whole business with the Johnson brothers was supposed to have been sewn up. Scott had left Liverpool and Michael and Grace had assured Craig and Ged that they wouldn't go after him if he stayed out of the way. He'd been home free. So why had the stupid bastard come back?

'I want to deal with him myself,' Sean said, breaking into Michael's train of thought.

Michael shook his head vehemently. 'No. Not a chance.'

'I'm dealing with him,' Sean insisted.

Michael squared up to him. It wasn't often that he and Sean were at odds, but he knew he was right on this one. 'You're going to do what you promised Sophia you'd do and stay away from this shit. You're going to stick to the restaurants, and you're going to leave Scott to me.'

Sean started to protest but Michael interrupted him. 'You've just woke up from a fucking coma, mate. You almost died. We need to take care of Scott as soon as. We don't have time to wait for your recovery.'

'I could take that little prick out with half an arm,' Sean snapped.

'Yeah, I know. But you're not going anywhere for the foreseeable future. I know you want revenge, but that's the beauty of having a brother, isn't it? And trust me, no one wants to make that fucker pay more than me.'

Sean leaned his head back against his pillows. 'Fine,' he snapped, wincing with the effort.

———

Grace sat opposite her sister-in-law in the small cafeteria and placed two cans of Diet Coke on the table. Sophia had said only two words to her since they'd come face to face ten minutes earlier, and that was to agree to go to the café to talk in private and that she'd like a cold drink.

'So, shall we clear the air?' Grace suggested.

Sophia shrugged. Grace had experienced Sophia's fiery Italian temper on many an occasion, but the two women had always had a close relationship and they adored each other, even if they didn't always see eye to eye.

'He's going to be okay, Sophia. I know how scared you must have been, but he's okay.'

'No thanks to you and Michael,' Sophia hissed.

'Oh, come on, Sophia. You know better than anyone what a stubborn sod Sean can be. Do you honestly think Michael and I have any control over what he does? He's a grown man, for God's sake.'

'Well, maybe Michael doesn't. But you do, Grace. You could have talked him out of it.'

'Sophia—' Grace started.

'You promised me once that you would help him go straight. You promised you'd keep him away from that life.'

Grace sighed. A long time ago, when Sean had got out of prison for the last time, Grace had helped him set up his first restaurant business. She remembered the conversation she'd had with Sophia at the time, over a few glasses of brandy. The two of them had talked about the future and Grace had agreed to do what she could to keep Sean away from a life of crime. But she'd never made any promises.

'I told you I would help him do that, and I have done. You know that. But he is a grown man who makes his own decisions. For some reason, he wants back into the action and maybe you need to ask him, or yourself, why that is.'

'Are you suggesting it's *my* fault my husband got shot?' Sophia snapped.

Grace sighed. Sophia was clearly, and understandably, still very emotional 'No. I'm not suggesting that at all. But you blaming me and Michael for this isn't going to do anyone any good. All it's going to do is make the atmosphere difficult for everyone. Don't you think Michael already feels guilty enough? That bullet was meant for him, and I for one would rather focus on finding out who was responsible than squabbling amongst ourselves.'

Sophia sipped her drink but she remained silent.

'You married into this family, Sophia. For better or for worse. You knew who the Carters were and what they did for a living.' Grace stood up. 'I'm going to see your husband now. The next time you see mine, I'd appreciate it if you greeted him with something more welcoming than a scowl.'

Then Grace walked out of the café leaving Sophia alone.

Grace knocked on the closed door of Sean's hospital room. She'd been advised by the nurse that it needed to remain open for the remainder of the visit and Grace provided her assurance that it would be. Michael and Sean had been speaking alone for over ten minutes and she assumed they'd already had all the privacy they needed and had discussed what needed to be discussed.

'Come in,' she heard Michael call and she pushed open the door.

For someone who'd almost died and had only woken

from a coma a few hours earlier, Sean looked surprisingly well.

'Hey you,' she said as she walked across the room to him.

'Hiya, Grace,' he said with a smile. As she drew closer to him, she saw how tired and drawn he looked. No doubt all the activity of the past few hours was starting to take its toll on him now. She bent down and kissed his cheek. 'It's good to see you,' she said quietly.

'It's good to be seen,' he replied.

Grace sat down opposite Michael while Sean laid his head back against the pillow and closed his eyes. She looked across at her husband and he nodded to her. Grace knew that meant Sean had given Michael the answers he'd been looking for. She was desperate to know too, but the door was now open, and Sean was flagging with each passing second.

Grace took Sean's hand in hers and squeezed. 'We'll go and let you get some rest, Sean.'

His eyes snapped open. 'No. You don't have to,' he said wearily.

'We'll come back tonight and see you again,' Michael assured him.

'But those nurses will kill us if we tire you out too much, not to mention Sophia. Anyway, the girls are on their way,' Grace said, referring to his two youngest daughters, Nicola and Beth. 'You don't want to waste all your energy talking to us two, do you?'

Sean's eyes were rolling in his head now as he struggled to keep them open.

'The nurse gave him some morphine before I came in,' Michael said. 'It must be kicking in.'

'Let's go then,' Grace said as she stood up.

'See you later, Bro,' Michael said as he gave Sean a brief kiss on the forehead.

———————

Grace listened intently to Michael's replaying of his conversation with Sean as they drove to pick up Belle from school. She was as shocked as Michael had been that the shooter was Scott Johnson. Why would he be so stupid as to come back to Liverpool and shoot one of the Carters?

'I wonder if Craig and Ged knew anything about this?' she asked as Michael drove.

'I wouldn't put it past that pair of snakes,' he replied.

Grace, however, wasn't convinced that they had anything to do with their younger brother's actions. It was true that Craig and Ged were a pair of lying scumbags who couldn't be trusted, but they were also self-serving and hell-bent on self-preservation, no matter what the cost. So Scott killing Michael, who she believed had been the intended target, served absolutely no purpose. In fact, it was the quickest and surest way to get them all killed. No, the more she thought about it, the more Grace was convinced that Scott Johnson had acted alone.

'What are you going to do?' she asked as she placed a hand on his thigh. Ordinarily, she would be involved in the decision-making and the planning, but this was too personal for Michael. And there was a part of her that didn't need to know the detail.

'I'll find him and kill him,' he said matter-of-factly.

'Alone?'

He shook his head. 'No. Me and Connor,' he replied.

Grace suspected there was an element of him regretting the way he had handled his son Paul's murder, even though Grace still thought he'd done the right thing. He had simply shot Sol Shepherd in the head instead of making him suffer. Connor also felt he'd missed an opportunity to make the man responsible for his brother's murder pay, and she wondered if this would be some sort of reckoning for them both.

'What do you think?' he asked her.

'Whatever you need to do, love,' she replied with a faint smile. Then when it was over, maybe it was time for her and Michael to finally hand over the reins to the next generation?

Michael lifted her hand to his lips and kissed her fingertips. 'I'll get it sorted quickly and cleanly. I promise.'

'I know you will.'

Chapter Forty-Three

Leigh Moss threw the folder onto the desk in the investigation room and turned to her team. 'CPS have given us the green light to charge Wilkinson and Fox, but they say we don't have enough evidence for any of the others. It's a fucking joke!'

'That's not a bad result, Ma'am,' DS Whitney said.

There were murmurs of assent.

Leigh leaned against the desk and let out a long breath. 'I know that. But we know there were more of them involved, and it kills me that we couldn't make them all pay for what they put that poor girl through.'

She watched the bobbing of heads around the room and knew that her team weren't the ones who deserved to bear the brunt of her frustration. They all felt the same as she did and she knew it. It hurt when they couldn't bring the perpetrators to justice and they felt it as a team. The Bridewell Blades crew weren't as stupid as they looked, and there had been unsophisticated, yet effective, attempts made to clean Kacey Jones' body before she was dumped at the hospital, resulting in limited DNA evidence being found except on the main perpetrators, Wilkinson and Fox. Charging two of the Bridewell Blades crew for rape and wounding was a good result, but good results weren't enough for victims like Kacey Jones. They deserved perfect results. And the poor girl still had the trial to endure. Leigh would bet her house that none of the perpetrators would plead guilty.

'It sticks in the throat though, Ma'am,' Detective Constable Shaw added. 'That Bridewell lot are animals and they all need putting away for life. It's a shame we couldn't charge more of them.'

Leigh nodded. She had been wondering if her team could consider a joint operation with the OCG Task force. They wanted to bring the Bridewell crew down as much as her team did. She would speak to the DCI and see what she thought.

She looked around the room at the tired and expectant faces. This investigation had been a tough one for all of them, not only because of the hours they'd all had to put in, but also because it had been such a harrowing one.

'Notwithstanding the CPS decision, you've all done an amazing job on this case. Now get home to your families and I'll see you all tomorrow.'

'Thanks, Ma'am,' they chorused before they started to file out of the room.

Leigh looked at the folder on the table and sighed. She rubbed her temples and could already feel the headache coming on. She should go home like the rest of the team and start the paperwork tomorrow. But she couldn't face going home to her empty house. Rattling around the place on her own made John's absence from her life even starker. She missed him so much. Despite how different they were, no one had ever made her as feel as comfortable, safe and looked after as John did.

Despite what he had done, she still loved him.

She shook her head. Thinking about John was a waste of her time and energy. She could never forgive what he'd done and the fact that he had lied to her about it throughout their entire relationship. It didn't matter how much she missed his incredible hugs, his attempts at cooking, the way he made her laugh or how safe and comforted she felt with one of his huge arms draped over her when she woke in the night, because, as painful as living without all of that was, she could never trust him again. And without trust, they had nothing.

Chapter Forty-Four

Danny picked up his watch from the bedside table and clipped it onto his wrist. He turned to Jake, who was lying in bed with his arms behind his head. Danny knew that he had a big day ahead of him, as he, Connor and Michael were going to deal with the prick who had shot Sean.

'I won't be long. I'll see you at your mum's in about an hour, okay?'

Jake nodded absent-mindedly. 'Okay.'

'I'd do this tomorrow. But she won't stop calling if I don't go today.'

Jake frowned as he turned to him. 'How long are you going to keep doing this, Dan?' he asked. 'She clicks her fingers and you go running. How much money are you even giving her?'

Danny swallowed. 'I'm only giving her a hundred quid a week. If I give her it all at once, she just burns through it in a day and then she's on the blower for more anyway.'

Jake sat up. 'So? Fuck her! You don't owe her anything, Dan.'

'She's my mum, Jake,' he said with a sigh.

'You keep saying that, but she has never been any kind of mum to you from what you've told me. I don't get why she has such a hold over you,' he snapped.

Danny closed his eyes and sucked in a breath. The constant lying was becoming exhausting and he knew it was only a matter of time before Jake stopped believing that he was only paying Glenda out of the goodness of his heart. The truth was, he had been giving her money hand over fist these past few weeks. It was becoming an almost daily occurrence that she'd phone him wanting more. She was so out of it on crack, she didn't even know what day it was most of the time. He had to think of another way out of this situation, and soon.

'I just can't stand to see her struggling, that's all,' Danny replied. 'I won't be long.'

'Why don't you have one of the lads drop it off for you?' Jake suggested.

'Because I don't want anyone knowing I'm related to her, Jake. If you saw her now…' He shook his head. 'She's an embarrassment.'

Jake's face softened at his words and placed his warm hand over Danny's. 'Okay. You'd better get going then. I'll see you at my mum's.'

'I'll be back as soon as I can,' Danny said before leaning over and kissing him on the forehead.

· · ·

Half an hour later, Danny was standing outside the door to his mother's flat for the second time that week. At least it was a Sunday and the nail salon wasn't open. One of the girls who worked there seemed to have a thing for him now, and he did his best to avoid her.

The door opened slightly and his mother's gaunt and haggard face appeared in the crack. 'Danny,' she said with a smile when she saw him. She opened the door wider. 'Come up, son. I've been waiting for you.'

Danny didn't usually go inside. He hated spending any time in the woman's company and he hated the way the stench and decay of her dirty flat lingered on him after he'd been there. But today he wanted answers. He'd had enough of Glenda's constant demands.

He stepped inside the hallway and followed his mother up the stairs and into her living room.

'Fancy a brew?' she asked with a toothless smile. 'I don't have any milk, but I'm sure there's a couple of teabags in the cupboard.'

'No!' He shook his head and stuffed his hands into his trouser pockets.

'Suit yourself,' she said as she sat on the mouldy old sofa. 'Did you bring my money?'

'I've brought you fifty quid,' he snapped.

'What? Is that all?' she shrieked.

'Yes. Because I already gave you a ton two days ago.'

'What? No, you didn't. That was last week.'

Danny sighed and shook his head. 'This has to stop, Mum. I'm not your personal fucking cash machine. I can't keep coming round here every five minutes to give you money. I'm not doing it anymore. I told you, I'd send you five hundred a month, and from now on, that's all you get. I'll have it dropped here on the first of every month, and then the rest of the time you leave me alone.'

'But I need more. I can't get by on that, Danny.'

'Well, you'll have to learn. Because it's that or nothing,' he said firmly.

'Well, then –' she sucked in air, smacking her lips over the few teeth she had left '– well, maybe I'll just have to tell all of your friends your little secret then. And Stacey. She'll be heartbroken when she finds out.'

At the mention of his sister's name, Danny lunged forward, grabbing Glenda by the throat and pushing her back against the sofa. 'I am warning you, Ma, one word to anyone and your little gravy train will come to an end. Without me, you'll have nothing, and don't you forget that. I am being more than fucking generous.'

She looked up at him and started to laugh and that made him angrier than ever. He thought about how easy it would be to squeeze his hand a little harder and put an end to all this right now. No one would miss Glenda Alexander. No one would care.

'Go on, Son,' she hissed. 'You're just like your father after all.'

He released her throat from his grip and stepped backwards with a shake of his head. 'What the fuck did you come back here for anyway? You were gone for fourteen fucking years.'

'Not quite,' she cackled as she rubbed her throat.

'What's that supposed to mean?' he snarled.

'Nothing.' She shook her head dismissively.

'So? Why now? Why bother coming here after all these years?'

'The old codger I was living with had a stroke. His daughters had always hated me, and they threw me out. I had nowhere else to go. So I came home. Where else was I supposed to go?'

'That's all?'

'And an old friend of mine told me that you'd just gone into business with the biggest security firm in Merseyside,' she admitted. 'And I knew you'd always look after your old mum, Danny Boy. You and me, we have something special, don't we? It was good when there was just the two of us. Remember?'

Danny felt the bile burning the back of his throat. 'You are an evil fucking witch. I would be happy if I never saw your miserable face again. Stay away from me. Stay away from Stacey. And if you don't stop with the constant demands for money—'

'What? You'll kill me?' She glared at him.

'I only wish I fucking could,' he snarled and then he threw the notes at her before turning around and walking out of her rotten, stinking flat.

Chapter Forty-Five

G race loaded the dishwasher while Danny wiped down the breakfast bar. She knew that, like her, he was trying to keep busy to stop his mind from working overtime. Michael, Jake and Connor had found where Scott Johnson was hiding out, and they had gone to pay him a visit. Danny had stayed behind when they'd left and had helped with Belle and Oscar's bedtimes. Grace found it comforting having him around and she enjoyed his company. She was glad of the distraction herself.

'Do you fancy a drink, Danny?' she asked as she picked a bottle of lager from the fridge.

'Yeah, go on,' he said and she handed it to him, before pouring herself a glass of Pinot.

'Do you ever get used to worrying about them, Grace?' Danny asked as he took a swig of his beer. 'I don't know about you, but I'd prefer to be there with them rather than sitting here waiting.'

Grace shook her head. 'No, I never stop worrying. But

also, no, I'd rather be here. I've been to enough of these things to last me a lifetime.'

'I can imagine.'

'Sometimes, I wonder how on earth I ever ended up here. If you'd known me when I was a teenager, when I met Jake's dad, I was so naïve and innocent.' She started to laugh. 'And look at me now. It seems like there's not a week goes by when we don't have to deal with someone staging a takeover. And if it's not that, there's the attempts at blackmail or extortion,' she said, noticing the change in Danny when she said those last few words.

He stared at her intently, sucking on his top lip as though he wanted to ask her something but didn't know how. Perhaps he didn't realise how many threats and idiots she and Michael had to deal with to keep the whole security business running smoothly.

'Is everything okay?' she asked.

He nodded absent-mindedly. 'What about blackmailers though? Do you think they ever stop? Is there ever enough money, or whatever else they want, to make them stop?'

'In my experience, no.'

'Then how do you stop them?' he asked.

'Well, there are two ways. One is the obvious way, which is to remove the threat – or "take care" of them as Michael would say.'

Danny nodded, understanding exactly what that meant.

'And the other way?' he asked.

'Well, it's much less messy and in my opinion much more effective, and that is to take away their power.'

'How?' he asked with a frown.

'By telling the truth. It can't always be done, obviously, but if it can – then that's your best bet.'

Danny continued to frown and she smiled at him. He was a grown man, but sometimes all she saw was a lost little boy in him.

'For instance, if a man was having an affair, a blackmailer might threaten to tell his wife. He has three options. Pay up and be on the hook for ever. Remove the threat by removing the evidence – which might include the person too. Murdering someone might be a bit extreme in that scenario, but let's face it, it's been done for less. Or he could tell his wife he's been having an affair and beg her forgiveness. If she had sense, she'd kick him in the balls and then kick him out, but that's beside the point. Which of those outcomes ends up best for him in the long run?'

'Telling his wife.'

'Exactly. There are plenty of situations where telling the truth isn't an option though and then you're back to options one and two,' she said as she took a sip of her wine 'So, which is it to be for you?'

He blinked at her. 'What?'

'I assume this isn't a hypothetical situation, Danny. So, what are your options? How are we going to deal with this particular threat?'

'We?'

Grace shrugged. 'I kind of feel invested now. Besides, you're too important to Jake for me to allow someone to blackmail you. I assume he doesn't know about whatever it is?'

He shook his head. 'It's nothing really. I shouldn't have

even mentioned it. I was just asking,' he said dismissively, but Grace knew he was hiding something.

'Jake's father tried to blackmail me once,' she said.

'What? Why?'

'It's a very long story, but basically, he threatened to frame Jake for an armed robbery. He had a gun with Jake's prints on it.'

'But...' Danny shook his head. 'His own son?'

'Yep. Nathan was a narcissist. He loved Jake, in his own way, but nothing came between him and what he wanted. Not even his own son.'

'What did he want?' Danny asked. 'Money?'

'No. Me! Or so he claimed. It was a way to keep me in line.'

'So you removed the threat?' he asked.

'Yes. Him and the gun. But I would have preferred an easier solution. Sometimes removing their power isn't an option. The only way to have done that would have been to call his bluff, and I couldn't have risked Jake like that.'

'I knew Jake's dad wasn't the best, but I had no idea...' Danny said.

'Oh, that's just the tip of the iceberg. But my point is, we are all vulnerable to being exploited by other people. So, what is going on with you?'

Danny shifted in his seat.

'Is this anything to do with your mum?' Grace asked him.

'Why would you think that?'

She noticed he didn't deny it. 'Because she turns up and

now you're being blackmailed. And I wouldn't put it past her. So, what does she have on you?'

Danny shook his head and she could see the heat creeping up his neck as he looked down at his feet.

'Have you hurt somebody you shouldn't have?' she asked.

His head snapped up. 'No. It's nothing like that.'

Grace frowned at him. 'Is it illegal?'

He shook his head.

'Jesus, Danny. I feel like we're playing charades. Just tell me what it is and let me help you. Because it's either that or we're going to have to bump off your mother – which I am completely down with, by the way,' she said with a grin.

Danny looked up at Grace Carter and felt like he was sitting in a confessional. This woman had a way of seeing into his soul. He weighed up his options and realised that she was right. He had three choices, and two of those were unthinkable. Being at his mother's disposal for the rest of her life was as frightening as the thought of bumping her off. So he supposed he only had one option left.

Danny took another long swig of his beer as he prepared to tell Grace about his real father. 'Have you ever heard of Alan Price? His case was massive in the nineties.'

'Yes, I remember. He murdered that little girl.'

'Well, he's my real dad,' he said, the word 'dad' sticking in his throat.

'What? I thought David Alexander was yours and Stacey's dad?' Grace asked.

'Everyone does. Even Stacey. Only me and my mum know the truth.'

Grace blew out a breath. 'Jesus, how long have you known?'

'Since I was five,' Danny said, willing himself not to cry. The memory of finding out that the man he believed to be his father wasn't at all, was a painful one for him.

'I don't understand. He's been in prison for years.'

'I know. He went to prison seven months before I was born. My mum had only been with him for a few months when she got pregnant with me. She thought he was the one, but then a few weeks later he was arrested and charged with all of those offences against those kids. And the murder of the little girl.'

'Bloody hell,' Grace said. 'Your mum must have been terrified. That case was huge. I remember it being talked about everywhere. You couldn't turn on the telly or open a newspaper without seeing his face.'

'Yep. But then my good old mum did what she does best – self-preservation. She met my poor chump of a stepdad, took him home for a night of passion and convinced him that I was his. A few years later, Stacey came along and we were all really happy for a few years. But nothing David ever did was good enough for my mum. Their relationship started to turn to shit and during one of their many arguments, my mum told him who my real dad was, while I was sitting right there in front of them.' Danny looked down at the floor as the waves of anger, shame and sadness washed over him. He'd never spoken about this to anyone before.

'Oh, Danny,' Grace said. 'You poor thing. What did David do when he found out?'

'I can't remember exactly. But he left us soon after that. And as far as I knew, it was because of me. My mum told me that when he found out he was raising the son of a monster, he'd been too disgusted to even look at me again. So he fucked off and we never saw or heard from him again. Me and Stace missed him at first. He'd been a nice dad. We always played footy in the garden and he made the best jam roly-poly ever. But it wasn't long before we learned to hate him as much as our mum did. Him leaving was the start of her drinking getting worse. Things were never the same after that.'

'So Stacey doesn't know why her dad left or that he wasn't your dad too?' Grace asked.

Danny shook his head and took a deep breath to force down a sob. 'No. No one knows who my real dad is.'

'But why didn't you tell her when she got older? Didn't she always wonder why her dad left?'

Grace's words were like a barb to Danny's heart. He'd felt guilty his whole life for driving Stacey's dad away, and for not telling her that he was the reason why. And now Grace saw that too. How could he justify never telling his little sister the truth? That was self-preservation too, wasn't it? Didn't that make him just like their mother?

'My mum made me promise never to tell anyone. She told me that if anyone ever found out, they'd be disgusted by me, just like she and David were. They would only see the monster in me – because evil like that, well, it's in the genes, isn't it? That's what my mum always said anyway.'

Danny finished speaking and looked up at Grace, expecting her to tell him to get out of her house. He thought he would see the same venom and disgust on her face as his mother always had whenever she spoke about his father. Instead, Grace surprised him by standing up and walking around the table to him. Then she wrapped her arms around him and kissed the top of his head.

'You poor kid,' she said softly. 'When they were handing out parents, you really got the shittiest of the bunch.'

Danny buried his head in her shoulder, inhaling the citrusy smell of the expensive perfume she always wore. Then Danny Alexander did something he hadn't done since he was five years old. He cried.

Grace's heart broke in two for him. She recalled Alan Price's court case well. She had been eighteen at the time and because it had happened in Liverpool, it had been a regular topic of discussion at The Rose and Crown. The trial had lasted for weeks and there had been armed police outside Liverpool Crown Court when he'd first appeared, such was the venom the city had for him. He was eventually sentenced to life for murder, kidnap and a string of sexual offences against children. And while Danny's father might be a well-documented monster, his mother wasn't much better in Grace's opinion. All his life she had led him to believe that he was somehow damaged simply because of who his father was. The truth was, if Danny was damaged, it was because of his terrible childhood with her and his stepfather, and not his DNA. And to convince him that the man he'd believed was his father until he was five years old had left because of him was unforgivable. Grace would bet everything she owned that he left because Glenda was a lying, manipulative cow, but she knew that Danny wasn't in the right frame of mind to be convinced of that just now. David Alexander wasn't exactly a hero in this story – clearing off and leaving his children with their horrible mother. Grace wondered if any adult in his young life had ever not let Danny down.

Danny sat staring down at his empty bottle of lager. He wiped his eyes with the sleeve of his hoodie, making him look twelve years old rather than twenty-eight.

'Is that what Glenda is holding over you? That your biological father is Alan Price?' Grace took a deep breath. She would like to personally take care of Glenda Alexander and bury her in a deep ditch where no one would ever find her. The fact that Danny had carried this secret shame alone for almost twenty years made her want to cry for him. It wasn't his shame to carry at all, and it seemed he'd never even considered that.

'Then she has nothing on you, does she?' Grace said matter-of-factly.

He stared at her. 'But what if she tells everyone?'

'Well, she won't. Because believe me, Danny, she comes out of this story far, far worse than you. And so what if she does? We don't choose our parents. Who your father is has absolutely no bearing on who you are. You've never even met the man, have you?'

He shook his head. 'No. But Stacey—'

'Stacey adores you,' Grace interrupted him. 'You two

having different fathers will make not one bit of difference to that.'

'But she'll find out I'm the reason her dad left.'

'Danny,' Grace said with a sigh and deciding it was time for some tough love. 'You're not five years old anymore. I understand you have always believed what Glenda has told you, but I think we can both agree she is a self-serving, narcissistic liar, can't we?'

He stared at her but didn't answer.

'So, what is more likely? That Stacey's dad left because of that, or because of a five-year-old boy, whom he loved like his own son? Did David say goodbye to you?'

Danny thought for a moment and then he nodded. Tears filled his eyes. 'He came up to my room and he told me to look after Stacey. He told me to keep practising my penalty kicks.'

'So he asked you to look after his baby girl? Would he do that if he was disgusted by you and thought you were a monster?'

Danny blinked at her. 'I've never thought much about that night. Afterwards, my mum convinced me that he didn't… She told me and Stacey that he never loved us. She said that was why he never came back.'

Grace wondered exactly what Glenda had said to her husband to make him leave his two children and never return, because, from what Danny had said, up until that point he'd seemed like he was a decent enough father.

'You don't have to tell anyone, Danny. I'm not going to, and I doubt your mother will either. But you probably should. If you see any future with Jake, don't you think he deserves to know? And Stacey should too. If only so she has some understanding of why her father left – and that it wasn't anything to do with you.'

Danny leaned back in his chair. 'You think they'll be okay with it?' he asked.

'Of course they will. There's nothing for them not to be okay with. At least not with you anyway.'

'I suppose. Don't you get fed up of always being right?'

'Never. Can I give you one more piece of advice?'

'How could I refuse?'

'Tell Glenda to stay the hell out of yours and Stacey's lives and don't give her another penny. If she refuses, I'd be more than happy to tell her for you.'

Danny smiled. 'I will. And thank you, Grace. I thought after people found out who I really was, they'd think I was … well, you know.'

'But who you really are hasn't changed at all, has it?'

He smiled again and this time it reached his eyes. Grace felt a wave of emotion rush over her.

'Now, how about you make us a nice cup of tea each while I take Bruce for a quick walk?' she said breezily as she stood up. 'If we keep drinking, we'll be pissed by the time the boys get back.'

'Sounds like a deal,' he replied.

Chapter Forty-Six

Michael Carter edged the stolen Ford Mondeo slowly down the gravel track. He had switched off the headlights when they had turned into the caravan park. The engine thrummed quietly in the silence. When the caravan was in sight, he pulled into a cluster of trees and switched off the engine. He turned to look at his son Connor in the passenger seat. They were both dressed similarly in black jogging bottoms, hoodies and gloves.

'You ready?' he asked.

'Yep.'

'Let's try and stick to the plan if we can. We want this quick and clean.'

'Yeah.'

Michael could see the change in Connor's demeanour. He was psyching himself up for what they were about to do. The tension crackled in the air between them like a recently lit firework that was waiting for the spark to set it free. A few years earlier, Connor and Paul had made a living doing this kind of thing for gangsters and criminals all over the UK. Michael had known they were involved in it but he had never asked questions. They were referred to as 'The Cleaners' and had earned themselves a shitload of money, as well as a reputation for being professional and discreet.

Nevertheless, when they had gone into partnership with Jake Conlon, and started to focus on business closer to home, Michael had been relieved. They had reminded him so much of himself and Sean back in the day, and because of that he'd known, better than most, the toll that kind of employment took on you – both physically and mentally. He had wanted more for his boys.

Michael felt a surge of grief come out of nowhere, almost taking his breath away. He wondered if Connor felt Paul's absence as much as he did right now. He sat forward, trying to shake the feeling from his bones. Now wasn't the time.

'Grab the bag,' he said to Connor as he put the car keys in his pocket.

Connor took the black holdall from the back seat of the car. Then the two men stepped out of the vehicle and headed towards the caravan. As they drew nearer, they saw the soft, flickering light from the television. A figure dressed all in black stepped out of the shadows and Michael silently acknowledged his stepson Jake, who had driven ahead and parked the Land Rover, which they were going to use to get back home, in a clearing nearby.

'Is he in there?' Michael asked quietly as Jake approached.

Jake nodded.

Michael put his hand on the back of Jake's neck. 'You ready?' he whispered.

'Yeah.'

'You think he's awake?' Connor whispered as they edged towards the caravan.

'Don't know,' said Michael. 'But why don't you two head around the other side in case he hears and tries to make a run for it.'

'Okay,' Connor replied.

As they reached their target, Connor, Jake and Michael parted ways, the two younger men walking around the back of the old tin box while Michael climbed the two steps to the caravan door. He took a small toolkit from his jacket pocket and pulled out the thin blade that was perfect for picking locks, particularly old knackered ones like this. In a few seconds, he'd picked the lock and the handle gave way beneath his hand. Slowly and quietly, he pulled open the door and stepped inside.

Scott Johnson was asleep on the sofa. In the dim light from the television screen, Michael saw the gun clutched in his hands, pressed close to his chest. Michael made a split-second decision, crossed the caravan in one quick stride and pulled the gun from Scott's hands. Scott blinked awake and screamed in fright as he saw Michael standing over him. Michael clamped his large hand over Scott's mouth. 'Shut the fuck up,' he hissed as he brought his face closer to Scott's.

Just then Connor came running into the caravan, throwing the holdall onto the floor in the middle of the room, with Jake following close behind.

Michael glanced behind him and indicated that it was fine to proceed to the next stage of the plan. He turned his attention back to Scott, who stared at him wide-eyed. The sound of Scott's soft cries hummed against Michael's palm as he kept his left hand firmly over his mouth. Michael raised the gun in his right hand and pressed the cold steel against Scott's temple. Scott winced, confirming Michael's suspicion that there were bullets within.

'I'm going to move my hand, but if you make a sound, I'll shoot you in the face. Understand?' he growled.

Scott nodded and Michael slowly withdrew his hand and sat back, the gun still trained on the youngest Johnson brother. Meanwhile Connor had removed his chosen weapon from the holdall and held it aloft. Scott's eyes widened even further when he saw what it was, and he let out a quiet sob.

Connor pressed the button on the cordless drill and it whirred to life, the sound almost deafening in the small confines of the caravan. Michael's knee was between Scott's legs, pressed against his groin. He looked down in disgust as he felt a warm wetness against his trousers and realised that Scott had pissed himself. Connor released the button and all was quiet again.

Michael glared at the quivering mess in front of him. 'If you're going to run around shooting people, then you really should grow a pair of balls, lad,' he said.

'I'm sorry,' Scott whimpered as tears started to run down his cheeks.

'A bit late for that now, isn't it?' Michael said as he slid off the sofa and sat back on his haunches. 'You're going to die, Scott. There's no escaping that. You shot my brother and you left him to die in the street like an animal so there's no way I'm going to be able to let you walk out of here.'

Scott's skin had turned a strange shade of pale grey by this point and he started to tremble uncontrollably while shaking his head violently from side to side. 'No. No,' he mumbled.

Michael grabbed hold of his face with his free hand, his fingers squeezing either side of his cheeks as he held his head still. 'Don't worry. You still have options. I'm not a monster,' he said with a smile. Releasing Scott's face, Michael unzipped the pocket of his jacket and pulled out the hypodermic needle. 'There's enough brown in here to send you off to meet your big brother Billy. You'll feel great for a few seconds, and then you'll drift off to sleep and never wake up. We'll make it look like a suicide.'

Scott stared at him as though he'd lost his mind and Michael understood that agreeing the method of your own demise was a decision that most people would recoil from. However, he was about to present Scott with the alternative.

Michael looked at Jake and Connor. His son continued standing there in silence, holding the battery-powered drill in his hand while he glared at Scott Johnson.

'I want answers first though, and if you give me some that I'm satisfied with, I'll stick you with this.' He shook the needle gently before placing it back in his pocket. 'But if you mess me around, or I think you're lying to me, then my sons will happily drill holes in you until you do answer. They'll start with your kneecaps and then see where we go from there.'

Scott tried to sit up as he began to retch. Michael stood up and moved out of the line of fire. The last thing he wanted was to be covered in someone else's vomit. He handed the gun to Jake who tucked it into the large front pocket of his hooded jacket.

Michael turned back to Scott, who was now a gibbering, trembling wreck. 'So, which is it to be?' Michael asked.

Scott looked up at him. 'Fuck off!' he spat before wiping his mouth with the back of his hand.

Connor stepped forward. 'Our way it is then?' he said with a grin.

Scott shrank back, his body pressed against the back of the sofa. 'No,' he screamed.

Michael put his hand on Connor's shoulder. 'Let's see if he answers my questions first,' he said.

Connor stepped back while Michael pulled up the nearby chair and sat in front of Scott.

'Where is our money? You stole two hundred grand from my brother when you shot him. Now where is it?'

'In the bedroom. In a wardrobe.' Scott tilted his head towards the door at the back of the caravan.

'All of it?' Michael asked.

'Most of it. I only spent a few hundred quid,' Scott stammered.

Michael turned to Jake, who went into the bedroom Scott had indicated. A moment later, he came out holding the bag of money aloft.

Michael turned back to Scott. 'Good. Now that we have that out of the way, let's get to the important stuff, shall we? Why did you shoot my brother?'

Scott looked down and his bottom lip trembled.

'Was that bullet meant for me?' Michael asked.

Scott looked up again and sniffed loudly before nodding his agreement.

'Why? I had nothing to do with Billy. You were in the clear. Free to go and live your life any way you chose. Away from your idiot brothers. So why risk all that to shoot me?'

'My brothers are all I have. I wanted your family to know how much it hurts to have someone taken away from you. I knew that losing you would hurt them all,' Scott said between sniffs.

'Well, I suppose I am pretty fucking awesome,' Michael said, and Connor and Jake laughed in the background. 'How did you fuck up so badly though? I mean, I'm not the one in hospital recovering from a gunshot wound, am I?'

'I thought he was you,' Scott mumbled.

'Fuck! That's a whole new level of stupid right there. If you're going to try and kill someone, you should at least make sure that you're shooting the right fucking person.'

Scott wiped the snot running from his nose and looked from Michael to Jake and Connor.

'Are you wondering whether my boys are going to kill you, or I am?' Michael asked, but he didn't wait for an answer. 'Because I haven't decided yet.' He leaned back against the chair. 'How did you know I was even supposed to be there that morning? Nobody knew except the men I was meeting.'

'I followed them for months,' Scott said.

Michael frowned. 'You were following them?'

'I knew I couldn't follow you. There are too many

people around you and some of them know what I look like. I knew you did business with the Kellys because my brothers told me that Jimmy prefers to work with you rather than anyone else. So I knew if I followed them, eventually they'd meet up with you.'

Michael had to admit that was a clever move. Maybe Scott wasn't such an idiot after all. 'So did you just carry that gun and wait for your moment then?'

'No,' Scott snapped. 'That day, I followed you, or at least I thought your brother was you. He got into your car. He looks like you. He even dresses like you. I knew you were supposed to meet them that morning and I knew you always met them somewhere quiet and out of the way where a gunshot would be less likely to be heard.'

'How did you know I was supposed to be meeting them?' Michael asked with a frown. He always met the Kelly brothers on different days and at different times.

'You think you mix up your meets with them, but actually you follow a pattern. It seems random, maybe even to you, but I worked it out. You only ever meet them on a Monday, Tuesday or Wednesday. You always choose a different place, a different time and a different day each week except for the second week of the month when it's always a Monday afternoon.'

Michael blinked at him in surprise. Scott was right. The second Monday of the month was the day that he always met with Luke and Danny at Cartel Securities to go over any issues and review the rotas. He usually met Jimmy Kelly and his nephews before or after because they delivered drugs to some of their bouncers and he was able to tell them who would be working, and when.

'You're not as daft as you look, are you?' Michael said as he stood up. 'No common sense, like. But you're pretty smart. It's a shame your brothers fucked up your life. You could have gone far.' With a shake of his head he turned to Connor and Jake. 'I'll wait in the car. Make sure you torch the place when you're done. I want nothing left but ash.'

'Will do, Dad,' said Connor.

'What?' Scott shouted. 'You said…' He looked frantically around the three men.

Michael turned to him. 'I didn't like your answers,' he snarled.

'But I told you the truth,' Scott snivelled.

'Then you should have lied.'

With that, he picked up the holdall full of cash and left the caravan, walking across the grass to where Jake had left the Land Rover. The stolen Mondeo would be left where they'd parked it. It was a recently retired private taxi and therefore a petri dish of DNA, but they'd worn gloves to ensure it was clean of their prints.

Michael had brought the syringe full of high-strength heroin with every intention of being ready to use it. If Scott had co-operated, he would have been prepared to give him a painless death. He didn't know what he'd expected to hear from him, or even what he'd wanted to hear. But he'd thought that somehow there might be an explanation that he could live with. Unfortunately for Scott, his confession had done nothing to alleviate Michael's feelings of anger and guilt. Seeing the man who had shot Sean, and who was the reason he was lying in a hospital bed in Intensive Care, had made him realise that a quick and painless end wasn't going to be an option. Besides that, Jake and Connor had wanted to deal with Scott too, and if Michael was being honest with himself, they were in charge now. They always listened to him and he suspected they always would, just as he still listened to his own father. But Liverpool belonged to his sons now. It was their city and he owed it to them to let them run it their own way.

Michael was relieved when Connor and Jake approached the Land Rover just twenty minutes later. Jake jumped into the passenger seat while Connor climbed into the back, placing the holdall at his feet. Michael didn't need to ask if they had cleaned the weapons and tools they'd used before placing them back into the bag. He knew they would have wiped them down with alcohol solution and rags, before tossing the evidence into the fire. They were professionals.

'How did it go?' he asked as he pulled out of the clearing.

'Fine. He didn't last long,' Jake replied.

Michael didn't need to ask what that meant. 'Did he say anything else of note?'

'Nope,' Jake said.

'Lots of crying and saying he was sorry. That was all,' Connor added.

'Stupid fucker,' Michael said with a shake of his head. 'Why didn't he just stay away and get on with his life?'

There were some people for whom he never felt an ounce of remorse, no matter how much pain he or his associates had inflicted on them. But for some reason, Scott Johnson wasn't one of them. Michael wondered if that said more about Scott or him. Perhaps he really was getting too old for it all.

Glancing in the rear-view mirror, he saw the orange glow of the Johnson family caravan burning in the distance and wondered how long it would be before one of the neighbouring caravans noticed and called the fire brigade. The Johnsons' caravan was tucked away at the far end of the site – no doubt because it was such an eyesore. Connor and Jake had used a can of petrol to ensure the fire burned as fast and as fiercely as possible. Hopefully, the caravan, and its inhabitant, would be burned beyond recognition before the blaze was put out.

Chapter Forty-Seven

G race and Danny anxiously watched the clock as they waited for the three men to return.

'They should be back by now, shouldn't they?' Danny asked as he chewed on his thumbnail.

'They've only been gone four hours. The drive to the caravan park is at least an hour each way. They'll be here soon.'

'You think it's gone okay?'

'I think we'd have heard if it hadn't. No news is always good news, Danny. Trust me.'

As she spoke, Bruce's ears pricked up and he let out a deep bark. The sound of the front door opening followed immediately after, and Bruce scampered out into the hallway to greet his visitors.

'Hello, boy,' Grace heard Michael say and the tone of his voice made her breathe a sigh of relief. A few seconds later, Michael and Jake walked into the kitchen. Crossing the room in a few strides, Michael walked straight to Grace and wrapped his arms around her.

'Where's Connor?' she asked.

'We dropped him at home,' Michael replied.

Jake sat next to Danny and put an arm around his shoulder.

'Did everything go okay?' Grace asked.

'Yep. Not a problem. Clean and efficient,' Jake said matter-of-factly.

'The boys were consummate professionals,' Michael said.

Grace smiled and rested her head on Michael's chest, thankful that he and the boys were home in one piece. Now that Scott Johnson had been taken care of, she and Michael would have some decisions to make about their future and the future of their business.

Jake threw his car keys onto the coffee table and flopped onto the sofa beside Danny with an exaggerated groan. 'I'm fucking starving. Shall we order a pizza?' he asked. They had stayed at his mum and Michael's for an hour talking about plans for the future. Michael had offered to cook for them but Jake suspected he and his mum really just wanted the place to themselves.

Danny checked his watch. 'It's almost midnight. Will they still be delivering?'

'That place up the road will if I say it's for us.'

'Okay then.'

Jake ordered the pizza while Danny grabbed two cold beers from the kitchen. He handed one to Jake, sat back down and stared into space.

'You okay?' Jake asked.

'Yeah.' Danny took a long swig of his lager, not making eye contact.

'I don't believe you. What's up? I never asked how it went with your mum this morning. Did something happen?'

Danny turned so he was facing Jake on the sofa. Jake saw him swallow and his own heart lurched in his chest. What was Danny looking so worried about?

'You know I've been going to see her once a week to drop some money off to her?'

'Yeah?' Jake wondered if Danny was about to tell him that he'd been going somewhere else instead.

'Well, the truth is, it's been more than once a week. She phones me nearly every day asking for more. And the reason I drop everything and go and give her more is because she's been blackmailing me.'

'What?' Jake snapped. 'Blackmail? Your mum?'

'Yeah.'

'With what? What the fuck does she have on you? And why couldn't you tell me about it?'

'I couldn't tell you because I thought it might change the way you see me. Nobody knows except me and my mum. And now your mum too.'

'My mum?'

'Yeah. I was talking to her tonight and, I don't know, she

295

has a way of making you tell her your darkest secrets, doesn't she?'

'Tell me about it,' Jake snorted. But then he remembered that Danny had a secret and he was desperate to know what was so terrible he hadn't been able to talk to him about it. 'So, what is it? What's so bad that you couldn't tell anyone about it? Not even Stacey, or Luke … or me?'

'Have you ever heard of Alan Price? He was convicted before we were even born, but his case is well known.'

Jake shook his head. 'Rings a bell, but I can't think why.'

'Google him,' Danny said. 'Go on.'

Jake frowned but he did as Danny asked and took out his mobile phone. Typing Alan Price into the search bar, he saw the numerous articles and links regarding the notorious paedophile and murderer who had received a life sentence twenty-eight years earlier.

After reading one of the articles, Jake looked back up at Danny. 'Okay. He's a vile piece of shit. But what about him?'

Danny closed his eyes and put his head in his hands. 'He's my dad.'

Jake hadn't been expecting that. 'Fuck!' he said with a low whistle. 'I thought you and Stacey had the same dad? David?'

Danny looked up again. 'Yeah, well, that was what my mum wanted everyone to think. Until she told me and David the truth when I was five. He left after that and my mum had always convinced me it was my fault. I thought it was.'

Jake shook his head. 'I still don't understand how she's

blackmailing you though.'

'Because I didn't want anyone to know who he was,' Danny said quietly. 'In case they thought I was anything like him. I don't want people to look at me and see that piece of shit.'

Jake put his hand on the back of Danny's neck. 'You're nothing like him.'

'I know,' he said quietly.

Jake saw the tears in Danny's eyes and in that moment, he wanted to make the person responsible for his pain suffer. 'I can make sure she never utters another word to anyone – ever, if that's what you want?' he offered.

Danny shook his head. 'No. Don't do anything like that, Jake. I'll take care of it.'

'Okay. But what are you going to do?'

'I'm going to tell Stacey the truth about why her dad left. And then I'm going to tell my mum that I don't give a fuck who she tells about who knocked her up almost thirty years ago. When I saw her this morning. I told her I'd still give her a few hundred quid a month. I was prepared to still do that to keep her quiet, but it stops now, Jake. I don't want her in my life. In *our* life.'

'Good,' Jake said with a smile. 'She doesn't fucking deserve you.'

'So you don't see me differently then?' Danny asked.

'No, of course I don't, Dan,' Jake said. Danny blinked at him and Jake wondered if he should tell Danny that he loved him. It was true, but he'd never told anyone other than Paul that before. He pulled Danny's face to his and kissed him instead.

Chapter Forty-Eight

Craig Johnson lay on his bunk and glanced at the mobile phone in his hand.

'Try again,' Ged suggested.

'I've tried fourteen fucking times, Ged. It's not connecting,' he spat.

'Maybe he's just in hiding? He's smart, our kid. He's ditched his phone and he'll be hiding somewhere.'

Craig looked across the room and glared at his brother. Was Ged completely stupid, or was this just an attempt at some sort of self-preservation? 'He's not in hiding. He's fucking dead, and we both know it, Ged.'

'You don't know that.'

Craig wanted to shout at him. He wanted to vent some of the rage he felt inside. But he was fast losing brothers, and the truth was, Ged was the only person in his life now that he could trust. 'Sean Carter woke up, mate. That means Scott is gone.' He choked down the tears that threatened to spill out. First Billy and now Scott. Scott had been the best of them and they had let him down badly.

For a few moments, the two brothers lay in their dark cell in silence.

'We were shit brothers to him, you know?' Ged finally said, his voice thick with emotion. 'Billy was the only one who had any time for him really.'

'I know, mate,' Craig replied. 'He could have been so much better than any of us. Remember how excited he was when he got accepted into Cambridge?'

'Yeah.' Ged laughed quietly. 'Came home with that big goofy grin on his face, waving his letter around. Daft bastard.'

'Till Bradley pissed on his dreams and told him there was no way he was going anywhere,' Craig remembered.

'Yeah.'

'We should have stuck up for him. We should have made Bradley let him go.'

'I did stick up for him,' Ged said with a shake of his head. 'Me and Billy both did. But you...' Ged trailed off and let out a long sigh.

'I know,' Craig said. The truth was he had always backed his eldest brother Bradley, even when he knew he was in the wrong. But he had been the head of the family and what he said was law. That was how it had to be. If only Craig had known what a lying, two-faced cunt his brother really was, things might have been different.

'What are we gonna do now? I don't think we can count on Grace's protection anymore, do you?' Ged asked quietly, his voice sounding small and childlike.

Craig thought about his answer. On the same day he'd been beaten up, a few weeks earlier, Ged had been attacked too – dragged into a cell by four men and assaulted. He didn't have the same kind of wounds that Craig did though – Ged's wounds were of an entirely different kind and would take much longer to heal. His brother had been a different man ever since. Craig realised that he was the head of the family now. Bradley had only ever been out for himself and he had landed them all in the proverbial shit. It was too late for Craig to protect Billy and Scott, but he would protect Ged from any more pain.

'We're going to be fine, Ged. I promise you.'

'How, Craig? Without the Carters' protection, we're sitting ducks.'

'Let me worry about that, mate. I promise you, I'll sort it,' he said, his voice full of a confidence he didn't feel.

'Okay,' Ged answered.

Craig lay on his bunk. What he was thinking was dangerous. There was a chance he would go down for life – but it was the only way he could see out of his and Ged's predicament. Tomorrow, he would speak to Big H and arrange a phone call with Jake Conlon and Connor Carter.

Chapter Forty-Nine

Jake took the bottle of Chivas Regal from the drinks cabinet in his office and poured four glasses. He looked around the room at the three men and smiled. He didn't know what he'd do without them – his best mates and business partners. Connor was as close to him as any biological brother could be. Luke had proven himself to be a trusted ally and now that he was family too, it had made them even closer. Then there was Danny Alexander. Jake had never believed that he could love any man as much as he'd loved Paul Carter, until Danny had walked into his life.

Each of them took a glass from the table and they sat in his office in silence for a few moments enjoying their well-earned Scotch.

'So, what are we going to do about the Johnson brothers?' Connor asked, breaking the silence.

'I'm not sure they can be trusted to behave themselves,' Luke said. 'Especially once they find out about Scott.'

'I agree,' Danny said solemnly.

'Are you suggesting what I think you are?' Jake asked with a raise of his eyebrow.

Connor put his glass down on the table and sighed. 'It's risky. But I don't know what else to suggest, Jake. I mean, every time we think we've dealt with them, they keep on coming back for more. They have been nothing but a royal pain in our arse.'

'But taking out all three of them is going to look suspect, isn't it? Especially after Scott,' Luke replied.

'There will be nothing at all to link us to Scott Johnson,' Connor interrupted him. 'Trust me. And the gun that he used to shoot Sean has been destroyed.'

Jake nodded in agreement. Connor and Michael had dealt with Scott together and they were both professionals.

'But he's still dead, isn't he? It will still look suspect if the other three are killed shortly after he is,' Luke went on.

'What other choice do we have if we want to shut them up for good?' Connor asked.

Jake knew that Connor was right. The Johnson brothers had caused them nothing but aggro, but you couldn't just wipe out a whole family and not have questions asked.

'I'm not disagreeing, but we need to be careful about it. Maybe we make one of them look like an accident?' Jake suggested.

'Craig and Ged share a cell, don't they?' Danny asked.

'Yeah,' Connor replied.

Danny sat back in his chair, deep in thought.

'What are you thinking, Dan?' Jake asked.

'I'm thinking frightened men do stupid things,' he said.

'So we need to act fast, but maybe we can use it to our advantage.'

Jake looked at them all. It seemed they were in agreement that the Johnson brothers needed to be silenced for good – one way or another.

Chapter Fifty

Leigh Moss turned to her sergeant, Mark Whitney. 'Are you ready for this?' she asked him.

'Can't hurt, can it?' he said with a grin. 'Let's go then, shall we?'

The two of them climbed out of the car and walked towards the Bear's Head pub. It was the newest headquarters for the Bridewell Blades crew, particularly Jerrod and Devlin, since it had been taken over by new management and reopened a few weeks earlier.

Mark pushed open the door and held it open for Leigh. 'After you, Ma'am.'

Leigh walked inside and saw the Devlin brothers sitting at a table near the back, with at least half a dozen of their minions hanging around them. She braced herself, feeling like she was walking into a lion's den. Except that the King brothers were no lions – more like weasels. Besides, Mark was with her, and he was an ex-boxer who could handle himself if the need arose.

''Allo, 'allo,' Devlin King shouted to a chorus of laughter. 'I think you two must have the wrong pub. We don't serve your kind in here.'

'That's okay. I wouldn't drink in here if it was the last boozer on earth. The place has really gone to the dogs. What do you think, Mark?' she asked as she turned to him.

'Couldn't agree more,' he replied.

Jerrod King stood up and walked across the room to meet them in the centre of the floor. 'So, if it's not to drink, then just what brings you two pigs in here today then?' he snarled to a chorus of pig noises from his band of mindless cretins.

'We're just here to deliver a not-so-friendly warning, is all,' Leigh said with a smile.

'And what's that?' Jerrod sneered.

'That me and my team are watching you and your pathetic little crew, Jerrod. You *will* make a mistake soon enough, and when you do, we will be all over you so fast you'll be crying for your mummy.'

Jerrod squared up to her. 'Is that a threat, Detective?'

'No, shithead! That is a promise,' she snapped before turning on her heel. She signalled to Mark that they were leaving and then they walked out of the pub with Leigh's heartbeat pounding in her ears.

'Well, who knows if that did any good, but it was certainly fucking worth it to see the look on that gob-shite's face,' Mark said as they reached the car.

'They will screw up soon, Mark. I know it. They're too bloody cocksure of themselves not to.'

'I'm sure you're right, ma'am. I cannot fucking wait to bring that lot in. Especially those King brothers.'

'You and me both,' she agreed. 'Now, let's get back to the station and see what fresh hell this day has in store for us, eh?'

'You have such a way with words, Boss,' he said, laughing as they both climbed into the car.

Devlin King bounced around the Bear's Head like a kangaroo on speed. 'Who the fuck does that busy think she is?' he shouted. 'Fucking coming in here, Jerrod!'

'Calm the fuck down, Dev!' Jerrod warned him. 'She's just pissed because she's got nothing on us. And she never will have. So sit the fuck down. Because we've still got work to do.'

Devlin scowled at his older brother, but he did as he was told and sat down at the table.

'Now, are we all set for tonight?' Jerrod asked.

'Yeah,' said Benno. 'Ten of us will be waiting for those fuckers when they get back to their offices, while you two sort the dog fight.'

'Why do we need a fucking alibi anyway?' Devlin interrupted. 'I thought we wanted the Carters to know it's us that's going to bring them to their knees?'

'And they will. When it's time. But for now, little brother,' he said in a patronising tone that made Devlin want to punch him in the mouth, 'we want them to think that we're still licking our wounds. They don't think we've got the balls or the manpower to take them on, so let's let them keep thinking that. And while they're looking for someone else to blame, we'll keep chipping away. I've told you, Dev, we need to play the long game.'

'Whatever!' Devlin said with a sigh as he leaned back in his chair and shoved his hand down his tracksuit bottoms. 'I wish you'd let me go with the lads tonight. I'm fucking bored of dog fights.'

'They might recognise you, soft-shite!' Jerrod snapped. 'Just stick to the fucking plan.'

'And Danny and Luke will definitely be there tonight?' Benno asked.

'Yep. Our cousin's fella works for them and he's arranged it so that one of their dealers will be making an unexpected drop of money tonight. They'll take it to their office, that's what they usually do.'

'Sound. Then we'll do them over and take whatever money we can get our hands on,' Benno replied with a grin.

'They won't have a fucking clue what's hit them.' Jerrod started to laugh and everyone else joined in. All except Devlin, who sat sulking in his chair.

Chapter Fifty-One

Danny Alexander walked into Jake's office at The Blue Rooms and found him sitting behind his desk talking on the phone. Jake looked up and winked and Danny felt a familiar stirring in his groin.

The keycode lock that Jake had installed a few weeks earlier had made their evenings in work much more enjoyable. He found himself thinking about the previous night after Luke and Connor had left and couldn't help but feel the heat rising up his neck. He closed his eyes and tried to think about something else. There was no time for that, even if the look in Jake's eye suggested he was thinking the same thing too.

Danny closed the door behind him, sat down opposite Jake and waited for him to finish on the phone.

'I wasn't expecting to see you until later,' Jake said with a smile as he ended the call.

'Well, I've had a very interesting phone call, and I thought you'd want to know about it asap.'

'Oh, from who?'

'Ste Mac.'

'Gary Mac's lad? He's on remand, isn't he?'

'Yeah. He's one of the lads who keeps an eye on the Johnsons for us.'

'What did he want then?'

'Craig Johnson spoke to him this morning. He wants to talk to you and Connor. He has some sort of arrangement he'd like to talk to you about, apparently. He's got a mobile. He's asked you to call him tonight after lock-up, then he'll be able to talk to you in private with no distractions.'

Jake checked his watch. 'That's in an hour, isn't it?'

Danny nodded.

'Any idea what this arrangement is?' Jake asked.

'No. He wouldn't say anything other than he needed to speak to you or Connor.'

Jake sucked air through his teeth as he considered the proposal. 'What do you think?' he asked Danny.

Danny sat back in his seat and felt the emotion swell in his chest. He was honoured that Jake sought his advice and opinion on important matters. It meant that he saw him as more than just his boyfriend. Danny had been worried that given who Jake was, when people found out about the two of them, they would assume that Jake was the one with all the power and the one who made all of the decisions in their relationship – both business and personal. If he was honest, he'd wondered himself if that was how it would all play out between them. But Jake had always made him feel like an equal partner.

'I think it's worth hearing what he has to say, at least.'

'I'll give Connor a quick ring and let him know. But you're right, it wouldn't hurt to hear him out.'

'I'll get you a burner just in case he's trying to pull a fast one.'

'Thanks. Always looking out for me, aren't you?' Jake said.

'Well, I can't have anything happening to you, can I?' Danny replied.

'Oh? And why's that?'

'You know why.'

'Tell me anyway,' Jake said as he leaned forward in his seat and rested his elbows on his desk.

'Stop fishing for compliments,' Danny said with a roll of his eyes. 'I'll nip out and get you that phone. I'll be back in half an hour.'

———

Craig Johnson sat on the bed in his cell staring at the mobile phone.

'Do you think they'll phone then?' Ged asked him.

'Course they will,' Craig said confidently. However, he wasn't as convinced as he sounded. The reality was that Jake Conlon and Connor Carter could take him and his brothers out without breaking a sweat or losing a wink of sleep. As far as he could see, this was his and Ged's only chance of survival. He'd gone to see Big H earlier that morning and he'd told him that Ste Mac was the man he needed. He was the one with a direct link to the Carters. Ste had told him that it was Jake and Connor he needed to speak to now. It seemed there was a subtle changing of the guard taking place and Grace and Michael were taking a step back. Ste had agreed to phone his boss, Danny, and put Craig's request forward. Craig was pleased about that. From what he'd heard, if anyone could convince Jake, it was Danny.

Craig had told Ged his plan. As expected, Ged hadn't taken it too well at first, but Craig was able to convince him that it was the only way forward. If he and Ged were ever going to get out of this place in one piece then they had to at least try.

The vibration of the phone next to him made him jump. It was coming from a withheld number, which was a good sign.

Craig took a deep breath and answered it. 'Hello?'

'You wanted to speak to me?' Craig recognised Jake Conlon's voice.

'Yeah. Thanks for ringing.'

'I haven't got time for fucking pleasantries. What do you want?'

'Firstly, I want you to know that me or our Ged didn't have anything to do with recent events. And if we had known what our brother had planned, we'd have talked him out of it.'

Craig waited for a response but he got none. All he heard was breathing on the other end of the line. Jake Conlon wasn't stupid. He would say as little as possible.

Craig went on. 'We understand that there will be repercussions and we accept that. But me and Ged hope that we can keep our arrangement. You will have no trouble from us. I swear that on my kids' lives. We'll keep our heads down and get on with our stretches. This can be the end of it as far as we're concerned.'

That last statement obviously struck a chord and Craig winced at his error.

'As far as you're concerned? How fucking charitable of you!' Jake snarled.

'I meant in as far as we wouldn't be seeing any retribution, that's all. As far as we're concerned, the person who caused all of this misery is sitting not two landings above us. We appreciate that you might want some assurances from us that we're going to hold up our end of the bargain.'

'Such as what?'

Craig swallowed. 'I understand that me and my brothers could be considered a problem to you. I give you my word that Ged and me won't cause you an ounce of bother, but I can't give the same assurances for Bradley. But I can deal with him for you. Ged and I will deal with him, in exchange for us keeping the same deal we had.'

Jake laughed on the other end of the line. 'Really? You're going to do that to your own brother? Fuck off!'

'We will. *I* will. The way I see it, Jake, it's either going to be all three of us, or just him. So I'm hedging my bets and picking just him.'

'You expect me to believe anything that comes out of your mouth?' Jake snapped. 'You've already proved you're not to be trusted.'

'Well, this is where your insurance policy comes in. Are you recording this conversation?'

'No,' Jake snapped.

'Well, you might want to record this next bit.'

He heard a shuffling on the other end of the phone.

'Go on,' Jake said.

'My name is Craig Johnson and I'm making this statement from my cell in Liverpool prison. I am not under any duress. I am going to kill my brother Bradley Johnson by stabbing him in the neck.'

'How is that my insurance policy? You expect to do that and not have anyone see you? You'd go down for it anyway.'

'I'm going to start a fight with him. Ged will be my witness. Bradley is going to come at me with the knife and I'll turn it on him. Self-defence. It was me or him. I'll get a few extra years for manslaughter, especially with that new, expensive brief I've got. But if you pass that recording onto the police then I'll get life for premeditated murder. That's your insurance, Jake. I will deal with Bradley tomorrow and then all three of us will be out of your hair for ever.'

'Not Ged though? Why does he need to fall in line? I'd have nothing on him.'

'Because he's a good brother. He's loyal. Why would he screw me over like that? He would have no one left in the world without me. So, what do you say? Shall I make a move on Bradley?'

There was a moment's silence before Jake spoke again. 'You do realise I could have one of my men kill Bradley and pin it on you now?'

'Yes,' Craig replied. He had thought of that. 'But the way I see it, if you don't take my offer, then I'm a dead man walking anyway. At least this way me and Ged would be indebted to you. So, what do you say?'

Jake sat in his office opposite Danny. The burner phone was on the desk in between them as they listened to Craig Johnson on speaker phone.

Jake ran a hand over the stubble on his chin as he considered Craig's proposal. He wanted the Johnson brothers out of his life, but he also knew that killing the three of them while they were in prison and not bringing any heat onto themselves was easier said than done. He could allow Craig to take care of Bradley – that would eliminate their main concern, that Bradley might some day start telling people he didn't murder Billy after all. He could hope that Craig and Ged kept to their word, but if they didn't, they could be dealt with at a later date. It seemed like a win-win, and a way to resolve their problems without getting any of their hands dirty in the process. Using his brain instead of his fists, as his mum would say.

Jake looked at Danny and raised his eyebrows in a bid to gauge his reaction. He trusted Danny's opinion on such things.

Danny stared back at him and nodded.

'When I hear of your brother's demise, then I'll consider our previous deal back on, Craig,' Jake said. 'But not a minute before. So I suggest you act fast.'

'Consider it done,' Craig replied.

Jake ended the call. He looked across at Danny. 'Do you think he'll go through with it?'

Danny shrugged. 'Who can say? He sounded pretty determined though, didn't he?'

'Yeah, but … killing your own brother though? It's one thing to talk about it, but actually doing it…'

'You told me Craig was the only one with any nous about him. And let's face it, he's right about one thing, isn't he? It's either one of them or all of them. And from what I've heard, Bradley Johnson has fucked his brothers over time and time again. I'm surprised one of them hasn't done him in before now, to be honest.'

'Well, only time will tell if he pulls it off. Let's give them a few days and if nothing has happened, we'll review.'

'Sounds like a plan,' Danny said.

Jake checked his watch. 'I'll nip round to Connor's and let him know the score.'

'Want me to come with you?'

'Nah. You get on with finishing your rounds and I'll meet you at my place later.'

Danny stood up. 'I won't be late. I've only got a few people left to see.'

'Isn't Luke with you tonight?' Jake asked. They usually did their weekly rounds together.

'No. He had to go and see someone about a new contract.'

'Oh. Need me to come with you?' Jake said with a frown, feeling suddenly protective of Danny, which was daft really when you considered that Danny was as hard as nails and had a team of bouncers at every venue he was

318

visiting. Suddenly, Jake's head was filled with thoughts of Paul and how he'd been taken from him in the blink of an eye. Paul Carter had been as hard as they came, but that didn't really matter when someone put a bullet in your neck, did it?

Danny laughed, snapping Jake from his thoughts. 'It's fine. I'm a big boy. I'll see you later.'

'See you later.'

Chapter Fifty-Two

Jake sat in Connor and Jazz's living room waiting for Connor to come downstairs from his shower. Jazz was in the kitchen making them both a brew and baby Paul was fast asleep upstairs.

Jake looked around the room of their new house in Mossley Hill. It wasn't far from his mum and Michael's house. It was similar to the one Jake had once lived in with Siobhan and Isla: detached with four bedrooms and a huge garden. When he and Siobhan had split up he'd gone back to his apartment on the waterfront. It was much smaller but he'd felt less lonely there right in the middle of the city centre. It was handy for the club too. Now he wondered if the flat was getting too small. Danny spent almost every night there. Isla stayed two nights a week too. Jake had been thinking about asking Danny to move in with him. Although it was a big step, it felt right. They practically lived together already anyway. But maybe they needed to look for something a little bigger?

'Everything okay, mate?' Connor said as he walked into the room, his hair still damp from his shower. He gave Jake's shoulder a squeeze before sitting on the sofa opposite him. 'Did you speak to Craig Johnson?'

'Yeah. That's what I'm here to talk to you about.'

Jazz came into the room carrying three mugs of tea. She handed one to Jake before sitting on the sofa next to Connor.

'Thanks, Jazz,' Jake said with a smile.

'So, what did that prick have to say for himself then?' Connor asked as he blew on his tea to cool it.

Jake spent the next few minutes telling Connor about his conversation with Craig. He watched as his best mate's face darkened during the course of the conversation until he was full-on scowling by the end of it.

'So, we're just going to let Craig and Ged off with this?' he snapped.

'Well, to be fair, they didn't actually do anything this time. It was their brother—'

'They're all the same,' Connor interrupted him.

'I don't exactly call agreeing to murder your own brother getting off with it, Con, do you?' Jake snapped back. He rarely disagreed with Connor on anything and it didn't feel right when they were at odds.

'I can't believe you would consider making any type of deal with them, Jake. They've proved they can't be trusted, over and over again.'

'What have we got to lose, Connor? The fact is, they don't *need* our protection in prison. They just need our lads to back off them. *If* Craig keeps his word and kills Bradley, then it saves us a job. It removes the only credible threat to me and you if the man convicted of Billy's murder is dead. It also gives us leverage over Craig because we would have proof it was premeditated murder.'

'And if he doesn't go through with it?' Connor said, his arms folded across his chest.

'Then we stick with the original plan.'

Connor sat on his sofa in silence and Jake could tell he wasn't entirely convinced.

Jazz sat forward and put her mug of tea on the coffee table. She placed her hand on Connor's thigh. 'I think Jake has a point,' she said.

'What? So now you're agreeing with him too? For fuck's sake, Jazz,' Connor said.

'You're letting your anger over what happened to Sean cloud your judgement, Connor. But the man responsible for that is gone. What Jake has agreed will solve your problems, and it does it in a way that doesn't have any comeback whatsoever on either of you. How is that not a win-win for us all? You have a family now. You have to use your head and not be led by your need for revenge.'

Connor looked at her and Jake saw the anger dissolving from his body. He smiled to himself. God, she was good.

'You sound just like his ma,' Connor said with a half-smile as he indicated Jake.

'Well, then I must be talking sense,' Jazz said with a smile.

Just then the sound of Paul crying blared through the baby monitor.

'I'll go. You two boys can carry on arguing if you like,

but if you're finished, phone that Indian you've been promising me for the past hour, Connor,' Jazz said as she stood up and left the room.

'She speaks sense, your missus,' Jake said. He had been grateful for Jazz's intervention. She had a way of putting things across that made people listen. He supposed she was a lot like his mum.

'I know, mate. I just don't trust those Johnson pricks.'

'Neither do I. But we hold all the power here, Con. We don't need to trust them, we just need to sit back and let them fight amongst themselves. They have nothing on us.'

'You're right. I know you are…'

'But you wanted them gone? I get that. But this is the safer way to deal with them.'

'When did you start thinking things through?' Connor said with a laugh. 'It's fucking annoying. Between you and Jazz, I'll be lucky to get in a decent scrap ever again.'

Jake laughed with him. 'On that note, hadn't you better order her Prawn Jalfrezi? Or she'll kick your arse when she comes back down.'

Connor rolled his eyes and picked up his mobile phone. 'You staying for something to eat?' he asked.

Jake checked his watch. Danny wouldn't be home for a couple of hours. 'Yeah, go on. I'll have a Beef Madras and garlic naan.'

'God, Danny's going to love you later.'

'Yeah, there's this thing called toothpaste. You should try it some time.'

Connor threw a cushion at Jake's head as he dialled the local takeaway. Jake caught it and threw it back. He was glad they were on the same page again, and all felt right with the world.

———————

Jake, Connor and Jazz had just finished their curries and Connor was clearing the dishes when Jake's phone rang. He answered it to one of their bouncers, Timmo.

'Everything okay?' Jake asked him. It wasn't like one of them to call him directly – they usually dealt with Danny or Luke.

'Boss,' Timmo said, breathless. 'We need a hand down here. Things are kicking off and there's only me and Danny and Murf here.'

Jake felt the adrenaline starting to course around his body. 'Where are you? Where's Danny now?'

'At the Cartel office. Danny is here somewhere. They came out of nowhere, Jake. One minute I was talking to him and the next four of these fuckers had jumped on his back.'

'Who? Danny?' Jake asked as stood up, readying himself to leave.

Timmo was too distracted to answer. Jake could hear the carnage unfolding in the background. 'Shit!' Timmo shouted. 'Just get us some backup,' he said and then the line went dead.

Jake could feel his heart pounding in his chest. If something happened to Danny... He couldn't help but think of Paul again – shot in cold blood as he was leaving the gym. He'd been taken from them in a split second. Full of life and energy one minute, and then gone the next. Jake had once thought he was invincible. He'd thought they all were. But now he knew that nobody was.

'What's up?' Connor asked, his face full of concern.

'There's trouble at the Cartel offices. I think Danny's hurt.'

'Fuck!' Connor hissed as he jumped up and started to pull his trainers on. 'Let's go.'

'You got any weapons handy?' Jake asked.

'Golf clubs in the boot. Dusters in my gym bag in the hall. Come on.'

'Be careful, both of you,' Jazz said as she stood up and gave Connor a quick hug.

'We always are, babe,' Connor replied.

'Now go on. Go and make sure Danny is okay,' she said as she ushered them out of the room.

Jake could hardly concentrate as he walked through Connor's house. Connor pressed something into his hands and Jake looked down and saw the knuckle dusters he'd mentioned.

'Come on, Jake. He'll be okay, but we need to get there now, mate. Focus.'

Jake's head snapped up. Connor was right. Now was not the time for emotion. He took a deep breath and tried to steady his breathing but his blood continued to thunder in his ears. He needed an outlet for the anger and adrenaline coursing through his veins.

'It looks like you'll get that kick-off after all,' he said to Connor as he headed for the front door.

Ten minutes later, Connor's car screeched to a stop outside Cartel Securities. Jake and Connor jumped out of the car and ran towards the building. Connor ran straight over to a group of men outside who were laying into Timmo and started smashing heads open with the golf club in his hand. Soon, he and Timmo had overpowered them. Jake ran past. He had to find Danny. A big lad with a skinhead came charging out of the building towards him and Jake punched him in the temple with his iron-clad fist, knocking him unconscious. He turned and saw the large black van pulling up outside. The doors slid open and he breathed a sigh of relief. The cavalry had arrived. 'Let's wrap this up before someone calls the busies,' he shouted to his men as they piled out of the van.

Jake ran inside the building. Where the fuck was Danny? Timmo had said four of them had jumped him. Four men with weapons. Danny wouldn't have had any on him. He didn't do his rounds carrying weapons with him, it was too risky. He was supposed to be the legitimate face of Cartel Securities. Jake heard shouting from the back office. He ran towards it, wondering what he would find and whether Danny would be hurt – or worse. He felt the bile rise from his gullet, burning the back of his throat.

Rounding the corner, he saw three bodies on the floor. Danny Alexander stood in the centre of the room, wiping the blood from his face with the back of his hand. He looked up and saw Jake standing there. 'I wish you'd showed up about ten minutes earlier,' Danny said as he walked towards him. 'I could have done with a hand.'

Jake ran over to him. 'Are you okay?' he asked. As he

reached Danny, he was aware of the injured men making a run for it and he didn't plan on stopping them. They had taken enough of a beating for the night and Jake would find out who was behind the attack soon enough. He took Danny's face in his hands, inspecting him for injuries. He had a huge gash over his eye and a split lip and grazes on his chin. Jake imagined he was going to look much worse once his bruises started showing in a few hours, but he was okay. Then he looked down at Danny's white shirt and his heart leapt into his throat as he saw that the whole stomach area was stained a deep crimson.

'Dan,' he said as he put a hand on his stomach. 'What the fuck?'

'It's not mine,' Danny assured him.

Jake pulled Danny towards him and wrapped his arms around him.

'Ow.' Danny winced. 'Easy, tiger. It's not my blood, but I think I've broken a rib or two.'

Jake released his grip and took a half step back. 'I thought...'

'I'm okay,' Danny insisted. 'But we need a clean-up crew here.'

Connor came running into the back office. 'Everything all right?' he asked.

'Yeah,' Jake said as he stepped back further and released Danny from his embrace. 'But we need to sort this mess out.'

'I've already called the cleaners. They'll be here within the hour. Everyone has walked or been carried out, still breathing,' Connor said pointedly and Jake let out a sigh of relief. That meant there were no bodies to deal with. That was all they needed.

'We need to get out of here and get him sorted,' Connor said as he looked at Danny.

'I'm fine,' Danny breathed as he clutched his ribs. 'The blood's not mine. Nothing that a bath and a back rub wouldn't sort.' He started to laugh but the action made him wince in pain.

'Come on, Rambo,' Jake said as he put an arm around Danny's waist for support.

'I'll go and start the car,' Connor said.

Danny clung on to Jake as the two of them walked slowly out of the building.

It was two hours later when Jake finally climbed into bed beside Danny, who was propped up against some pillows eating Crunchy Nut Cornflakes from the box and watching *Taskmaster*. It was one of his favourite shows and he winced every time he laughed.

'Why are you watching something that makes you laugh so much?' Jake asked with a roll of his eyes.

'Because I've just been beaten up and when I thought my boyfriend had run me a nice hot bath to soak in, he forced me into a frigging ice bath instead. So I need a little light relief,' he said with a grin.

'A hot bath would have felt good for about ten minutes but then it would have made everything worse. And I wouldn't have had to force you if you'd just got in there like a grown-up. Ice for the first forty-eight hours. Then I'll run you two hot baths a day if you want,' Jake said.

'Your intimate knowledge of dealing with broken ribs and swollen limbs is pretty scary, you know.' Danny smiled at him.

'Yeah? Well, your lack of knowledge is fucking terrifying. God help me if I ever need you to look after me after a scrap. Sticking me in hot baths and rubbing deep heat all over me.'

Danny shrugged. 'Heat feels good, that's all I know.'

Jake shook his head. 'Ice heals. And I don't want you out of action for any longer than you need to be.'

Danny stared at him. 'I bet you don't,' he said, his eyes narrowed and a wicked grin playing on his lips.

'I actually meant for work purposes,' Jake said with a laugh. 'But, yeah, that too.'

Danny put his box of cereal on the floor. 'I'm not completely out of action,' he said, turning his body towards Jake and wincing in pain. 'There are parts of me that are feeling just fine. In fact, better than fine.'

'Is that so?' Jake laughed. 'You've probably got a couple of broken ribs, sunshine. It's not happening. Trust me.'

Danny bit his lip to stifle a groan as he manoeuvred himself closer. Jake put an arm around him, careful to avoid his bruises. 'I shit myself when I got that message from Timmo. He said you'd been attacked by four of them, and then he couldn't see you anywhere.'

'Yeah, well, I shit myself when they jumped us. They came out of nowhere. Do you think they were after the money?'

'Who even knew you'd be there with the money though?' Jake asked. Danny had ended up collecting a payment at the last minute from some of their dealers and very few people should have known about it.

Danny shrugged and Jake saw the pain on his face. He'd had broken ribs himself in the past and remembered how every movement felt like breathing glass.

'We can think about it tomorrow,' Jake said. 'Try and get some kip.' He reached over and picked up the television remote to turn it off.

The two men lay in darkness facing each other, Jake with his hand resting on the back of Danny's neck. 'I love you, Dan,' he said quietly. 'If anything ever happened to you…' He couldn't finish the sentence. He didn't know how to.

'I love you too,' Danny replied. 'And nothing's going to happen to me.'

Jake closed his eyes and wished he could believe that.

Chapter Fifty-Three

Danny lay on the sofa, propped up by cushions, flicking through the television channels. It had been three days since the incident at Cartel Securities. He'd been checked over by a private doctor, the type that didn't ask too many questions, who'd confirmed that he had two broken ribs as well as significant bruising. Jake had refused to leave him on his own for more than a few minutes, but today he had to go back to work. For one thing, they still needed to find out who was behind the attack. Danny watched as Jake picked up his watch from the sideboard and slid it onto his wrist.

'What time will you be back?' Danny asked.

'I'll be done in a few hours. But don't worry, I'm not leaving you to fend for yourself. The cavalry will be here in a minute.'

'What? Who's on their way? I'm sure I can cope for a few hours, Jake.'

'You can hardly walk, Dan. Anyway, she insisted,' he said with a grin. 'And no one says no to my mum.'

Danny groaned inwardly. The embarrassment of Grace Carter babysitting him was almost too much to contemplate. 'Your mum! Jake! Why is your mum coming to babysit me? I'll be fine.'

Jake walked over and sat on the edge of the sofa near Danny's feet. 'She's not babysitting you. She's coming to keep you company, and if you're lucky, she'll make you the odd cup of tea and some dinner.'

'But Jake – your mum?'

'What about her? She's fucking boss at looking after the sick and wounded. Trust me.'

'Yeah, but she's your mum. She has to look after you. She doesn't have to play nursemaid to me. I'm sure she has a million other things she'd rather be doing.'

'You're the worst fucking patient in the world, do you know that? Have you ever let anyone take care of you?' Jake asked.

Danny blinked at him. He'd never thought about that before. But there had never been anyone to look after him. He'd looked after Stacey, but there had been no one to take care of him when he was sick or injured. He wasn't used to being cared about and that realisation made him feel incredibly sad. He'd spoken to his own mother the day before, and naively told her that he had a couple of broken ribs, hoping for what, he didn't know. But, as usual, all she had been interested in was whether he could get any money to her. It had made it all that easier to tell her to go to hell, because he would never give her another penny. He told her he didn't care if she told the whole world that his real father was a paedophile and a child killer, and she had slammed the phone down on him. Danny was intending to tell Stacey the truth the next time he saw her. He only hoped that she'd take it as well as everyone else had.

Sensing the change in him, Jake put a hand on Danny's leg. 'There is nothing she'd rather be doing, mate. I didn't ask her to come here, she offered to. She's been on the phone twice a day to see how you are. You're one of us now, lad, whether you like it or not, so you'd better start getting used to it.'

Danny swallowed. 'That's kind of what I'm worried about,' he said without thinking.

'What do you mean?' Jake asked, his eyes narrowed.

'That I'll get used to all of this,' he said with a half-smile, trying to make a joke of it before the conversation became even more awkward than it already was.

'And so what if you did?' Jake asked with a look of genuine bewilderment on his face.

A knock at the door interrupted their conversation and Jake stood up to answer it. A few seconds later, Grace Carter walked into the room, carrying some magazines and a huge flask.

'I'm going, Mum,' Jake said as he kissed her on the cheek. 'I'll see you later. Be nice to my mum,' he said with a wink as he turned to Danny. Then he left.

Grace walked over to Danny and placed a stack of glossy car magazines on the coffee table right beside him.

'Jake said you like reading these. And Michael has made you a pan of his famous cure-all chicken soup,' she said as she held up the flask. 'I'll stick this in the kitchen unless you fancy some now?'

Danny shook his head. 'I'm good, thanks, Grace.'

She smiled and walked out into the kitchen leaving Danny sitting on the sofa and wondering what he was going to talk to her about all afternoon. Danny admired Grace. He got on well with her, but he didn't often spend more than half an hour alone in her company. The last time he had, he'd ended up bawling like a baby and telling her all about his real dad. And if he was honest, she was kind of intimidating. What if he said something completely stupid? What if, by the end of the afternoon, she wondered what the hell her son saw in him?

'I'm making a coffee, Danny, do you fancy one?' she shouted from the kitchen.

'Yeah, go on then,' he shouted back.

A few minutes later she came in carrying two steaming mugs of coffee and placed one down on the coffee table, making sure it was well within his reach. She sat on the end of the sofa, her hand casually resting on his feet as she raised her cup to her lips and blew on the hot liquid.

'So, what do you fancy watching, Danny?' she asked with a smile.

'I was going to watch the new *Star Wars*,' he said. 'But we can watch whatever you like.'

'Oh, I love *Star Wars*. My dad took me to see them in the pictures when I was a kid. I haven't seen the latest one.

Stick it on then,' she said with such enthusiasm that Danny smiled too. He picked up the remote to search for the film and Grace made herself comfortable, tucking her feet underneath her.

When the film was over, Grace and Danny tucked into the soup, which Danny had to admit was the best chicken soup he had ever tasted in his life. The last few hours had passed quickly and he wondered why he'd been so worried about spending time with Grace. Although she could still terrify the life out of him, she was an easy person to be around. She made anyone in her company feel like they were the most important person in the world. He had seen this skill of hers in action many times before, so he wondered why he'd thought the afternoon would be any different.

'That was gorgeous,' Danny said as he wiped up the last dregs with a piece of crusty bread and stuffed it into his mouth.

'I know. Michael hardly ever makes it either. It was sitting on the stove all last night and he wouldn't let me near it,' she said with a laugh.

Danny frowned at her. 'Why not?'

'Because it was for you. Don't tell him I nicked a bowl off you. Although he'll make you another batch at the weekend.'

Danny stared at her, open-mouthed. He was lost for words. Michael Carter had made a pan of soup – from scratch – just for him. It was such a thoughtful thing to do, and it didn't fit at all with the man Danny thought he knew.

Grace frowned at him. 'What is it?'

'Nothing.'

She placed her bowl on the table and turned so she was facing him. 'Well, it's definitely something. I can't quite figure you out, Danny.'

It was his turn to frown now. 'What do you mean?'

'I mean that looking in from the outside, you have it all. You're smart and successful. You're good-looking. You're hard as nails. You're one of the most powerful men in this city. You go about your business with confidence and certainty. I trust you and there's not many people I'd say that about.'

'Sounds like you have me pretty well figured out then,' he said, trying to lighten the mood.

Grace laughed. 'I thought so too. But now I can see the truth.'

Danny swallowed. Where the hell was this going? Did Grace Carter see that he was really a pretender? He wasn't worthy of her trust. He didn't belong with them, and he never would.

'For some reason, you think that you don't deserve any of it,' she said, staring at him, her eyes piercing his soul. 'Why is that?'

He shook his head. 'Maybe I don't,' he admitted, and was shocked that he'd said those words out loud.

'Jake's dad was a terrible father. He was cruel and arrogant and he only ever cared about himself. He was never there when Jake needed him. He missed every single

338

important moment in his son's life. I used to worry that Jake would end up just like him.'

'You don't have to worry, he's nothing like that,' Danny said.

'Well, he can be a bit arrogant,' she said with a laugh. 'But he has every reason to be, in my incredibly biased opinion. Anyway, my point is that none of that was Jake's fault. Jake was the most lovable kid in the world. He was funny and kind, and so cute you wouldn't believe, but Nathan never saw any of that because he was a complete narcissist.'

'I'm not sure why you're telling me this, Grace,' he said.

'Because of what you told me about your dad. But also because I've had the displeasure of meeting your mother, Danny, and she is just like Nathan. And people like that will try and fuck you up and make you believe that it's your fault when they do.'

'It's not the same though. She's my mum. Aren't mothers genetically programmed to love their offspring, or something?'

'For the most part, yes. But some aren't. Some people just aren't wired to love anyone. And Glenda Alexander is one of those women.'

Danny shook his head. 'I know what you're trying to say…'

'I understand this is hard to accept. You've believed your whole life that there was something wrong with you. It's hard to let that go.'

'She didn't just not love me. She hated me, Grace. She left us with that fucking animal.'

'Do you love Stacey?' she asked.

He frowned. 'Of course I do.'

'And you expect Luke to love her and treat her with respect?'

'Yeah.'

'So why don't you deserve that then? Your mum left Stacey too.'

'She knew I'd look after Stacey.'

Grace sighed. 'I promised I would never get involved in Jake's love life, Danny, and he will kill me if you tell him, but I have to say this.'

Danny stared at her. She was about to tell him that he wasn't good enough for her son, and she'd probably be right.

'I have never seen Jake look at anyone the way he looks at you. He adores you, Danny. I see that every time I see the two of you together. His whole face changes when you walk into a room. If you are not deserving of affection, then why does my son seem to love you so much? Why do Stacey and Luke love you? And besides, my husband does not make chicken soup for just anyone. He makes it for his family, and that's it. But last night, he spent two hours in and out of the kitchen making it for you. Tell me why he would he do that if he didn't care about you? You have to learn to let people in, Danny, or you will end up pushing them away.'

Danny felt a tear run down his cheek and he wiped it away. Thirty minutes earlier, they'd been laughing about Oscar's latest mishap and now they were having the deepest conversation Danny had ever had in his life.

'I've never had a family, Grace. I don't know how to do

this. I love the way you all look out for each other and I would love to be a part of that, but I can't. I'm scared that eventually I will do something to fuck things up and then it will all be gone. If I keep you all at arm's length, it will be easier to walk away. I can't let myself believe that any of this is real. Does that make sense?'

'Perfect sense. But we are real, Danny. And you're already a part of it. Believe it or not, we all care about you. All of my children adore you. You're practically Luke's brother. Michael made you soup, for Christ's sake. So, I think you're kind of stuck with us, sunshine. I can guarantee that the sooner you accept that, the happier your life will be.'

Danny smiled at her. Grace had a way of convincing people of anything. She often referred to her ex-husband Nathan as being full of charm and charisma, but actually she was too. Was it any wonder that Jake had turned out the way he had?

Perhaps Grace was right? Despite what Jake's ex-wife Siobhan had done in the past, she was still welcomed into the fold. Grace spoke very highly of her and she managed their wine bar in Lytham. Besides, Grace Carter wasn't one for empty promises and blowing smoke up people's arses to make them feel better. She was a woman of her word.

Danny leaned back against his cushions as Grace cleared the dishes and he wondered whether he really was one of them now. That thought made him smile. They knew all there was to know about him, and they loved him anyway. That someone as amazing as Jake could love him was mind-blowing to him. That must count for something. Maybe he wasn't the monster his mum had always tried to convince him he was? Maybe he wasn't going to fuck this up after all? He felt the emotion swelling in his chest and he swallowed it down. The last thing he wanted was to start bawling his eyes out in front of Grace Carter again. Even if this time they'd be tears of joy.

Chapter Fifty-Four

Jake walked through the corridor of Cartel Securities to the office in the back where Luke and Connor were waiting for him. He entered the room and sat down.

'How's Danny?' Luke asked.

'Apart from being the worst fucking patient in the world, he's okay. He should be back on his feet in a couple of weeks,' Jake replied.

'Good. Me and Stacey will call round and see him later, if that's okay?'

'Of course it is,' Jake replied. 'You're welcome any time. Anyway, is there any news on who we're looking for?'

'Nothing concrete,' Luke said. 'But we're pretty confident it's those Bridewell kids.'

'Oh? I didn't recognise either of the King brothers. What makes you think it's them?' Jake asked. He hadn't been as involved in the search as much as he usually would because he'd been busy looking after Danny, but he wasn't sure the Bridewell Blades were behind the attack.

'Well, it wasn't exactly a well-thought-out operation, was it? They were all over the place,' Connor said. 'We know they weren't happy with us refusing to go into business with them. They're motivated purely by money.'

'Well, who the fuck isn't?' Jake said.

'I know, but … well, who else would it be?'

'Okay. If you think this was just about the money, how would those dickheads have even known Danny was carrying money? The pickup was a last-minute arrangement. Nobody except a few of our own men knew about that.'

'So, you think it was one of our own?' Connor asked.

'No.' Luke shook his head.

'Why not?' said Jake. 'Haven't you almost doubled the workforce of Cartel Securities in the past twelve months? Who knows if one, or a few of them, hasn't got fed up of grafting for their money and saw an easy way to make a decent wedge.'

'I still think we should have a little chat to the King brothers,' Connor suggested.

'Okay. But I also think we need to find out who else knew that Danny was picking up that money.'

'That's easily done,' Luke said. 'I'll have a word with the lads and see who knows what.'

'Good. And when you find out who it was, I'd like to deal with them personally.'

'Of course,' Luke replied.

'I have other news too,' Connor said.

Jake looked at him. 'What's that?'

'Bradley Johnson was stabbed to death this morning.'

'By Craig?' Jake asked.

Connor nodded and Jake let out a low whistle. 'So he really went through with it, eh?'

'Seems that way,' Connor said. 'And when the time is right, we'll take care of Craig and Ged too, right?'

Jake nodded. Despite Craig following through on his promise, the Johnson brothers had gone back on their word too many times for them to be trusted. 'Yeah. But the two of them aren't going anywhere for a long time. So let's bide our time. Then they'll never see us coming.'

'Sounds like a plan,' Luke said.

'You got to get back to Danny?' Connor asked.

'No, my mum is with him. Why?' Jake replied.

'You fancy paying the King brothers a little visit?'

Jake smiled and stood up. 'Why not?'

Luke started to laugh. 'What's so funny?' Jake asked.

'You two going to deal with the King brothers. Isn't that the definition of using a sledgehammer to crack a walnut?' Luke replied.

'What do you mean, us two? You're coming too, soft lad,' Jake said with a grin. 'If it was them behind the attack on Cartel the other night, then I'd say it was perfectly justified. Wouldn't you?'

Luke stood up too. 'I suppose so. Wouldn't hurt to put on a show.'

Connor smiled at them both. He always enjoyed a good scrap. 'Let's go then,' he said and the three men walked out of the room.

A few hours later, Jerrod and Devlin King were hanging by their ankles over the balcony of the twelfth-floor flat where Jake, Connor and Luke had found them. Connor held Jerrod while Luke held onto Devlin. Jake leaned over the balcony and looked at the two of them as they screamed to be pulled back up. They'd been asked politely if they'd had anything to do with the attack on Cartel Securities and had responded with a mouthful of obscenities, which was how they came to be in their current predicament.

'The pair of you just shut the fuck up and answer my questions,' Jake snarled. 'And if you tell me the truth, they might pull you back up.'

The two of them stopped wailing for a moment and looked at him.

'Where were you both on Sunday night?' Jake asked as he popped a piece of chewing gum into his mouth.

'What? I don't fucking remember,' Jerrod snapped.

'Well, fucking think,' Jake snapped back. 'Because in a few minutes, my colleagues' arms are going to start shaking with the weight of holding you two fuckwits. The lactic acid will keep building up until they can't stand the pain of it any longer. And when that happens, well, it's only a matter of seconds before you two go splat.'

'We were on the estate,' Devlin screamed. 'We'd arranged a dog fight and afterwards we all got stoned.'

'Yeah,' Jerrod agreed.

'Hmm.' Jake looked down at them. 'What time was this dog fight?'

'What?' Devlin screamed.

Jake smiled at Connor and he flexed his arm. 'That shoulder still giving you grief, Con?' Jake asked.

'It was eight o'clock,' Jerrod shouted and Jake saw the wet patch soaking the crotch of his grey tracksuit pants.

'Oh dear. I think you've pissed yourself, Jerrod,' Jake said with a laugh.

'Let us up,' Jerrod screamed in response. 'We haven't fucking done nothing.'

Jake looked at Luke and Connor. 'Pull them up,' he said begrudgingly. He had enjoyed watching the two of them squirm. They were a pair of horrible bastards and the more he learned about them and their crew, the more he disliked them. But they didn't need two dead bodies in the car park below.

Jerrod and Devlin were pulled back over the balcony and dropped onto the floor. They scrambled to their feet and back into the flat as Jake, Connor and Luke walked in behind them.

'If we find out you two or your motley crew of fuckwits had anything to do with the attack on some of our bouncers the other night, we'll be paying you another visit, but next time, we won't be so accommodating,' Jake snarled at them.

Jerrod and Devlin nodded at them as they trembled in fear.

'Nice chatting with you, lads,' Connor said with a grin, before walking out of the flat with Jake and Luke close behind.

Chapter Fifty-Five

Leigh Moss poured the remainder of the bottle of Chardonnay into her wine glass. It was so full that she had to sip some before she could carry it through to her living room. But she didn't care. After the week she'd had, she figured she deserved a whole vat of wine.

She sat on her sofa with a heavy sigh. She looked around and suddenly it was if she was only just noticing how bare the place was. She had no photographs on display. No souvenirs or mementos from holidays or trips away. She'd had so few of them anyway. She couldn't even recall the last time she'd had a holiday. She'd never had any real friends to do anything like that with. She had work friends, but that was different. There had never been anyone whom she could call up in the middle of the night who would drop everything and rush to her side. The closest thing she'd had to that recently was Grace Carter. The irony of that wasn't lost on her. While she'd been with John, they had gone to Grace and Michael's house a few times for dinner, and whenever she was there, Leigh had been envious of the closeness they all shared. They had always made her feel included, even if she could never really be one of them. Leigh's work had always been her life and whilst that had once been enough, suddenly it wasn't any more.

She felt a wave of sadness washing over her as she remembered how John had suggested they have a holiday in Italy in the autumn. He'd been there lots of times and loved the place. He'd made it sound so exciting and romantic that she'd hastily agreed and they'd booked it online there and then. What a fool she'd been making plans with him!

She felt a tear running down her cheek and swatted it away.

There was no point thinking about what could have been. It was over now.

Leigh glanced around the room again. There was nothing of her true self in the place. It made her think about John's house – full of photographs of his three sisters and their children; of his parents; of his holidays away with his family or his mates. His house had felt like more of a home to her than her own ever had.

She leaned back against the sofa and took a large sip of wine. Her stomach growled with hunger but she couldn't face warming up a microwave meal. John had always been happy to cook for her. It was never anything fancy. But it always tasted good.

The tears were running down her cheeks now and she didn't even bother wiping them away.

John Brennan could rot in hell for all she cared.

Leigh Moss prided herself on being a woman who had principles. But she was coming to realise that was maybe all she did have.

On the other side of the city, John Brennan walked into Jake Conlon's office at The Blue Rooms. He had to do a double-take when he saw Jake sitting at the desk, his head bent low as he scrutinised whatever was on the paper in front of him. Jake Conlon was a dead ringer for his father Nathan, whom John had worked for back in the day.

'All right, John,' Jake looked up and said with a smile.

'All right,' John replied as he took a seat.

'What did you want to see me about?' Jake asked.

John took a deep breath. Was this really all he was good for? It seemed so. 'As you know, I'm in between jobs at the moment, and I wondered if you had any work that needed doing?'

Jake frowned. 'Does my mum know you're here?'

'No. But I don't work for your mum anymore. She's no longer interested in the kind of services I offer.' If Grace and Michael were intent on taking a step back and trying to go legit, that meant, as far as John was concerned, there was no place for him in their new world.

'I've always got work for someone with your particular skillset, John, you know that. But are you sure you want back in?' Jake said as he leaned forward and planted his elbows on the desk.

'Why wouldn't I?' John snapped.

Jake shrugged. 'I thought that you and that copper—'

'Well, we're not,' John interrupted him.

Jake stared at him.

John looked at the man sitting across the desk. When Jake's father had been killed seven years earlier and Jake had taken over, John had stopped working for him and branched out on his own. Jake had made it clear that he didn't want his dad's old mates hanging around and John had been happy to leave. Jake had been an obnoxious, arrogant little shit at the time, who hadn't known his arse from his elbow. But in recent years, John had seen the change in the younger man. Jake had grown into a respected and fearsome leader. He was vicious, but he was also reasonable and he was fair. He used his head when he needed to, and more extreme methods when they were called for. He took after his mother much more than his father these days and John was happy to work for a man like that.

'Then consider yourself no longer between jobs,' Jake said with a grin. 'It's good to have you on board, big fella.'

John sat back in his chair and smiled. 'You got anything for me to do tonight?'

Jake laughed. 'You are eager to get back in the action, aren't you?'

'Eager to have something to do, more like,' John admitted.

'I've been there, mate,' Jake said. 'I've got some money needs collecting from Jimmy Kelly. I was going to go myself but, seeing as you're at a loose end...'

'Consider it done.'

'And if you're in the mood for giving someone a good slap, the King brothers have been causing problems for the local Indian restaurant. The owner is an old friend of Sean and Michael, so I promised him we'd have a word with the racist little scrotes. Take some of the lads with you too. I'll let them know you're back and that they'll be answering to you from now on.'

'Sounds good to me, Boss.'

Jake laughed. 'You've known me my whole life, John. No need to call me Boss.'

John laughed too. 'Old habits and all that.'

'It's good to have you back where you belong, John.'

'It's good to be back.'

Chapter Fifty-Six

G race smoothed the dress over her thighs as she sat on the chair on the front row. Liverpool Town Hall was a beautiful wedding venue and Jazz had done an amazing job with the understated arrangements.

'This reminds me of our wedding day,' Michael said quietly against her ear.

She smiled, a flush creeping up her neck. Their wedding day had been one of the happiest days of her life. Despite the fact that they'd arranged it in less than six months, it had been perfect. But then, as long as Michael had been there, they could have got married anywhere and it would have been perfect. She turned and looked at her handsome husband as he held their two-year-old son on his lap. The sight of him in a tuxedo gave her butterflies. Sometimes she could hardly believe how much her life had changed since she'd met him.

Just seven years earlier, Grace had wondered if she

would ever escape the clutches of her psychopathic ex-husband Nathan Conlon. She'd been a single parent to her only child, Jake, and her only goal in life had been to make sure that he was safe and happy. Now she had two more children and a stepson as well as a daughter-in law – in about fifteen minutes' time – and two grandchildren. And, of course, she had Michael. She had sworn she would never marry again after divorcing Nathan, but she was glad she'd changed her mind. After all, Michael Carter was a man worth breaking that oath for. He made her happier than she had ever believed was possible.

Oscar fidgeted on Michael's knee and he whispered something in their son's ear that made him burst into a fit of giggles. He was an incredible father as well as an incredible husband. Their daughter Belle was on flower-girl duties. She had talked non-stop about her pretty dress for the past six weeks.

Grace looked up to the front of the room and smiled as she saw Connor standing there in his tux, waiting patiently for his bride-to-be. Jake stood beside him – his best man. She loved to see the boys dressed up in suits too. She and Michael were so proud of the men they had become. She knew that they would be missing their brother Paul today, but she believed that he was watching over them all.

Jake turned his head and winked at someone on the end of the front row, and then a huge smile lit up his face. She didn't need to look to know that it was Danny Alexander he was gazing at. The two of them had become inseparable since they'd told everyone about their relationship, and it made Grace's heart feel like it would burst to see how happy her son was. She liked Danny a lot, and he was the perfect partner for Jake in every sense of the word.

Connor fidgeted and looked at his watch. It was almost time for the main event. The atmosphere in the room suddenly changed and John Legend's 'All of Me' started playing through the speakers.

Grace turned in her seat and it took all of her willpower not to start bawling when she saw the wedding party walking up the makeshift aisle. Belle and Jake's daughter Isla both beamed proudly in their beautiful cream dresses as they scattered rose petals with each small step.

Jazz looked completely stunning, and she had a smile that could have lit up a thousand rooms. She had made Connor's life so much richer in so many ways. She had given him their beautiful son, and a reason to go on when Paul had been murdered. Grace loved her as much as if she were her own flesh and blood. She felt a fat tear run down her cheek and she quickly wiped it away with her hand. She felt Michael's strong hand on her shoulder and he gave her a gentle squeeze.

She turned to him and smiled. 'This is the start of the whole next chapter for our family.'

'I know.' He smiled back, lifting his hand and wiping another tear from her cheek with the pad of his thumb. 'But it's time to let them spread their wings, Grace.'

She nodded. Then she leaned her head on his shoulder as she watched her family at the front of the room. She felt like she could burst with happiness and pride. But she couldn't help feeling a twinge of sadness, knowing that she was witnessing the birth of a whole new era. None of their lives were ever going to be the same.

Epilogue

Six weeks later

G race Carter walked into the sitting room with two glasses of wine and handed one to Jazz, who was sitting on the sofa.

'Thanks, Grace,' she said with a smile as she took the drink.

Grace sat beside her daughter-in-law and took a sip of her wine.

'I wonder if the boys are enjoying the match. Have you seen the score?'

'No,' Jazz said with a shake of her head. 'I've heard about nothing but the derby all day, I've had enough,' she said with a laugh.

Grace laughed too. It was true that the Merseyside derby was a big event for the men in their family and they had all gone to Anfield to watch it in the executive box they'd recently purchased.

'It's nice to have some girl time,' Jazz said as she too sipped her wine. 'No point spoiling it with football talk.'

'I couldn't agree more,' Grace said. 'Anyway, I have something much more important and interesting to talk to you about.'

At this, Jazz tucked her feet beneath her and gave Grace her undivided attention. 'Oh?'

'Have you thought any more about what you and I were talking about the other week?'

Jazz lowered her glass and smiled. 'About getting back to work?'

Grace nodded.

'Yeah, some. And I think you're right about not starting at the bottom, Grace. I know I don't have much experience, but I understand the business side of things. I think I could be an asset in the right role. But I don't know what that is yet, and I was going to mention it to you again. Where is there a gap that I might fill?'

'Well, that's the thing. You know how Michael has been talking about moving out of Liverpool and taking a step back from some of the businesses?'

'Yeah?'

'Well, he's finally convinced me that it's time to make the move.'

'What?' Jazz asked, her eyes wide in surprise. 'You and Michael are leaving?'

'We're not going far. Just out to Birkdale probably.'

'But you're leaving the business?' Jazz asked.

'Some of it. We'll still be responsible for the restaurants

and the wine bars, but we're going to leave the other side of the business to the lads.'

'Do Jake and Connor know about this?' Jazz asked.

'They know that Michael and I are taking a step back at least. But they have proven themselves more than capable of running operations themselves over this past year. They've grown up so much, and I'm sure, where Connor is concerned, that has a lot to do with you, Jazz. You're a good influence on him.'

Jazz's cheeks flushed pink. 'Thank you, Grace.'

'It's true.'

'Well, I try,' she said with a grin as she took another sip of her wine.

'But I haven't told them about our plans for Cartel Securities yet.'

'And what are they? How does this fit in with a job for me?'

'Luke and Danny are going to remain the Managing Directors. They'll still be responsible for the day-to-day running of the business.'

'Well, that makes sense,' Jazz agreed.

'But you realise the CEO position of Cartel Securities is the real seat of power, Jazz?'

Jazz narrowed her eyes at her. 'Well, of course. That's why you and Michael are the CEOs.'

'The bouncers allow the drugs to move through the clubs. They protect the dealers. They ensure the merchandise is received and transported safely and securely throughout the North West. Jake and Connor control that side of the business, and that won't change, but the smooth operation of that business relies on the strategic arm of Cartel Securities. There needs to be someone overseeing the logistics and making sure that any potential obstacles and barriers are identified and dealt with.'

Jazz swallowed as she continued to watch Grace intently. 'I get that.'

'So you understand that I need someone in that position who can think on their feet? Someone with a cool head who will think through problems instead of charging in all guns blazing? Someone who can make difficult decisions but will always put our family first?'

'Of course.'

'Does that sound like anyone you might know?' Grace asked, wondering if Jazz had realised where she was going with this.

'Sounds like you,' Jazz said and started to laugh.

Grace laughed too. 'You agree it's a job for a woman then?'

Jazz stopped laughing and looked at her. 'I never really thought about it, but I suppose that makes sense. Us women have a different way of looking at the world.'

'Exactly, which is why I want you to take over, Jazz.'

Jazz almost spat out her wine. '*Me*?'

'I know you would always have Connor and Jake's best interests at heart. You're tough and you're smart. I can't think of anyone I would rather hand the baton over to than you.'

Jazz stared at her. 'Grace! I don't know what to say,' she stammered. 'When I asked for a job, I didn't mean yours.'

'I know you didn't. But I have been waiting for the right

person to come along so I could finally take a breather. So, please, just say yes.'

'But what about the boys? What about Michael? Is he okay with this?'

'Michael thinks it's a great idea. And the boys will be fine about it. So, what do you say?'

'I'm not sure if I have what it takes to be the next Grace Carter,' she said as she looked down at her wine glass.

'You don't have to be. Being the first Jasmine Carter will do just fine.'

Acknowledgments

As always, I would like to thank the wonderful team at One More Chapter for believing in me and bringing these books to life, most especially Charlotte Ledger and Kim Young, whose support of the Bad Blood series has helped it go from strength to strength. I'd also love to thank my amazing editors, Emily Ruston, for helping to make Grace Carter the best badass ever, and Jennie Rothwell for her input and guidance in shaping the vision of the next chapter of the Bad Blood series.

Most of all, I'd love to thank all of the readers who have supported me and who have bought or read my books. You have made my dreams come true.

I couldn't do this without the support of other authors too, and the crime writing community are a particularly lovely and supportive group of people. But, I'd like to give a special mention to Mary Torjussen and Amanda Brooke for always being willing to lend a listening ear.

To all of my friends who put up with my constant

writing chatter. There are too many to mention, and I love you all! A huge thank-you to my family for their constant love and support.

And finally, but most especially, to Eric – who supports every crazy decision I make, and my incredible boys – who continue to inspire and amaze me every single day.

Read on for an extract from Traitor in the House...

OLD GAME

When several young prostitutes are found murdered in Liverpool, DI Leigh Moss knows there is only one person she can turn to for help with the case. Gangland queen, Grace Carter, knows the streets of Liverpool better than anyone and can ask questions Leigh can't…but will Grace help?

NEW RULES

Grace doesn't trust easily, but when she discovers that her family might be linked with the gruesome murders, she decides to give Leigh a chance. But helping Leigh is risky and as Grace is dragged deeper into the murky world of vice, her own life is put in danger.

Can these two sworn enemies work together? Or is that a line they will never cross?

Chapter One

DI Leigh Moss watched as the forensics team processed the crime scene. Their painstaking work would ensure the preservation of any evidence and, if luck was on their side, find something that would point them to the killer. Although Leigh didn't hold out much hope. This was the third murder in a month with the same MO, and so far they didn't have a scrap of evidence to identify the killer. What they did have was a serial killer who was targeting working girls.

After the second victim had been found two weeks earlier, the DCI from the Major Investigation Team had approached Leigh to collaborate on the investigation. Both victims had been well known to Leigh's Phoenix team, Merseyside Police's specialist rape and sexual offences unit, and both had also once been residents of Sunnymeade children's home. Sunnymeade had been closed down only two years earlier after an undercover investigation revealed a scandal of systematic abuse going back decades.

The latest victim, Nerys Sheehan, was also a former Sunnymeade resident. A young woman of twenty-one, with ash-blonde hair and eyes the colour of steel. She was as thin as a rake, and the couple of times Leigh had previously met her she'd had the urge to force a good pan of scouse down her. Nerys had been a likeable girl, with a dry sense of humour and an easy-going manner. After she'd ended up in A&E one time too many, one of the Police Constables from the unit had put her in touch with a local refuge. Nerys had managed to get clean and sort herself out, but it had only lasted a few short months before her pimp found her, and had her back on crack and back on the game within the week.

Leigh's heart broke when she thought about some of the women and girls they saw on a day-to-day basis. Each of them had a story to tell. All had been victims of some form of abuse, usually at the hands of the very people who were supposed to protect them. When she'd resigned from the Organised Crime task force, Leigh had planned to join the high volume crime team and spend the next part of her career dealing with burglaries and thefts. It had been her way of trying to minimise her usefulness to Grace Carter and her family now that she was even further indebted to the woman. A few months earlier, Grace and her firm had rescued DS Nick Bryce, Leigh's then boyfriend, from the clutches of an Essex gangster by the name of Alastair McGrath, who would have surely killed Nick if he'd had his way. But when the Assistant Chief Constable had approached her himself, and told her there was an opening in for a DI in the Phoenix team, she hadn't felt able to say no. Before she'd become a police officer, and after Grace had saved her from being murdered by Nathan Conlon, Leigh had worked with victims of sexual abuse and it was a cause still close to her heart. Whilst many people looked at a working girl and simply saw a prostitute, or a drug addict with loose morals, Leigh saw a woman who had survived through nightmares that such people couldn't even comprehend.

Thankfully, most of her colleagues in Phoenix thought the same way, and they did the best they could for the women they came into contact with. But for the most part, their best was never enough, and certainly not in the case of young Nerys or the other two young women who had met a similar fate. Leigh shuddered as she recalled her own past and how a few more months as Nathan Conlon's mistress might have led her down a similar path. Nathan was Grace's ex-husband and he had once been one of Liverpool's biggest gangsters. He had been as vicious as he was charming. Leigh had fallen for him hard and had thought her world had ended when he'd tossed her aside as soon as he'd got bored of her, as he'd done with most women. As much as she'd like to, Leigh could never forget just how much she had to thank Grace Carter for.

But there was one thing Nerys had in her favour, if you could call it that now that she was lying cold and broken on the ground just a few feet away. During a brief stint when Nerys's pimp had been inside and she'd managed to get herself off the crack, she'd worked at a knocking shop on the dock road – the aptly named Number 69. The place was well known to the Phoenix team. It was a well-established

Liverpool institution that had been around since the Sixties. Leigh's team raided the place from time to time, but for the most part, the punters and the employees of Number 69 caused little trouble and the management generally looked after their employees, ensuring they were paid a fair wage and worked in good conditions. It was a much safer place to work than the cold, hard streets of Liverpool.

It was often said that prostitution was the oldest occupation around and Leigh knew that there was no way of eradicating it entirely. Unfortunately, so long as women and girls were seen as a commodity, there would be men, because it was largely men, who would exploit that fact for their own ends. Places like Number 69 at least allowed some semblance of safety and enabled the girls to earn a decent income, and for that reason, Leigh and her team were willing to focus their attentions elsewhere. And with budget cuts, as well as policing some of the most deprived wards in the country, their attentions were always needed elsewhere. They never seemed to have the manpower or enough hours in the day to deal with everything that Liverpool's seedy underbelly threw at them.

The vibration of her mobile phone pulled Leigh from her thoughts. Pulling it out of her pocket, she glanced at the screen to see Grace Carter's number. Leigh answered it quickly. As much as it went against every instinct she had as a detective, she knew that if anyone could help her to shed some light on this case, it was Grace Carter – and Leigh was about to give her a reason to.

'Grace, thanks for calling me back,' Leigh answered.

'No problem. What's wrong?'

'It's delicate. Can I call round?'

'Here?'

'Is that a problem?'

'Not for me. But you're usually very reluctant to come to the house. Is this something I need to be worried about?'

'Maybe,' Leigh started. 'Probably not. To be honest, Grace, I need your help.'

There was a moment's pause and Leigh could imagine Grace frowning as she considered her request. If she refused then Leigh would have to mention the link between young Nerys and the Carter family, but she would rather do that in person if she could. The last thing she wanted was for Grace to go into defence mode before Leigh had even had a chance to plead her case.

'Okay,' Grace finally responded. 'Will tonight do? The kids will be in bed by eight. Call round then.'

'That would be great. I've got things I need to attend to here anyway. And thanks.'

'No problem. See you later,' Grace replied before ending the call.

Leigh slipped her phone back into her inside pocket and made her way back towards the crime scene as she saw one of the forensics signalling her. Her DS, Mark Whitney, was already there, peering at the victim's arm as the forensic officer held it outstretched.

'What is it?' Leigh asked as she reached the two of them.

'We can't be sure, Ma'am. But it looks like a tooth,' Mark answered.

'A tooth?' Leigh echoed as she brought her face closer to inspect the small white fragment which was embedded in a welt on the victim's wrist. 'Could it be our killer's? It's tiny. Is it a fragment?'

The forensic shook his head. 'We'll confirm when we do the post-mortem. But it looks like it's a child's.'

Leigh's blood ran cold. 'A child's tooth? What the hell?' she said with a sigh.

Mark shook his head. 'No idea, Ma'am.'

'She didn't have kids, did she?' Leigh asked, wondering if that was a snippet of information she'd forgotten.

Mark shook his head. 'Nope. Not as far as we know anyway.'

'Well, let's wait and see,' Leigh said to the forensic, who nodded and then resumed his work with his colleagues. 'In the meantime, check missing persons and make sure there are no kids missing too,' she said to Mark. 'God forbid.'

'Will do,' Mark replied as his own mobile phone started to ring and he slipped away to answer it.

Leigh closed her eyes and rubbed the bridge of her nose. This case got more sinister with each victim. There had never been any hint of any children involved up until now. She wondered if there was a perfectly innocent and reasonable explanation for the deceased to have a child's tooth embedded in her wrist when she was murdered – but couldn't think of a single one.

Traitor in the House is available in ebook, audio and paperback now.

ONE MORE CHAPTER

YOUR NUMBER ONE STOP

FOR PAGETURNING BOOKS

One More Chapter is an
award-winning global
division of HarperCollins.

Sign up to our newsletter to get our
latest eBook deals and stay up to date
with our weekly Book Club!
<u>Subscribe here.</u>

Meet the team at
<u>www.onemorechapter.com</u>

Follow us!

 @OneMoreChapter_

 @OneMoreChapter

 @onemorechapterhc

Do you write unputdownable fiction?
We love to hear from new voices.
Find out how to submit your novel at
<u>www.onemorechapter.com/submissions</u>